15.95

The Unlikely Missionary

by
Elizabeth Brady

THE UNLIKELY MISSIONARY
Copyright © 2005 by Elizabeth Brady
http://www.unlikelymissionary.com/

ISBN 1-59113-698-9

All rights reserved. No part of this publication may be reproduced, stored in a retrieval system, or transmitted in any form or by any means—electronic, mechanical, digital, photocopy, recording, or any other—except for brief quotations in printed reviews, without the prior permission of the author.

This is a work of fiction. Names, places, and incidents are products of the author's imagination or are used fictitiously. Any resemblance to actual persons, living or dead, or to events or locales, is entirely coincidental.

Printed in the United States of America.

Scripture taken from the HOLY BIBLE, NEW INTERNATIONAL VERSION. Copyright © 1973, 1978, 1984 by International Bible Society. Used by permission of Zondervan Publishing House.

Page 4: "All that I do…" reprinted by permission of the publishers and the trustees of Amherst College from THE POEMS OF EMILY DICKINSON, Thomas H. Johnson, ed., Cambridge, Mass.: The Belknap Press of Harvard University Press, Copyright © 1951, 1955, 1979, 1983 by the President and Fellows of Harvard College.

To Christian, Izzy and Mack

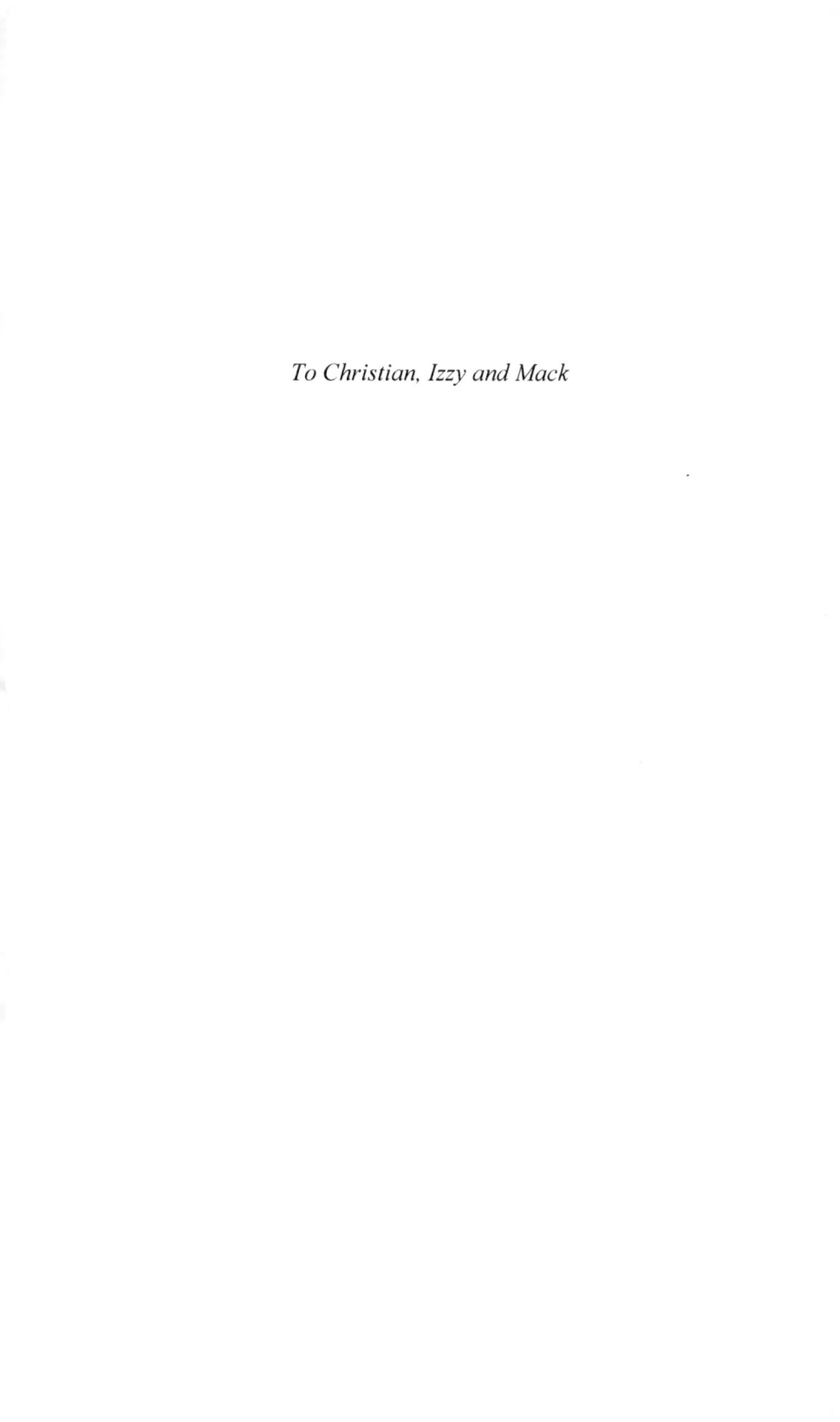

Acknowledgements

I would like to thank the many people who have encouraged and challenged me in the writing of this story: Ken and Nancy Walma, Allison Joyce, Kevin Walma, Ken Walma, Joyce Kraska, Ann Brady, Martha Pool, Catherine Smith, Mary Odom, Caroline Bauerschmidt, Dawn Cox-Hette, Allison Mercante, Tammy Nunez, Emily Henderson, and the ladies at Christ Episcopal Church in Covington. But, special thanks goes to Dr. Myrna Grant, my former graduate supervisor and mentor, for reading my manuscript in one sitting. Her confidence inspired me. And to my husband, Chris, who bought me the iMac, opened the blank document page, sat me down in the chair and said, "Write."

All that I do
Is in review
To his enamored mind
I know his eye
Where e're I ply
Is pushing close behind
Not any port
Nor any flight
But he doth there preside
What omnipresence lies in wait
For her to be a Bride

—Emily Dickinson c.1880

Prologue

I never wanted to be a missionary. I just wanted to go to Africa. In my northern Virginia Episcopal church background I could recall one missionary couple visit our church. They stood in the communal coffee hall between services next to their slide projector patiently waiting to be introduced by Father Jarvis. I remember thinking, in my teen estimation, that they exuded an incongruous confidence for a couple so poorly dressed and coifed. But, I watched the slide show and enjoyed the photos of their Land Cruiser and the woman wearing an African dress looking tanned and windblown and somehow freer in the bush than in suburbia, and I decided that I wanted to do that, too. It was not a burden to share the Gospel, but an intense desire to *be* there. I knew that someday, somehow I would have my own windblown picture taken in Africa.

Many years later my spiritual life had been deadened by too much alcohol and unhealthy living. It dawned on me late one sober night during my senior year of college that I would actually have to leave the safe confines of college hedonism and do something. It was during these late nights that I began to pray again and the thoughts of Africa returned to me stronger than ever. I phoned Father Jarvis out of the blue one fall day from my college apartment in North Carolina and shared my thoughts of Africa with him. He astounded me by taking me seriously and acted as if he had expected my call. But he also challenged me to search my heart because some might think that Africa was an escape, a way of further delaying having to grow up. He committed to pray for me and recommended that I apply to a non-denominational missionary group called Protestant Mission International because he was familiar with their short-term missions program designed for people to serve for a year or less. He promised that if the mission agency accepted me the church would find a way to fund my mission trip.

I have often wondered if Father Jarvis thought that was the last he would hear of Katherine Tierney's "call" to Africa and simply checked my name off a list of pastoral phone calls and moved on. But our phone call changed my life.

After I had applied to PMI and had to consider the possibility of becoming a missionary, I accepted the invitation of a friend and began attending a large charismatic church on the outskirts of town. The congregation was diverse and the live band that played every Sunday was full of college students I recognized but we had run in different circles. On a crisp October evening Pastor Jay invited people to the altar. I had never gone forward because I had been baptized and confirmed in the Episcopal church, which confessed Jesus as my Lord. But for some reasons I understand, and others I probably never will, I heard the Gospel message from Pastor Jay like I had never done before. I felt physically propelled toward the front and made a public confession of my faith. After the service several classmates came up and hugged me and told me they had been praying for me. And, John Gruber invited me for coffee.

John was in his mid-thirties and handsome. He was a divorcé with no children and owned a successful insurance business. He began picking me up on campus and taking me to lunch with the business crowd. We began attending church together on Wednesday evenings and Sundays followed by delicious food and lingering conversation. We fell in love and everything was wonderful except for the fact that Africa still beckoned. He asked me to marry him and I said I would, after I got back from Africa.

Before Thanksgiving I received a slim letter from PMI provisionally accepting me, pending funding and attending missionary training the following summer, as a short term missionary. I was to assigned to a far-away place called Fada N'Gourma, Burkina Faso, for one year beginning in July. I was to serve in the office there as an Administrative Assistant to the Director of PMI for that region. I went to the library and pulled out an atlas to look up Burkina Faso, a sub-Saharan landlocked country in West Africa of 2.5 million souls.

A few weeks later a letter arrived directly from Burkina Faso. I stood at the mailbox and stared at the envelope. The stamps were brightly colored and seemed curiously upbeat for a continent so full of famine and strife. One of the stamps had an intricate line drawing of a scorpion that was exotic and yet spooky. The other stamps were drawings of pink flowering trees. The letter was from Malcolm Falk, the director I would be reporting to in Burkina Faso. He included a list of things I should bring and said that he and his wife, Anna, were looking forward to my summer arrival. I tucked the letter in my purse and carried it everywhere. And sometimes when I was sad or confused I would take the letter out and re-read every word and stare at the stamps and know in my heart that God was calling me there.

John drove me home to Fairfax, Virginia, to spend the Thanksgiving holiday with my family. My Mom had outdone herself and the table was overflowing with lovely decorations and food but the conversation was strained. My parents didn't know whether to be more concerned about the engagement to the divorcé from small town North Carolina or the upcoming year as a missionary in West Africa. John was tense because he was getting tired of hearing about Africa. And, I was conflicted because I loved John in Beauville but sitting at my parents' table I suddenly felt embarrassed to be with him and then felt sad that I felt that way. My younger siblings didn't help by calling him John Boober under their breath and stifling their laughter when John talked of an upcoming revival at the church in Beauville.

Graduation arrived in May and in June John drove me to Raleigh for missionary training. Things had become more strained between us, I think he thought when I saw the pear shaped caret diamond that Africa would melt away in the promise of a nice home and gifts, but it didn't. He carried my two trunks to the room and I walked him back to the car. We stood in silence watching the other families arrive. He started to ask me something and then stopped. I didn't ask him what was on his mind because I already knew and I was tired of trying to assure him that I loved him even though I was leaving. He held my hand and twirled the engagement ring around my finger between his thumb and forefinger. We kissed and hugged and he left. I watched him pull away and I felt relieved.

And so I spent the next three weeks being shuttled back and forth between the unairconditioned dormitories to the rolling hills and tidy buildings that made up the PMI campus. We attended lectures, had psychological evaluations, signed "healthy lifestyle" pledges, and shared our testimonies. It was a very positive experience and frankly it was a crash course in missions for me as I had very little understanding of what modern missionaries actually did. Like any other sector, missions had evolved over the years and had become very vocational. I met teachers, doctors, nurses, engineers, linguists and other professionals who would fill specific roles. They were serious people and that was an adjustment for me, who was used to people for whom all of life was potential fodder for caustic comment and humor. Many of them had hard edges, their hearts made heavy by the suffering they had witnessed around the world. My edges were hardened, too, but the wall of ice that had separated my heart and conscience until this past year had begun to melt in slow drips.
    "You're an unlikely candidate," the short-term coordinator, Henry, said to me in his office when I went to pick up my airplane tickets on the last day of training. His office was covered with photos of him on the beaches of Liberia and now he was behind an empty desk looking slightly uncomfortable in a tie. He leaned back in his chair and regarded me. "Your application kind of came out of left field. To be honest, I didn't know what to make of it when I received it. But, I've been at this long enough to know that God works in surprising ways." He handed me the plane tickets. "I try not to get in the way."
    "I feel like I kind of stand out in this group," I admitted to him.
    "You do," he smiled. "But it's good for us to be reminded that God calls His servants, we don't."
    I took the shuttle back to the dorm for the last time and packed my trunks. My roommate had left a note saying that John had phoned three times. I crumpled it and threw it in the trash. The shuttle dropped me and another trainee named Sarah off at the airport where we were taking the same domestic flight to JFK airport in New York.
    "I can only check your luggage through to Paris, you'll have to pick it up and recheck it before your flight to Burkina Faso," the check-in attendant informed me.

"Okay," I shrugged. I had know way of knowing that would pose a problem.

In JFK I parted ways with Sarah. We didn't know each other very well, but suddenly we were the only people in the world we knew. We hugged and wished one another good luck. I boarded a TWA flight bound for Paris.

1
Left Baggage

My flight landed in Paris at the Charles De Gaulle airport before dawn, but my connecting flight to Burkina Faso wasn't scheduled to leave until ten that night. Even though I had plenty of time, I had rushed to load my two trunks and cosmetics case onto a Smarte Carte and took the elevator downstairs to find UTA, my connecting airline. I parked myself in front of the UTA desk as if it might disappear at some point throughout the day. The sign was dark, apparently I was the only person traveling on the flight who had arrived 15 hours before check in time. I put my feet up on my trunks and looked at my watch: it was still only 7:10 a.m. local time but it felt like I had been there for hours.

The cleaning lady wheeled her cart past me and gave me a sharp nod. It was unsettling to be alone. I would take another overnight flight tonight to where? I had been so confident of my call to Africa, but suddenly alone in the airport I felt deeply vulnerable. I leaned my head back and closed my eyes.

I pictured John. John Gruber. John Caleb Gruber. *God-fearing hick*, my mother called him. Sometimes I felt she was right and other times her attitude offended me. I must've dozed off very quickly for suddenly I was jolted awake. The cleaning lady was standing directly in front of me tap, tap, tapping the handle of her feathered brush on my trunk.

"Non, Madame! Do not sleep. There are thieves," she whisked her brush around with dramatic flair. "People will take your belongings, you must watch," she said to me in English.

I looked around for the potential villains but saw no one. "Merci," I said.

Left Baggage

She dropped her brush back into her cart and moved on. But, the area was completely deserted so every few minutes she wheeled her cart past my aisle to check on me. I looked at my watch again: More than 14 hours to go. Clearly I needed a diversion.

I wheeled my cumbersome Smarte Carte back into the elevator from which I had come and took it up to the main level. With the trunks stacked one on top of the other I could barely see over them so I navigated by peering around the side. There were cafés and duty free shops surrounding an area of white bistro tables where I parked myself once again.

I exchanged my last $20 for French francs in a nearby machine. After the fee, it gave me about $12 worth of francs. So I wheeled myself over to a food counter and ordered a ham baguette and coffee. I didn't realized how hungry I was until I began eating. I wheeled back and ordered a fresh chocolate croissant. I finished my food and sat at the white tables. I watched all the different people and tried to listen in on their conversations to figure out which languages they spoke.

I watched as group of Africans approached the tables and sat down. There was one man, three women and several small children. They were all draped in fantastically colored robes and the women's gold bracelets jingled when they moved. I watched the group talking and laughing and one of the women looked my way and smiled a gorgeous smile. They were beautiful, confident women. And suddenly, without warning, my confidence crumpled and I was completely overwhelmed with the realization that I had nothing to offer these women. What had I been thinking? I had been so focused on the call, on preparing to leave that I had thought little about where I was actually going. I felt young and naïve.

I threw away my trash and wheeled away from the table and circled around the concourse. Every possible fear about my upcoming mission washed over me and I felt as if I had made the biggest mistake of my life. I had a man at home who wanted nothing more than to marry me but no! I had to pack myself off to the bush to do what? Who did I think I was? And, a thought that had never occurred to me before was death. What if I contracted some strange tropical

Chapter 1

disease or was bit by a poisonous spider in my sleep? What if I never made it home again?

And then I spotted a newsstand with my old friends *Marlboro Lights* in a neat row behind the cash register. I spent the rest of my cash on a pack of cigarettes and quickly wheeled myself to the elevators and back down to my hovel. I ripped open the pack and could barely light the cigarette my hand was shaking so badly. I took a long drag and slowly exhaled. I closed my eyes, "I'm sorry, Lord, I know I'm not supposed to smoke but it feels so good." I tucked the gold cross necklace my Mom had loaned me into my sweater and smoked one cigarette after another.

I looked at the glacier of cigarette butts in the ashtray and then at my watch. It was now almost 11:00 a.m. in Paris. I counted back six hours on my fingers. It was 5:00 a.m. in Beauville. I wheeled my Smarte Carte over to the nearby payphones. I dialed the international operator and placed a collect call to John. I needed to hear a familiar voice; I needed to feel needed.

"Hello?" the familiar, yet groggy, voice came through after he accepted the charges.

"It's me," I burst into tears. "I'm sorry to wake you up."

"Oh, darlin' it's okay," he comforted me. "Where are you?"

"In Paris."

"You sound so close."

"I'm scared."

"Hey, God has called you to do great things. Don't be afraid now, ya hear?"

"Tell me you love me?" I tried to control my sobs.

"Of course I love you," he assured me.

"Only 384 days until our wedding," I snorted and wiped my nose with the back of my shirtsleeve.

"Yes, and it will be wonderful."

I couldn't think of anything else to say, I just needed to hear his voice.

"Are you going to be alright?"

"Yes."

Left Baggage

"Okay, baby, write soon—I've got a busy day so I need to get some more sleep."
"Okay."
"Bye, now."
"Pray for me?" but he had hung up. The line went dead. I reluctantly replaced my receiver.

I wheeled my Smarte Carte back to the orange seats and slumped back down. Since when was John so strong? Could it be that he was as eager to be away from me as I was he? Why couldn't we admit that to one another? And what was the matter with me anyway? A scant 24 hours ago I couldn't wait to get away from him. Now here I had only made it to France and I phoned him collect and in tears! Did this mean I actually did love him and was denying it because he wasn't what I expected my life long partner to be? I pondered this thought for a moment and decided that I was just needy. "Idiot." I chastised myself and lit another cigarette and propped my feet up on my trunks.

By the late afternoon the UTA area began to fill up. Two employees flipped on the sign illuminating *UTA* above the counters and milled around in the back organizing papers and typing on their computers. A few people were dotted around the seating area including an African man dressed in a powder blue button up shirt and polyester brown pants. He sat with his briefcase opened on his lap a few seats down from me and read over some notes on a legal pad.

I had now smoked more than half of the pack of cigarettes and had a fierce headache. I wheeled to the bathroom and water fountain and returned.

The man in the blue shirt slid three seats toward me and asked me in French where I was going with all those trunks. I told him Burkina Faso and he asked what I would be doing in his country. I answered in English, "I'm going to be a missionary."

He smiled, "So, you're going there to convert us heathens, yes?"

His comment pierced me and I felt embarrassed. I had thought of Africa as some far away place of lost and hungry souls but the people I had seen and met this morning were quite the opposite. "I don't know what I'm doing," I admitted and he laughed appreciating my honesty.

Chapter 1

"That's a very beautiful ring on your finger," he nodded towards my engagement ring.
"Thanks," I smiled but felt uncomfortable.
"Is it an engagement ring?"
"Yes."
"Someone loves you very much indeed."
"Merci," I smiled. Eventually he slid back down the row of seats and went back to his work. I held out my left hand and regarded the ring. It was a beautiful diamond. But, I felt self-conscious about it. It was supposed to represent a commitment and overwhelming love that I wasn't sure I felt. And people were overly impressed with its size and that made me even more uneasy.

I opened my cosmetic case and took out the velvet box. I slid off the ring and placed it carefully inside the box and tucked it deep inside the case. John would've been apoplectic to know I wasn't wearing the ring, but I needed to distance myself from the assumptions that it represented. I looked at my naked hand, there was a small wrinkle of skin and tan line where it had been but those would quickly fade.

I wheeled my cart into the elevator and took it one flight up to the main concourse where I had eaten earlier. I wheeled outside and leaned against a large iron flowerpot. It felt good to get some fresh air. I was in the departures area and watched the various travelers being dropped off. A gray Citroen pulled up and the parents got out and retrieved their luggage from the trunk. Their teenaged daughter kissed both of them and called, "Bon Voyage," and hopped into the driver's seat and zoomed off into the traffic leaving her parents on the curb. They looked at one another with what must be universal parental concern.

"She'll be fine," Dad assured Mom and nudged her into the airport with his suitcase.

I thought of my own parents and brothers and sister who came down from northern Virginia to visit me during missionary training. Mom wanted to meet on her turf: the champagne brunch at a downtown hotel in Raleigh, not at the inner-city dorm where I was temporarily living for training. Things had been strained between us

Left Baggage

for many years. I had been the wild child, the teenage rebel and suddenly I switched my colors to missionary candidate engaged to a charismatic Christian. It was hard to keep up.

I smoked my last cigarette and threw the pack away in a nearby trashcan. I had a headache and I was hungry but I didn't have any more cash. I figured I would eat on the plane later. I prayed for peace and courage and eventually made my way back downstairs to the UTA gate.

Two hours before flight time, just before eight p.m., I was the first person in line to check in. I heaved my two trunks onto the scales and the UTA attendant laughed. "You would have to pay thousands of Francs in excess baggage to take both trunks," she said in French.

"Excuse me?" I asked in my survival French.

"You are almost triple the 35 kilos weight allotment," she switched to English.

"But, I need all this stuff.," I explained. "I'm going there to live for a year. This is not a holiday."

She shook her head, "Non. There is no way you can take all of this baggage without paying excess."

I was on the verge of tears. I had no francs to pay excess baggage. I didn't have any credit cards. All I had was an envelope full of green paper "Monopoly" money that the mission had given me to exchange for the local currency.

"You should've had your baggage tagged for Ouagadougou in America. The European weight allotment is much lower than the American."

"I didn't know that," I gave her my best pleading look but she wouldn't budge. I relented and asked, "How much weight do I have to get rid of so that I don't have to pay any excess?"

She looked at her computer screen and then at my trunks on the scale, "You need to get rid of one whole trunk." She nodded her head towards the elevator; "Left Baggage is downstairs."

I wheeled my cart onto the elevator and took it another level down to Left Baggage. I maneuvered the cart into the bowels of the airport through a maze of lockers. I entered the Left Baggage area to find two men sitting behind the counter playing cards. They looked up and

Chapter 1

gave me a quick nod and went back to their card game. There were shelves behind them stacked with backpacks, suitcases, guitars and a variety of other travel things.

I pulled both trunks off my Smarte Carte and opened them. They were both so neatly packed! They represented months of preparation and not to mention expense. What could I possibly leave? Tears brimmed in my eyes as I looked at all the gifts of good wishes and Wal-Mart runs. I quickly decided clothes and toiletries had to be the priority.

I removed all the contents of both trunks and stacked them on the floor to the amusement of the bored Left Baggage attendants. They had stopped their card game and stood up to watch me. I quickly made my choices. In the first trunk I put priority items: clothes, underwear, pajamas, and shoes. I also tossed in my address books, Bible, journals, stationery, super-sized Pepto Bismal and anti-malarial tablets. In the trunk that would be left I packed linens, throw rugs, miniature lamps and pre-packaged curtains. The floor was left scattered with boxes of granola bars, miniature chocolates in seasonal wrapping, moisturized tissues, and paper towels with 4th of July décor. I scooped them up in my arms and stuffed them in the second trunk on top of the curtains. I simply had no room for them.

The final choice: my little brother's electric keyboard. He had given it to me in a moment of tenderness and I hated to disappoint him. I tried to fit it in the trunk but could not latch the buckles unless I took out half of my clothes. My daydream of sitting under a tree "tickling the ivories", as my Dad always said, entertaining new friends mocked me. I took out the keyboard and smashed it in on top of the granola bar boxes and slammed the trunk shut. Now sobbing, I heaved it onto the counter.

The attendant helped me with the trunk and then handed me a ticket. "You know there is a 24 hour limit?"

"I know."

"And then we have to destroy it."

"I know."

I had no choice. I closed my remaining trunk and heaved it onto my Smarte Carte. I picked up my cosmetic case and put it on top of

Left Baggage

the trunk. I took the elevator up one flight and went to the other attendant at UTA. She weighed my trunk.

"You are still over," she glanced at the first attendant I had tried. I looked at her. I pleaded with my puffy red eyes. "Please, I have already left one whole trunk downstairs."

She took the trunk and wrapped the boarding stickers around the handle. She looked at me, "Go. But do not say who assisted you."

"Thank you!" I wanted to kiss her. "Thank you."

I followed a group of Africans who had checked in before me up and down through a maze of escalators that connected us to our far-reaching satellite. I found one empty seat and sat down. I was exhausted. I admired the exotic clothes and hairstyles of the Indian and African women crowded in the boarding area. I was the only white freckled face and felt strangely vulnerable, I had never been in the minority before.

The same Burkinabé man I had spoken with earlier stepped through the crowd and approached me. "I thought you were going to Ouaga?" he asked me in French.

"I am."

"Our loading area is over there," he pointed over his shoulder. "This flight is headed to Singapore."

I burst into laughter in spite of myself. What would I have done if I had disembarked in Singapore! Could this day get any worse?

He picked up my cosmetic case and led me over to the proper boarding area.

"Thank you," I said as he handed me back my case. We held out our tickets for the attendant and I followed him on to UTA Flight 202 bound for Ouagadougou.

I watched from my window seat as we lifted up over the mercury-vapor lights that turned Paris into an endless yellow mirage. I felt so out of place; I was sure I had a neon badge on me that read, "Hello, I have never traveled internationally."

"Madame?" The flight attendant offered me a piece of French bread suspended by salad tongs. "Baguette?"

"Merci," I took the bread and broke off a piece and ate it.

Chapter 1

It was now pitch black outside. I would finally be in Africa in the morning, a place to which I felt sure that God had called me, as strange as it seemed to everyone else. I recalled the other single women missionaries I had met in the past weeks. They were obsessed with their singleness and yet few of them had ever dated. I wanted them to pray for my singleness, but that would've been insensitive with a diamond on my finger. I was edgy having quite drinking and smoking cold turkey at the beginning of survival training. The cigarettes were the hardest, I kept picking at not-yet formed sleep in my eye in the little mirror in my cosmetics case causing my roommate at one point to wonder about the state of my eyeball. "My eye is fine," I said. But, I wanted to say, "it's just a side affect of my addiction to nicotine and alcohol that is causing me to want to rip my eyes out!"

The flight attendant returned with miniature bottles of red and white wines. "Madame?" she held up both.

"Non, merci," I turned down the wine. I looked back out the window but could only see my tired reflection.

She returned again with dinner that was very tasty. I wasn't sure what the meat was, I thought I heard someone say 'goat' but my French was dubious and I was too hungry to worry about it. The meat was covered in a yummy white sauce and with the vegetables and several different cheeses I became contentedly full. I handed my tray back to the flight attendant and settled back into my seat. I was tired.

I fingered my Mom's cross necklace as I watched the activity in the cabin from the reflection in the window. I thought about the great missionaries who stepped off boats onto undiscovered shores and commanded the attention of all they met with the Gospel message. And then there was me who sat alone in the basement of the airport inhaling a pack of cigarettes. But, I didn't have a great burden to share the Gospel because I was still trying to figure out the message myself. I was just willing to answer a call. "Lord, be with me this year," I prayed. I leaned my forehead against the cool window and fell asleep.

The final leg of the journey flew us throughout the night south across the Mediterranean Sea and over the Sahara Desert to Niamey,

Left Baggage

Niger, where more than half of the passengers disembarked in the dead of night. From there we headed west to Burkina Faso where the plane touched down at Ouagadougou International at 6:35 a.m. local time.

It was misty so I couldn't see very far but I did spot the grounds crew roll the mobile stairs across the grassy runway towards the plane. Two flight attendants opened the cabin door and seconds later the earthy smell of leather, barn animals, and urine all baked together in the morning sun welcomed me.

I opened my cosmetic case and regarded myself in the little mirror. The man sitting next to me had slept the whole time so we had not spoken. He glanced at me and smiled, "I thought that was a tackle box," he said in a British accent.

"No, it looks like one though." My case was a plastic fluorescent green box with two collapsing layers that I had completely filled with makeup, hair combs, razors, lotions, and all manner of colorful, travel sized bottles that I would probably never use but they're fun to buy. I brushed my hair and put some face powder on and lipstick but it was hopeless, really. I had not bathed for two days, or eaten properly, and smoked too much, so I was dirty and I figured the mystery meat was to blame for making me constipated. Never have I longed for a hot shower so badly.

I walked down the mobile stairs onto the dusty grass runway and followed the single file line of passengers about an eighth of a mile through the hazy morning sunshine to the two-story cement block airport. It was very humid. Security guards in camouflage leaned against the walls with AK-47's strapped over their chests. The guards wore black berets that they took off to swat flies or wipe the beads of sweat off their brows and then toss them casually back on their heads.

We stopped and waited to be admitted through customs. Men were waved behind a black curtain on the right, women to the left. I stood for 45 minutes before my passport was checked and stamped and I was then waved into a cavernous booth. A woman security guard nodded at me as I slipped in and placed my carry-ons on the card table. She opened my cosmetic case and pulled up the drawers

Chapter 1

creating a bouquet of color. She seemed delighted by the discovery. She looked at me and smiled. I smiled back.

She lifted my Maybelline mascara out, "Ca?" she asked.

"Mascara," I said and fingered my eyelashes like I was applying mascara.

"Ca?" she lifted out a banana comb and I took it and showed her how it fit in my hair.

"Ah," she made a clicking sound from the back of her throat and nodded. She took it back from me and examined it further. She rifled through my case again.

"Ca?" she held up my powder compact. I took it and opened it and showed her how I powdered my nose. I clicked it closed and replaced it in the box.

She laughed and made that clicking sound again. We stood there in silence for a moment. I noticed she was still holding my banana comb.

"Do you want that?" I asked her.

She looked away from me and smiled. "Oui," she admitted softly.

"Okay." I closed my tackle box and draped my purse across my chest again. She was already waving the next woman in. I slipped out the other side of the curtain and joined the other passengers in front of the luggage carousel. There was some confusion and I overheard someone say that the carousel was broken.

Suddenly, through another black drape leading outside, a blue suitcase was unceremoniously tossed onto the cement floor. Then a black duffel bag, pink cosmetics bag, and so the luggage was delivered while we all scrambled to find our own.

I lugged my trunk outside, placed my cosmetic case and purse on top of it and looked around. Mopeds whizzed by with women in colorful dresses. Men wore navy blue polyester pants with pastel button-up shirts. Hundreds of mopeds grouped together at the stoplight and when it flashed yellow and then turned green they zoomed off leaving clouds of dust swirling behind them. Apparently I had hit morning rush hour in Ouagadougou.

I watched the light change to red again and the mopeds all slowed to stop at the light. The women were beautiful. Their hair was braided with beads and piled elaborately on top of their heads. Their dresses were tailored with big poofy shoulders and long skirts each with different designs in primary colors. The light flickered green and off they went in another swirl of dust.

The road was lined with corrugated tin market stalls as far as the eye could see. Men sat in the shade watching over their wares. Women brushed flies from their fruit baskets and many had babies strapped to their backs by a swath of fabric. Chickens and dogs wandered through the streets dodging bikes and mopeds. There was a buzz of life, of purpose, that surprised me.

A group of young boys approached me with several baguettes wrapped in a piece of brown paper. "Baguette?" They all asked me in unison and shoved it under my nose. "Baguette?"

I looked around hoping someone would come to my rescue. All I had with me were vouchers like Monopoly money that the mission agency had given me. I would be able to give the vouchers to my Director in exchange for the local currency. I shook my head and said, "No."

One boy cocked his head to the side and made a sad face. "S'il vous plaît, Madame," he rubbed his tummy.

I shook my head again. They moved on. The Director and his wife were supposed to pick me up. Maybe they had forgotten about me?

Two younger boys approached me. They circled around me, "Cadeau?" They held out their hands. "Cadeau?"

"I don't have a gift for you," I said in French.

"Cadeau?" The younger boy rubbed his tummy and dropped his chin to his chest. He looked up at me with a mischievous grin. I couldn't help but smile at his pluckiness.

A four-door white Nissan pick-up truck pulled up in front of me. A petite woman leaned out of the passenger's side window. "Katherine?" she asked.

"Yes!" I exclaimed.

"Welcome to Ouaga!" she opened her door and hopped out. She shooed the boys away and said something to them in a language I had never heard.

"What did you say?" I asked her.

Chapter 1

"I told them to move on in Gourmantché," she explained. "It always surprises them that a white person knows their native language."

"Oh." It surprised me, too.

"Normally they would be spoken to in French." She looked at me; "I'm Anna Falk, by the way."

"Yes, I'm Katherine Tierney," I held out my right hand. She shook it.

"Burkina should be a real shock for an American," she had a gentle laugh, it was more of a smile with a slight chuckle behind it.

"You're not American?"

"No, no, dear. We're proud western Canadians."

"Where are you from?"

"You wouldn't know it if I told you," she looked past me and smiled.

A deeply tanned man walked around the truck and stood next to Anna. He wasn't much taller than I. "I'm Malcolm Falk." He held out his hand and I took it. "Welcome to Burkina." He bent his head back and studied me through the bifocals of his glasses.

"Thanks," I smiled. "I'm glad I don't have to get on another plane."

"Yes, it was much easier when we took ships because it gave your body time to adjust to the time change and the climate." Malcolm was still looking at me. He didn't look *that* old to me. He smiled slightly as if he had read my mind.

"How are you feeling?" Anna asked.

"I'm tired but I think I'm okay."

"Did you have any trouble?" Malcolm asked me.

"Well, I had to leave one trunk in Left Baggage in Charles De Gaulle airport, but other than that it was fine." I reddened thinking of what an idiot I must've looked like in the airport yesterday—not to mention the fact that I might be in Singapore right now.

"Didn't you check your trunks all the way through to Ouaga?"

"No, I didn't know I could do that."

"Oh," Malcolm furrowed his eyebrows and looked very concerned. "The North American weight allotment is much higher

— 27 —

Left Baggage

than the European so normally you make sure to check the luggage all the way through to Ouaga to avoid that."

"I'm aware of that now, but it's okay," I just wanted to erase yesterday from my memory. "I still have one trunk and I think I managed to keep everything I really need."

"Well, we're going back to the Guest House where you can shower and we'll have an early lunch," Anna said kindly.

"That sounds good," I said wearily.

"We'll take it easy today and then tomorrow morning we'll pick up some food and supplies here in Ouaga. Tomorrow afternoon we will head home to Fada N'Gourma, it's about two hours east of here. So, tomorrow night you will be in your own bed, in your own house."

Malcolm lifted my trunk and slid it in to the flatbed. I climbed in the back seat of the four-door cab and Anna settled herself in the passenger's seat. A chorus of bleating moped horns greeted us when pulled onto the road and made our way across the rambling city to the mission's Guest House. Lean-to market stalls with corrugated tin roofs stood next to newer square cement buildings.

"What's with all the cement?" I asked Malcolm.

"Termites," he nodded. "They swarm and eat everything except cement."

At one point we turned down a mahogany tree lined street dotted with colonial homes that were obviously very grand in their day. They looked weathered and some were riddled with bullet holes.

"The French tried to recreate Paris when they colonized," Malcolm yelled over his right shoulder to me. "Senior officials and the President live in these homes now."

We stopped at a large intersection when suddenly a group of young boys appeared at all four open windows shoving long sticks of French bread into the windows. "Baguette!" they yelled in French, "Fresh baguette!" I watched Malcolm and Anna who just smiled and waved them away. Several people stopped their mopeds so close to us I could've reached out and touched their shoulders, they all nodded and greeted us. The light flicked green but traffic was delayed while a man tried to coax a large steer across the intersection. The mopeds

Chapter 1

swerved around him and the animal and finally Malcolm did the same. We continued on to the Guest House.

2
Ouagadougou (Waga-doo-woo)

"Ouagadougou seems to be a work in progress," I observed to Malcolm and Anna as we turned right onto an unpaved two-lane street that was sandwiched on both sides with high walls and iron gates.
"Yes, you could put it that way, Katherine," Malcolm chuckled. "There are not a lot of zoning laws or regulations in Burkina."
"Where are we now?"
"This is a residential area of ex-pats. Most of the embassies and international organizations are located in this section of town."
"Lots of high walls and iron gates," I noted.
"Lots of thieves," Anna stated.
We pulled up to a metal gate and Malcolm put the truck in park and hopped out and opened it. He got back in the truck and pulled into a gravel courtyard and parked the truck. The Guest House was a single story cement square with a flat roof. It had cobalt blue metal shudders that added a touch of pizzazz to the monotonous cement. We all got out of the truck and Malcolm walked back to shut the gate behind us. Anna waved away a small flock of black chicken-like birds.
"What are those?" I asked.
"Guinea fowl," Anna said. "They are all over the place and they are silly, squawking birds."
"This is a new Guest House, Katherine," Malcolm explained. He pointed next door to an older two-story house with a large wrap-around porch on the second floor. It was cement brick as well but an abundance of vines covered the walls and stately trees shaded it. "Ellen and Charles Simpson live on the second floor and the mission

Chapter 2

has administrative offices on the first floor. Charles practiced law in Canada and then began a second career as a missionary after he retired."

"Ellen runs the Guest House and Charles deals with all of the real estate, taxes, visas, and other governmental issues on behalf of the mission. I tell you, it takes a certain kind of person to deal with the bureaucracy in Ouaga on a regular basis, and he does an excellent job."

"I'm sure," I said and grabbed my cosmetics case and purse and followed Anna. Malcolm followed with my trunk. Anna opened the outside door with a silver skeleton key. We walked through a kitchen and eating area into a hallway with four closed doors. She opened the first door and we walked into my room. The only furnishings were a single bed, a nightstand and a Kelly green woven chair. A screened window covered in black iron thief-proofing looked out over the driveway. I could see the top of Malcolm's truck.

"It's simple but clean," Anna said. Malcolm put my trunk down at the foot of the bed.

"It's very nice." I knew it was a lame response but I had no idea what to expect.

Malcolm laughed, "This is luxury compared to where you'll live in Fada, Katherine."

"Malcolm," Anna waved him off. "Don't mind him." Malcolm was still chuckling when he left the room.

Anna showed me the bathroom adjacent to the room. It was completely tiled on the floor and walls. She showed me how to work the shower.

"It's actually part of the bathroom," she pulled the curtain around. "You stand in the area where it dips down into the drain and shoot the showerhead in that direction."

"Okay," I walked over to the door and held it open for her, "I don't mean to be rude, but I'm absolutely dying to take a shower."

She laughed. "See you at eleven-thirty for lunch."

I bundled my toiletries in my arms and shut the door behind me in the bathroom. I took off my clothes and dumped them in a pile on the floor. I pulled a starchy towel off the rack and wrapped it around me.

Ouagadougou

My hair was greasy and I smelled. I felt giddy thinking of how glorious a long, hot shower would feel.

I turned on the water and it trickled out of the showerhead. It was brown and ice cold. I turned the knob around as high as it would go and the trickle became a stream of brown ice water. I shut my eyes, took a deep breath and stepped full body under the stream. My body convulsed in shivers as I reached for the soap. I spit the rusty tasting water out of my mouth as I shampooed my hair. I had goose bumps the size of mosquito bites but I was clean. I turned off the water and wrapped three towels around me to warm up. I bit the towel to stop my teeth from chattering. If I had known I would not have a warm shower for a year I would not have come, it was torture!

I quickly dressed and brushed my wet hair. There was no mirror in my room so I had to use the little one inside my cosmetic case. It didn't feel like I had washed all the soap out of my hair and my skin didn't feel soft or smell fragrant like it normally did after a shower. I knew in my head that things would feel differently away from home, but I didn't expect to be affected in such an intimately physical way and it unsettled me.

We gathered for lunch on Ellen and Charles's second floor porch. It was shaded by leafy Flamboyant trees and had flowering plants and Elephant Ear planted in pots around the porch for additional shade. I walked to the edge of the porch and looked down at the Guest House where we were staying next door, the roof was completely flat and covered with pebbles. Beyond the compound wall there was a large open area where a group of boys were playing an intense game of soccer.

"My sons became quite good soccer players learning to play with the Africans," Malcolm came and stood next to me. "Some of the American missionary kids have even won scholarships to university."

"Really? What makes them so good?" I asked.

"The Africans are much faster, so the boys learned to play the game at a much quicker pace."

"How many children do you have?" I asked him, prompted by the mention of his sons.

"Two boys first and then two girls," he smiled.

Chapter 2

"I'm the eldest of two girls first and then two boys," I said.

"You're from a large family then, Katherine?"

"Yes, in fact, it was my brother McKenzie's keyboard that I left in the other trunk in Paris. I'll need to write him a letter soon and explain what happened."

"Yes, yes, I believe you will."

"Did you say there was a Guest House in Fada N'Gourma, too?" I asked.

"Yes, ours was built a few years ago. The hospitality ministry is very important in missions work. There are very few hotels outside the capital cities so the mission has Guest Houses set up in most compounds around the country where colleague missionaries, or any one, can stay for a nominal fee."

Ellen emerged from the house carrying a large platter of fruit and cheese. "Please, sit down," she put the platter down and hurried back into the house.

"All of the Guest Houses are equipped with kitchens because you're supposed to cook your own food but Ellen and Charles are especially kind to cook for us today," Malcolm explained as we sat down at the table.

"No, no," Charles waved a long, bony hand. He was very tall and thin with only a few stubborn strands of wispy gray hair remaining on the top of his head. His nose and chin were pointy and his eyes were sharp giving him a hawkish presence. "It is the Falk's that have set the example for the rest of us in the art of welcoming loved ones and strangers equally." He looked at me, "You don't realize it yet, but the Lord has put you in the company of angels for this next year." Malcolm and Anna both protested but he waved them off again. He looked at me, "What is your goal for this year?"

"On paper I am assigned to be Malcolm's Administrative Assistant in the church office, but I think at this point my goal is to survive."

Malcolm and Anna both laughed, "Oh, Katherine." Malcolm shook his head and took off his glasses, he wiped each lens with his napkin and put them back on.

Ouagadougou

Charles seemed irritated by my response. "Well, it's good that our American friend didn't arrive 20 years earlier by boat. There would've been no one to greet her, feed her, or drive her to her home. Not to mention the fact that her home is already built for her, furnished, and knowing our fair Anna, stocked with food. To top it all off she has indoor plumbing and electricity for most of the day. This is not survival, it is comparative luxury, young lady."

I wasn't entirely sure what to make of Charles, but what concerned me more at that moment was partial electricity. "Most of the day?" I asked Malcolm.

"The generator on the compound runs for 16 hours a day. From six a.m. to ten p.m." he winked at me and it reassured me. I was very thankful to be going with the Falks and not staying with Charles.

Ellen returned to the table carrying a large Dutch oven pot by its handles, her thumbs were stretched over a stack of bowls turned upside-down balanced on the top. She put the pot down in front of her plate and sat down. "Let's pray before my stew gets cold," she said and bowed her head and quickly prayed. She then passed the platter of fresh fruit and cheese around and then ladled a large portion of chicken stew into each bowl and passed them around. She surveyed the table to make sure everyone was eating and, looking visibly relieved that her task was accomplished, wiped her brow with a napkin and finally took a bite herself.

"Where did you get your cheese, Ellen?" Anna asked our hostess.

"A new grocery store opened up near the French Embassy. It's a little pricey, but I was really craving some cheese."

"Cheese?" I asked Anna.

"Oh, yes, Katherine, dairy products are very scarce and very expensive."

Clearly the adage "learn something new everyday" was to be my mission motto.

After lunch Charles brought out his guitar. He sang "Great is Thy Faithfulness" in a booming tenor while the rest of us listened. I tried to absorb the fact that I was actually here. Did it look the way I expected? Not really. And yet it was familiar. I watched the boys play soccer on the field. I looked at Ellen's little pots of herbs and

Chapter 2

flowering plants dotted around the porch and decided that the familiarity was in the living: working, playing, eating, universal tasks that we were all engaged in no matter where we lived.

Malcolm and Anna stood up. "It's time for rest hour, Katherine."

I looked at them, "Rest hour?"

"Well, it's called rest hour but it's actually three hours," Anna explained.

"You rest for three hours every afternoon?"

"Yes, Katherine." Malcolm smiled at me. "You don't have to rest, but the rest of the country does."

"It just seems like an awfully long time."

"You'll get used to it, trust me," Anna winked at me.

We all said thank you to Ellen and walked downstairs and next door to the Guest House. I retreated to my room laid down on my bed. The guinea fowl squawked incessantly outside my window and mopeds whizzed past bleating their wimpy horns. All of the smells and sounds were exotic and yet familiar at the same time. "Shouldn't I be feeling this amazing cross-cultural awakening or something profound? When do I start feeling like a missionary?" I asked myself. But I was simply exhausted. I slept until Anna woke me. It was dark and I felt disoriented.

"Come and sit with us in the kitchen for a little while," she said.

I followed her out and squinted in the fluorescent light. Malcolm sat in a woven love seat reading. "I guess the rest hour isn't long enough for you, eh?" he laughed.

I sat down in a chair. "I guess not."

"You need to stay up for a while to try to get on this time zone," he went back to his book.

"I didn't want Ellen to have to cook for us again so I'm just putting a light dinner together for us. I hope you'll eat something, Katherine?" Anna said to me from the kitchen.

"Oh, sure, thank you." What would I have done without Anna's help, I wondered.

We ate some soup and fresh baguette. I was quiet and barely ate. Anna watched me.

Ouagadougou

"You need to try to stay up at least another hour or so," she said to me.

"I don't know if I can make it. I think my two day travel extravaganza is catching up with me." I smiled at her, "I'm afraid I'm not much company tonight." I stood up to go back to my room.

"Tomorrow morning we need to buy some supplies and then I'd like to head out to Fada before rest hour," Malcolm said.

"Okay, goodnight." It took every ounce of energy I had to change into my sweats and a t-shirt before crawling in bed.

I was awake by 3:30 a.m. I lay there until dawn when I prepped myself by memory as the only mirror I had was the little one in my cosmetics case. The jetlag made me feel hung-over.

I pulled out my "missionary" wardrobe that my Mom had bought me from Sears. As it turned out they had a Safari line of clothes featuring a variety of African animals embroidered on the breast pocket of their polo shirts. She also bought me a selection of long cotton skirts because I was explicitly told women were still not to wear pants in the bush. I arrived at the breakfast table and sat down with everyone else.

I couldn't help but feel everyone kept looking at me. Maybe I was too self-conscious.

Ellen was the first to say anything, "Did you eat Mango yesterday at lunch?"

"Maybe. What is it?"

To which everyone at the table looked at me and laughed.

"What?"

"You have Mango rash!" Anna exclaimed.

"What is Mango rash?"

"Oh, it's just a red rash that you get on your face and neck. It's probably from eating local tropical fruit for the first time. It will go away in a few days and you shouldn't get it again," Ellen explained.

Everyone kept looking at me and smiling.

"What now?"

It was Malcolm who spoke up. "I'm sorry, I just have to ask, where did you get that shirt?"

"My shirt?"

Chapter 2

"Yes. Did you sew that elephant on it?"

"Me? No!" I looked down at my breast pocket, "No, my Mom bought me these at Sears."

"Sears?" They asked in unison.

"Yeah, I have five or six. They each have a different animal on the shirt pocket."

"Why would they sell shirts with African animals on them?" Malcolm asked.

"I don't know," I shrugged. "I guess all things African have become kind of trendy." Everyone stared at my left breast. "Is there something wrong with it?"

"It just seems so *American*, doesn't it?" Charles condescended.

"Why?" I asked.

"I don't know, just frivolous and silly. Sort of O-T-T, if you know what I mean."

"No, I don't. What's O-T-T?"

"Over-The-Top."

"Well, I guess when I'm here longer I'll start buying my clothes second hand and I'll fit in a little better." It was a smart comment and I shouldn't have said it, but Charles annoyed me.

"Perhaps so," he said and regarded me under his uni-brow.

And so I sat. My face sprinkled with Mango rash and everyone snickering at the lonely elephant on my breast. I slinked away after breakfast to hibernate in my monkish room. I lay down on the bed and stared up at the ceiling. Well, it wasn't the welcome I had expected, but what did I expect? I felt out of place. I tried to think on things that would give me courage. And suddenly I remembered John. His memory washed over me and I closed my eyes and remembered him holding me and wanting me. He seemed stronger, taller and generally more appealing at a distance. I held that picture in my mind and drifted off to sleep.

"Katherine?" I thought I heard. "Katherine?"

I opened my eyes and looked around. It was Anna outside my door. "Yes?"

"We need to go to the market now, we'll meet you out at the truck, okay?"

Ouagadougou

"I'll be right there." I glanced at my watch, it was almost 10 a.m. I got up and brushed my hair and teeth and met them outside.

"You look tired," Anna opened the passenger's door and climbed in the truck.

"I am," I said and got in the back seat behind her.

Malcolm exchanged a few of my vouchers the mission had given me for CFA, the local currency, or "Franc" of West Africa, to buy some groceries. We pulled out of the compound and I noticed someone in the flatbed out of the corner of my eye. I slowly turned around and realized that he had a gun. I leaned forward and said to Malcolm and Anna, "You all are aware that there is a man with a gun in the flatbed?"

Malcolm looked in the rear view mirror and Anna looked at me and smiled. "That's our guard."

"What do we need a guard for?" I sat back in my seat.

"We're going to be filling up the truck with all sorts of supplies and we have a lot of cash. It's just a precautionary measure."

I turned around and watched him. He waved and greeted every other person we passed while the AK-47 strapped across his chest occasionally clanked against the back window of the cab.

We stopped at the rambling outdoor market of thatched and corrugated tin roofed lean-tos and walked from stall to stall.

"You'll need to buy some fruit and vegetables here, Katherine," Anna explained. "They are much harder to get in Fada."

I spotted some lovely tomatoes and asked the woman how much she was charging. She blurted out, "800 Francs."

I looked at Anna, "Is that a good price?"

"No, and she doesn't expect you to pay that price. She wants you to haggle with her."

"500 Francs." I said to the woman in French.

She shook her head and looked thoroughly offended. "600."

I looked at Anna.

"Keep going."

"550," I countered.

The vendor shook her head again.

"Now, let's turn and walk away," Anna nudged me.

Chapter 2

We headed for the next stall when the woman yelled out behind us. "Madame!"

I turned around and she held up a plastic bag brimming with tomatoes, "550!"

I paid her and walked with Anna to the next stall. "That's a bit laborious for a bag of tomatoes, isn't it?"

"It's important to barter for everything." Anna picked up several cabbages and inspected them. "Africans say it's the western equivalent of arriving at a friend's home uninvited and asking, 'What's for dinner?'"

Anna handed the vendor three cabbages. I watched her barter back and forth. We walked away and the vendor yelled out behind us, "Madame!" Anna turned around and paid her with a 500-CFA note. And so it went through the entire market.

"I feel silly squabbling over what amounts to less than a dollar." I told Anna as we loaded our goods into the truck.

"Listen, I've been here 30 years and I still don't understand it, but I respect it and that's all you have to do."

We stopped at the new grocery store near the French Embassy that Ellen had mentioned. It was a simple cement building but there were shelves and refrigerated sections just like at home. And, every item had a price stamped on it so I was relieved not to barter. There were French cheeses and a large selection of European chocolates and biscuits.

Anna leaned over to me, "It's expensive, but buy a few nice things. You won't see anything like this for several months."

I purchased some Viennese cookies and several blocks of cheese. I also purchased several sticks of Toblerone figuring I had three or four PMS's to endure before I would see chocolate again. We loaded back into the truck and pulled into the fray of mopeds and bikes.

"Do you have everything you need, Mother?" Malcolm asked Anna.

"Yep, I think we're set." Anna had purchased a lot of staples like flour, sugar and canned goods that were all stacked up in the flatbed. Our guard sat on top of three layers of canned peas.

Ouagadougou

"I need to stop at the bank and then we can head back to the Guest House."
 Anna and I sat in the truck while Malcolm went into the bank. I rolled my window down all the way and watched the colorful bustle of activity. A legless man dragged his torso past our truck with his two strong arms. He looked up at me and flashed a disarmingly pearly smile as he made his way into the bank.
 Every other truck parked at the bank was a Toyota pick up or a Land Cruiser. All of them were white and had an agency or mission logo painted on the doors and a guard either sitting in the flatbed or standing next to the truck.
 "There aren't many ex-pats in Burkina." Anna followed my gaze. "If they're here they are with a mission or development agency or they are researchers."
 I noticed the street sign at the corner of the bank's parking lot. "Does that say Jimmy Carter Boulevard?" I read the sign out loud as I spoke.
 "Oh, yes, we're sitting at the intersection of Jimmy Carter Boulevard and Pope Paul IV."
 "Why would the Burkinabé honor Jimmy Carter?"
 "His organization has been helpful in assisting the government adopt democratic practices since it took over in 1983. That's when the name was changed from Upper Volta to Burkina Faso. The first democratic election is supposed to occur next summer."
 "Does Burkina Faso mean something?"
 "It means Land of the Upright Men in Mooré, the language of the Mossi tribe, the largest tribe in the country. We work and live with the Gourma tribe, a much smaller tribe in the East. Of course, they took over by staging a coup, but they have tried to implement some positive changes in education and health care," she rolled down her window further. "And, of course, the John Paul IV is to honor a visit made by the Pope a few years ago. When the French colonized they brought Catholicism with them. The French left in the 60's but the Catholics are still here and they have done terrific work in both education and health care, especially for disabled children."

— 40 —

Chapter 2

We watched Malcolm jog down the stairs in front of the bank and over to our truck. He said something to the guard, paid him and the guard hopped out of the flatbed and headed towards a different truck. Malcolm swung his leather bag through the window onto the seat next to Anna and then opened the door and settled behind the wheel.

"I saw James from SIL in there. I told him I'd leave our guard for him because we're heading back to the Guest House now and he's loaded with cash to pay for some construction they are doing."

I watched Anna tuck his bag on the floor between her legs and the passenger door.

Malcolm backed the truck out into the road and we were on our way. There were several mopeds around us as we stopped at our first traffic light. I noticed Malcolm glance in the rear view mirror. The light turned green and we took off. I noticed one moped pull up next to the left back quarter panel of the truck. I looked through the cab window and there was another on the right. I looked at Malcolm. He looked furtively in the rear view mirror. He couldn't speed up because of three mopeds directly in front of us. Suddenly the two mopeds sped off from behind us and the truck slowed. Malcolm pulled off to the right side of the road.

He got out of the truck and walked around the back. He appeared next to Anna. "They slashed our tires." He rubbed his chin and looked around.

"You're not serious?" She leaned out the window to look for herself. "Do you have some spares?"

"We've got one but I'll need to go buy another."

Anna got out and they both inspected the back right tire. I got out of my side and walked around the back of the truck to join them. There was a deep gash about four inches long. Malcolm knelt down and stuck his Swiss Army knife in the knurly gash while we watched. We looked up and saw a man lean into the passenger's side window and grab Malcolm's leather bag. He ran and hopped on the back of a waiting moped and the two zoomed off into the fray.

I looked at Malcolm, "Your bag!"

He watched the thieves disappear into the traffic.

Ouagadougou

I waited for him to explode. To yell! To cuss! To hop up and down and say how miserable life was and how unfair! How he'd dedicated his life to helping these people and they turn around and do that to him!

I looked at Anna. Surely she would be mad? Certainly she would blame him for releasing the guard? Would she tell him what a stupid idea that was? Now look at what happened?

"But," I looked back at Malcolm. "Shouldn't you call the police? Chase after them?" I looked to Anna; "Do *something*?"

"I need to go buy another tire so we can get back to the Guest House." Malcolm said to Anna. "You all stay here." He turned and jogged back towards the shops.

"How will he pay for the tire?" I asked Anna.

"The mission has a credit with the auto supplies store." She opened the door and climbed in her seat.

I joined her in the truck. She pulled out her thermos and filled up a plastic cup with hot tea and offered it to me. "Tea?"

I took it from her. "Thanks."

She filled one up for herself and sipped it. I felt edgy.

"Anna, what just happened?"

"Oh, thieves work in gangs. They probably watched us release our guard at the bank and followed us. They slashed our tires to distract us and it worked." She shrugged. "We had heard of it happening but it's never happened to us before."

We sipped our tea in silence.

"Shouldn't you call the police or something?"

"Malcolm probably will when we get back to the Guest House. But, we won't see the money again and they won't try to catch the thieves."

"Why not?"

"Because it's not really considered a crime to be a thief. It's not respected, mind you, but it's kind of expected that if you can't do anything else you'll become a thief."

"Why?"

"It's just survival," she sipped her tea. "Everyone is expected to do what ever they can to help their families and people survive."

Chapter 2

"Will you be reimbursed?"

"We'll talk to Charles when we get back to the Guest House," she nodded mostly to herself. "We'll take care of it."

I finished my tea and put the cup down on the seat next to me. I looked out the window again. Suddenly I felt all the smiles and the greetings from the Burkinabé were sinister: that they were really laughing at us naive white people, waiting to take advantage of us. I quickly rolled up the window and crossed my arms over my chest.

Anna looked at me over her teacup. "It's not easy, Katherine," she sighed. "It's a complex place with sets of rules we don't always understand. But, the Africans are strong survivors. Most of the people are gentle and gracious because life is so hard for them." She sipped her tea and gazed out the window.

I looked at her profile. The sun had wrinkled her face. Her hair was probably a soft red before the gray began to conquer. She didn't wear any makeup but her almond eyes lit up when she smiled. She seemed to me completely, utterly unflappable.

She looked at me again and smiled her kind smile. "A year seems like a long time right now."

I nodded, "Yeah, it does." I quickly looked away from her so she couldn't see the tears well up in my eyes.

"You won't want to leave," she whispered to me.

We sat in silence the next 92 minutes waiting for Malcolm to return.

Malcolm changed the tires on the truck and we returned to the Guest House. We unloaded our goods while Anna fixed us a snack in the Guest House kitchen. The three of us sat down at the table.

I looked at the slices of fresh tomatoes, three bottles of Fanta and ever-present baguette. I smiled thinking of how meager it would look at home.

"I know we've almost missed rest hour today, Mother, but I would like to depart after our snack," Malcolm looked at Anna. I glanced at my watch: it was almost two p.m.

"I don't mind missing my rest, I would like to get home, too," she said.

"May we hold hands to pray, please?" Malcolm asked us.

Ouagadougou

Anna took my hand and his.

"Lord, we thank you for your provision. We thank you for always taking care of us. And, we pray for those who need to take from others. Have mercy on us all."

I looked at Malcolm's leathery hand holding mine. It was deeply tanned with brown spots all over the knuckles. I looked at Anna's. Hers was fair but also deeply wrinkled and her nubby nails seemed to tell their own story. I wasn't sure if they had finished praying. I looked up to see that their heads were still bowed and their eyes were closed. I waited in silence.

Malcolm looked up, "Well, it's not much of a welcome to Burkina –but don't let it put you off." He broke off a piece of bread from the baguette and salted it. He looked me in the eye. "You know, Katherine, we need you here."

I was relieved to hear him say that after feeling so awkward. But then I felt uneasy being 'needed.' What did that mean? What if I couldn't meet their expectations? He watched me with his milk chocolate eyes; they were perfectly round like a Teddy Bear's and studied me with the same steady warmth. He popped the last of his bread into his mouth.

"I'm glad to be here," I admitted at last.

"Good," he said. And that settled it.

After our snack Malcolm went to speak with Charles while we loaded the truck. It was almost three p.m. by the time we pulled out of the gates and headed east out of Ouagadougou as the city was waking up from rest hour. Malcolm had tied a blue tarp over the flatbed that was full of food and building materials. "Fada N'Gourma means 'market of the Gourma's'," Malcolm explained as we came to a stop to allow a herd of miniature goats and a large steer cross the road. Two young boys waved sticks and hollered directions at them to coerce them across the road. "The Gourma's are a peaceful tribe." We left the last baguette seller and the bustle of the rambling capitol city behind as Malcolm zoomed into the bush countryside.

Every few miles we passed a compound of mud huts with thatched roofs built in a large circle. "The government has asked everyone to move closer to the main roads so that they can reach the people in

Chapter 2

times of famine or if they need medical assistance." Malcolm explained over his shoulder to me.

I nodded and continued to look out the window. "Who lives in these compounds?"

"It's normally a large extended family with a patriarch and all his wives, children and parents."

I watched a woman pumping water into a large tin bucket with an infant strapped onto her back by a swath of green and yellow fabric. A young boy ran waving a stick at two miniature goats as they disappeared around the side of a hut.

The sun baked land stretched on as brown and cracked as far as the eye could see. Baobab trees added texture to the landscape. Their knotted branches seemed to be confused as to which way they wanted to grow. One tree's branches had grown into the shape of a 'W' that resembled my Grandma's shaky cursive writing. Another we passed had decided to favor one side so the trunk bent to support its lopsidedness. There were also thorny trees without foliage that seemed to me to be downright cruel in this needy sub-Saharan climate.

Mud hut compounds lined the road as we headed into the suburbs of Fada N'Gourma two hours later. The traffic of women and children walking along the road increased so Malcolm slowed the truck and they both rolled down their windows. The air was warm and humid. Women nodded gracefully as we passed and Anna and Malcolm waved and nodded to everyone we drove by. "Choin-choin-chene," they said.

"Is that a greeting?" I asked.

"Yes, it's Gourmantché," Anna explained: "It means how are you, your husband, your wives, children, grandparents—everyone," she explained. "They will still greet you that way even though you're single."

"And I have no children?"

She smiled, "Yes, this society doesn't exactly know what to do with single women—we're seeing more in the cities now—but out in the bush there has really been no role for them."

Ouagadougou

I pondered this idea. Anna continued, "It's slowly changing, but a barren woman in this society has no place—it is justification for the man to take another wife or send her back to her father's home—the pressure is enormous." She nodded to herself. "In Niamey, which is a much larger city,"

"We had a lay over there yesterday morning," I interjected.

"Yes," she nodded. "The mission built a four-plex apartment building. One married couple and three single women lived in it," she smiled and shook her head remembering. "Well, during a church meeting the issue of polygamy came up and one of the local church leaders said, 'But that missionary lives in the new building with his first wife and three other wives.'"

"Really?"

"There are different cultural assumptions, ones that still surprise even us."

Malcolm slowed the truck, turned left and stopped in front of a burgundy colored metal gate with a sun-bleached sign that read, "Mission Protestante."

"We're home!" Anna exclaimed. Immediately a man popped his head out and then swung open the gate. He jumped up and down waving his machete in the air. Both Malcolm and Anna laughed and waved.

"That's Danjou," Anna enthused. "He lives on the compound with his family and helps us out with just about everything."

I watched Danjou pull the gate all the way back to let the truck through. His brown T-shirt hung on him barely attached over the shoulders by stubborn threads and his shorts, that were once pants, were cut off at the shin and he was barefoot. His outfit was reminiscent of Mr. Hulk's, post mutation. Danjou set about his work with the confidence that comes from being appreciated.

Danjou leaned into the driver's window to speak with Malcolm. His eyes startled me: they were brilliant blue. I tried to catch his eye to smile at him but he didn't look at me. We continued into the compound and he closed the gates behind us.

"His eyes are blue," I said to Anna.

Chapter 2

"Occasionally you will see a blue-eyed African. It could be a freak of genes or maybe Danjou has some white ancestors," Anna nodded. Whenever Anna spoke she nodded in the affirmative as if agreeing with the words once they reached her own ears.

Malcolm parked the truck in the shade of an expansive Flamboyant tree: its arms reached out welcoming us into its regal court, its wax-green leaves rustled in the breeze. I got out and stretched my legs and looked around at the collection of white mud-brick houses that made up the compound. The compound was about the size of a football field. The smell of open fires filled my nose.

"That's your house." Anna pointed back across the compound to a small, rectangular white mud brick house sitting next to the gate through which we had just come. All the windows were covered with iron thief-proofing.

I had never had a whole house to myself. "The whole thing?"

"Yes, until we have visitors. Then you may have to share a room if our Guest House fills up."

"Sure."

"Let me get the key and I'll show you your new home."

"I'll put Katherine's trunk on her stoop, Mother," Malcolm called to us.

I followed Anna to her house where we entered through a screened door with a ruffled yellow curtain into the kitchen, the door clapped gently shut behind us. I looked around while Anna rummaged through several different keys hanging on a hook. The kitchen was square but separated into two sections by a bar covered with orange Formica. There was a doorway in the opposite corner leading into the rest of the house and a large window over the kitchen sink that looked back over the parking area. Potatoes and onions dangled in netted bags from the ceiling and a gas lighter nestled in it's own custom holder to the left of the oven. The appliances were circa 1940's America but everything was well ordered and absolutely pristine.

"Okay, I think I've got the correct key," she announced.

"Your kitchen is spotless," I commented as I looked at the sink with two sponges standing at attention on their sides.

Ouagadougou

"I spend a lot of time in here," she nodded and I followed her back out the door and across the dusty compound to my house. She waved a flock of guinea fowl out of the way and they responded with shrieks and squawks.

"They're so loud," I said. I was amused to notice that the black chicken-like bird actually had little white polka-dots that seemed an incongruous touch of whimsy on God's part. "Polka-dotted, too?"

"Polka-dotted, loud, and stupid," she agreed. We walked through the opened gate of a simple wire fence around the house that made a yard. It was overgrown with bush grass in parts and other spots were bare. "I'm afraid the yard has been neglected since Elinor left—she was a keen gardener and built the fence to try and keep the animals from grazing on her herbs and vegetables," she said. "Danjou was going to cut back some of this bush grass for you." We stepped up on the stoop where my trunk sat with my cosmetic case and purse on top of it and Anna unlocked the padlock to the corrugated tin door with the second key. She pulled that open revealing a screened door. The tin door opened all the way and leaned against the house. "You only need to shut the tin door at night."

I followed Anna inside to a small pantry with shelves on two sides of the wall and a doorway leading into the kitchen. She hung the padlock key on a nail next to the door. "Keep the padlock key there, or you'll lose it."

"It's not very grand to walk right into your pantry but the house was designed for efficiency, not really for show." She waved her hand around, "It's a place to store your dry ingredients and other bulky items."

She turned left and I followed her into the long, narrow galley style kitchen. The retro refrigerator and the gas stove stood on either side of the kitchen sink that had a large window looking back over the whole compound. "Malcolm built some shelves for you." The cabinets didn't have doors but simple green curtains covered a variety of canned foods.

"Did you make the curtains, Anna?"

She inspected the stitches on the hem and dropped them back into place, "It was just a quickie job," she shrugged.

Chapter 2

She pulled open the fridge; "I put several bottles of Coke and Fanta in here for you and some cinnamon buns for breakfast."

"Thanks. Did you make those, too?"

"I have to make everything here, Katherine." She patted a tall plastic contraption on the counter next to the refrigerator. "This is your water filter. Just dump the water in the top and it filters down to the bottom."

I followed her into a sitting room. Several Gecko lizards looked at us from the walls and scampered behind curtains. There were two single beds pushed against the wall shaped in an "L" with wool blankets on top of them for decoration. There was a table with four folding chairs in front of the kitchen and then a small desk under the window of the far wall. "They are beds but they can act as couches until they are needed for guests." Plastic woven mats with designs of mosques covered the cement floors. Anna caught my eye. "They are Muslim prayer mats, they are the only type of floor covering we can find in the market here."

"It all looks very nice."

"We put some books in here for you as well," she waved her arm towards the hand made bookcase. "Someone sent us Louis Lamour's entire collection last year so that will start you off. Once you finish those we have most of the classics in our shed."

I walked over and examined the desk. It sat under the window that faced the compound wall and the Fada Road beyond.

"I still think of this as Elinor's house."

"How long did she live here?"

"She lived here for 20 some years until she retired back to Canada a few years ago. She was very frail and died last year. She wanted to die out here but Malcolm, her supporters, and the mission all wanted her to go home. She was sick and needed assistance. It's very sad, actually, when missionaries retire after spending their lives out here. When they return home they find many of their contemporaries are either dead or in Florida and it can be very lonely."

She sighed and continued, "Elinor sat at this desk many hours a day translating the New Testament into Gourmantché, the language of the Gourma's, she said it was the best spot in the house to write."

Ouagadougou

Anna looked at me, "The New Testament was printed last year just before her death."

"She lived in this house for more than 20 years?"

"Yes, we've had some visitors but you're the first one to live in it since she retired. The Geckos have really taken over in here and there are bats above your ceiling that flop around at night, so consider yourself forewarned. We found something like 80 Gecko eggs when we cleaned your house out a few weeks ago and I'm sure there are more we didn't find. But, they won't hurt you, and they do eat a lot of bugs, but they leave a lot of droppings in their wake."

Anna walked up to Elinor's writing table and adjusted the piece of orange and green cloth that served as a tablecloth. She smoothed the corners, "It's strange to think about, really."

"What's that?" I wondered.

"That Elinor did the work the Lord wanted her to do in this life and now she's with Him in a new life." She looked at me, "I'm sure He welcomed her as a good and faithful servant."

I wasn't sure how to respond to Anna. I had never heard anyone talk about death, or heaven, in such a matter of fact way. But she wasn't looking for a response from me.

"Let me show you the rest of the house," she said.

I followed her down the narrow hallway that ran behind the kitchen and turned left into the bathroom. Anna kicked the door open, stood a moment and then walked inside.

"Is karate chopping the door a necessary exercise?" I teased.

"Well, it is if you don't like lizards falling on your head."

"Falling on your head?"

"I don't know why, but they seem to like to rest on top of the doors." She looked at me; "they're not very cuddly animals." Anna smiled, "We were dedicating the new church last year and one missed a step and fell off the ceiling and right down Gritty's dress!" She laughed mischievously, "Boy, did that surprise her!"

"Gritty?"

She waved her hand. "Gertrude—she goes by Gritty—and Stan Wauken live over there across the compound. You can't miss all of Stan's rusty water drums stacked on top of one another from some

Chapter 2

cockeyed invention of his that he never finished, but they're on holiday." She pursed her lips together. "They are due back any time now."

Her whole demeanor had changed. "Are they missionaries?"

"Oh yes, they've been out here as long as we have. They met out here as single missionaries." She softened. "They're Americans, too, so you'll have something in common."

She waved her arm around. "Anyway, here's the bathroom."

"It's huge!" I said.

"It was built as a second bedroom before it was a bathroom. I think indoor plumbing was installed about 15 years ago," she nodded.

A French style toilet sat in the corner with a knob that you pull from the top to flush. There was a standing sink with a fresh bar of pink soap and a shower in the corner. "Danjou will pump your water every morning from the ground well into a metal drum that sits on top of your house."

"Okay," I looked around.

"The water sits up on top of the house in the sun all day, so if you want a warm shower the best time to take one is during rest hour."

"That's good advice," I remembered my torturous shower yesterday in Ouaga.

She completed a circle ending in the bedroom that had a doorway leading back into the kitchen. A single bed stood in the middle of the room with a ballet pink mosquito net hanging above it from the ceiling. "We thought you might want to use this." Anna reached up and pulled the sides down to show me how to use the netting.

"Don't you use mosquito nets?" I asked her.

"No, we haven't used them in years."

"What about anti-malarial tablets?"

"Nope," she said. "Some of the medication is worse than getting malaria."

"I'm taking Chloroquine and it gives me terrible headaches."

"I know, but you need to take it," she tucked the netting in under the mattress. "Once you get in bed you tuck the sides in under your mattress, but during the day just keep it bundled on top of itself."

I watched her toss the sides back up.

Ouagadougou

A chest of drawers sat next to the wall. "These are empty," she pulled some of the drawers open to show me. "All four of my kids used this dresser," she patted the top and sighed. A neatly ironed embroidered cloth decorated the top.

"Where are your kids?"

"Well, three are back in Canada. But our eldest son, Daniel, his wife, and their kids are missionaries in Mahadaga."

"Where's Mah-dogga?"

"It's a bush outpost in the southern part of the country, near the border of Benin," she explained. "Actually, you'll visit Mahadaga in a few days."

"Really?"

"Yes, Janet, one of our colleague missionaries, purchased a car from another couple who just left on furlough and left the car with us. So, I think Malcolm wants you to drive her car, following us in our truck full of supplies, to deliver it to Mahadaga where they are all stationed. They are expanding the dispensary so we're going to deliver them some much- needed building supplies that Malcolm purchased in Ouaga. They are all extremely busy." She smoothed the cloth. "We were just waiting until you and Fiona arrived."

"Fiona?"

"Fiona Keys is a dear old friend. She served as a nurse here with us for many years before retiring back to Scotland. I think her flight comes in today and she insisted on taking a bush taxi out to Fada. She'll be staying with us here in Fada for a few weeks."

"Sounds good," I smiled.

I followed her back into the kitchen and spotted a neatly printed calendar nailed to the wall next to the stove. "You have made me feel very welcome," I waved my arm around the kitchen. "I really had no idea what to expect."

Anna looked around with satisfaction, "Well, I'm glad you like it." She headed towards the screened door. "Our colleague Philippe Godido, he is the President of the local church, and his wife Miriam have invited us all over to their home tonight for dinner."

"I didn't expect a social engagement my first night here."

Chapter 2

She chuckled, "We do stay busy with the Guest House and many visitors. It's an important courtesy for us to introduce you to Philippe."

I followed Anna out the door. We stood on the cement stoop and looked around. "The dinner fires are going strong," she breathed in deeply. It was after five. "Well, you'll want to take a few minutes to unpack and settle in. We will come back for you and walk to the Godido's together in about an hour."

"Thanks," I watched her walk across the compound to her house. I lugged my stuff into the bedroom when suddenly someone *clap clapped* their hands outside my door. I walked to the screened door to find a man standing there.

"Madame!" he exclaimed as I unlatched and pushed open the door.

"Oui?" I looked down to find a pig with its body sliced completely open and its muddy hooves and head still attached lay sprawled over his wheelbarrow. He waved swarming flies away from the bloody mess and smiled a toothless grin.

I held one hand over my mouth and nose and with the other I held up my index finger, "Un moment." I darted out of my gate, across the compound and banged on Anna's kitchen door.

"Yes, come in." she called from behind the ruffled curtain on her screened door. I pushed open the door.

"Anna, there is a man with a dead pig in a wheelbarrow at my door." I tried to catch my breath.

"Oh, it's the meat man."

"It's definitely a man with meat."

"Don't you want any meat?"

"It's covered in flies and disgusting!"

"Oh," she waved her hand, "it will be fine once you cook it."

"Well, I don't know what to order." I held up my hands, "I mean, the only meat I've ever had is from a store... it comes on these little pink Styrofoam plates wrapped in Saran wrap." She pulled off her apron and headed out the door. I followed her across the compound trying to defend myself, "I mean, I know what a *leg* is. That much I could figure out but I'm not sure where chops come from, you

— 53 —

Ouagadougou

know?" I had to jog to keep up with her, "What does 'chop' mean anyway, when you stop and think about it." I shrugged. She shot me a glance. I shut up.

We arrived at the meat man who was standing patiently next to his pig. He took off his baseball cap and bowed deeply as Anna approached. She looked over the beast.

She pointed to a red band on a back leg of the pig. "If the pig has a red band it means it was killed and inspected in the market today. If it doesn't have a band then don't buy it."

I nodded trying to hold my breath. She waved the flies away and gave the meat man instructions in Gourmantché. He made a clicking sound in the back of his throat and rolled the wheelbarrow away.

"I told him you wanted some chops and some ground pork. He will give it to Danjou to prep for you, okay?"

"Thank you very much."

"It's not going to be on pink Styrofoam."

I laughed uncomfortably. "I'm…I…well…I have a lot to learn."

She looked at me closely. "This is all really new to you, isn't it?"

"It is."

"Many of the short-termers that come through here are from Canadian farming families. It's just been in the last ten years or so that we're getting more from the cities. We find the adjustment to bush living for the city folks is much tougher," she mused. "The agrarian communities live much closer to the land, like the Africans. Instinctively they have much more in common than the city people."

"Well, than I'm even worse because I'm not from the city either! I'm from the D.C. suburbs of residential neighborhoods and strip malls. The only time I saw a farm was driving by in a car on family vacations."

She walked towards my gate and stopped and bent over a plant with long slender grass-like leaves. "This is mint, by the way," she pulled a couple leaves a handed them to me. "It makes lovely tea."

"Neat." I took the leaves from her and rubbed them together. A fresh spearmint smell tingled in my nose.

"You can make tea, can't you?" she smiled.

"That's water—in a kettle—boiled. Right?"

Chapter 2

She headed back to her kitchen.

I returned to my bedroom and unlocked my trunk. I organized my clothes in the dresser drawers and hung my skirts in the closet. It didn't take very long. I placed my cosmetic case on top of the dresser and left it open as a make-shift vanity table. I placed my purse with my passport, open-ended plane ticket and money in the empty trunk and locked it. I slid it into the bottom of the closet. There was a full-length mirror next to the closet. It was slightly warped so it made my head look enlarged; very unflattering.

I went back into the kitchen and poked around. I took out a Coke and opened it on the bottle opener conveniently hanging on a nail to the right of the sink. I could see Malcolm and Anna's house and the Guest House from my kitchen window. I sipped my Coke and watched Malcolm and Anna walk across the compound towards my house, Malcolm grabbed Anna's hand and squeezed it and she smiled at him. I met them on my stoop.

"Do you have your torch, Katherine?" Malcolm asked.

"My torch?"

"Your flashlight," he translated for me.

"Oh, let me go and get that," I darted to my room and retrieved the lime green flashlight, another Wal-Mart purchase.

"Is everything you own fluorescent green?" Malcolm asked as I joined them on the stoop.

"It's silly, isn't it? But, it seemed everything was either green or purple right now."

Both Malcolm and Anna looked at me with complete astonishment. "Why?" Anna asked.

"I don't know," and suddenly it seemed ridiculous to me, too. "I don't know."

"You always want to carry your torch at night, Katherine. When there is no moon it is extremely dark and there are no streetlights. Also, animals will generally run away from the light so it's good to carry it with you."

I stepped off the stoop behind them and followed them out of my yard and turned left. "Ah, what kind of animals?"

— 55 —

Ouagadougou

Both of them laughed, "Just don't look too closely, dear," Anna said. We walked past the church and then into a section of round mudbrick huts with thatched roofs. Every home had an open fire with dinner bubbling away in pots above the small flames. Little kids peered out from the hut doorways and women looked up and nodded as we meandered through. The ground was mud and various liquids pooled along the uneven path. Chickens pecked here and there while the more expensive goats were tied up. The familiar and yet mingling smells of urine, barn animals, burning wood, and leather all filled my senses. The compound was alive with chatter, with purpose, after all it was dinner time.

"What are they cooking?" I asked.

"Saabu," Anna nodded. "It's a heavy, gray mush made from millet. It's their staple and they eat it with a variety of sauces. It takes all day long to cook to achieve that consistency," she nodded. "We'll probably eat it tonight. The best advice I can give you is to swallow the Saabu, savor the sauce."

I followed Malcolm and Anna out of the residential section into an open field where a blue adobe structure stood near the back gate.

"We've basically cut diagonally through the compound," Malcolm explained. "The Wauken's run this pharmacy."

"I didn't think they were back from holiday yet," Anna said. "But, the door to the pharmacy is open."

I followed Malcolm and Anna inside the round structure. A Gourma man stood behind the counter with a white lab coat on with *Bob* embroidered in red on the breast pocket. He smiled broadly and greeted us. Malcolm introduced me to Etienne, a full time employee in the pharmacy.

"I didn't think his name would be Bob," I said to Anna.

She smiled, "No, it's Etienne. But, we get so many things secondhand I don't even notice it anymore."

Gritty shuffled out from a back room and Stan came out behind her and scurried around her to beat her to the counter. Malcolm introduced us and I shook their hands.

"Where'ya from in the States?" Stan asked.

Chapter 2

"I'm from Virginia, outside Washington, D.C.," he headed back to the back room. "Good to have you here," he called over his shoulder.

Gritty propped herself up against the counter. "So, how long are you here for?" she asked.

"A year."

"That's just a long vacation, you'll have just unpacked," she waved her hand.

"C'mon, Gertrude, it's a good amount of time." Malcolm chastised her. "Anyway, I need the help."

She snorted and looked around.

"Did you have a good holiday?" Anna asked.

"I'm glad to be back in my own bed. But, we've got lots of catching up to do," it was hard for me to read her, I couldn't tell if she were rude or just indifferent.

"We'll be heading off to Mahadaga in a couple days. Fiona Keys is coming and Katherine is going to drive the Corolla for us."

Gritty nodded. "Good."

Malcolm and Anna said good-bye and we stepped out of the pharmacy and continued our journey to Philippe's house.

"She was friendly," I joked.

Anna waved her hand, "Gritty is put upon. Don't worry about her."

We walked through the back gate of the compound and out onto a paved road. Mud brick huts were interspersed with square cement houses with completely flat roofs. We stepped up to the opened front door of one of the newer cement homes. Malcolm clapped twice. A tall, Gourma man with a salt and pepper beard filled the doorway, he wore a long kaftan with intricate embroidery around the neck. He and Malcolm clasped hands and exchanged greetings in Gourma, bowing their heads back and forth to one another. There was great warmth between the two men.

Philippe greeted Anna with equal genuineness and then turned to me. Malcolm explained to him in French that I had come to help him organize the office.

"Welcome," he said to me in English and bowed his head.

"Thank you," I said and bowed my head instinctively.

Ouagadougou

Malcolm and Anna slid off their shoes and left them on the stoop. I followed suit. We sat down on Muslim prayer mats arranged around a low wood table. It was a large open room with one chair and a single light bulb hanging from the ceiling. Philippe's wife Miriam and his two daughters came through a back doorway and served everyone a small white tin pot decorated with orange and red painted flowers. Miriam joined us on the floor but the girls disappeared through the back door again.

The conversation ensued in Gourmantché. I smiled and tried to participate but truly I had no idea what was being said. Occasionally Anna would look to me from her mat, her legs tucked neatly underneath her left side, and enlighten me.

"The new school building will be ready for classes in September," she said.

"Oh, good," I nodded.

The two teenage girls returned from the back of the house carrying two oversized tin bowls. They were also white with orange and blue flowers painted around them. They put them down near Miriam and left.

"Her daughters," Anna said.

One of the bowls was piled high with cooked spaghetti. It had a reddish tint to it as if it had some kind of sauce on it. The other bowl had a brothy sauce with pieces of white meat in it. Miriam worked her way around the table. She took the tops off of our little pots that contained Saabu and ladled the broth on top of it. She pulled two spoons out of her pocket and handed one to me.

"Merci," I smiled. Miriam smiled at me with that African smile that is hard to discern whether they are charmed or think you're a complete moron.

"Use the spoon to scoop some Saabu and sauce," Anna explained as she took her spoon from Miriam. "Just remember: swallow the Saabu and savor the sauce."

I followed Anna's direction. The Saabu was like eating tasteless oatmeal but the sauce was quite spicy. After we finished our Saabu Miriam carried the pot of spaghetti around. I watched everyone scoop out a portion with his or her right hand and eat it from their hand.

Chapter 2

After the meal was complete the daughters appeared again with a large pot of water and two towels. We dipped and dried our hands.

Malcolm and Philippe were engaged in a deep, and by all appearances, enthralling conversation. Suddenly there was a loud creak from the tin roof. I looked at Anna.

"What was that?" I asked.

She shrugged, "Sounds like the house is settling, it's relatively new."

Miriam clapped her hands together and leaned to the side. She said something in Gourma that sounded more like a song.

I looked at Anna, "She said the house gods are active tonight. They must know we have visitors."

Miriam clapped her hands again.

"Is she serious?" I asked Anna again.

"Oh, yes," she said and smiled at Miriam.

The daughters returned to collect the last bowls. Miriam stood up to signal that dinner was over. They walked us out into the night.

"Merci," I said and bowed my head like Malcolm and Anna. I flipped on my flashlight and waited for Malcolm and Anna to finish their goodbyes.

"There is a lot of activity out here," I commented to no one in particular as we walked home.

"Oh, yes, Katherine," Malcolm said. "It's much cooler at night and especially when there is a moon a lot of business is accomplished. The Africans don't keep a nine to five schedule, at least not in the bush."

We walked down the street along the outside of the compound wall and then turned left on the Fada Road and walked until we came upon the burgundy gates.

Men and women on bicycles rang their bells and called out, "Bonsoir!" Moped lights illuminated our path and then they scooted past leaving us in darkness again. As we reached the main gates the ground began to rumble.

"What is that?"

"Probably a convoy of trucks," Malcolm explained as we all stepped off the road and stood next to the gates. We could see other

Ouagadougou

people move off the road and hop off of their bicycles. The rumble intensified when three semi-tractor trailer trucks came barreling down the narrow street flinging small pebbles and dust in their wake. They were heading East towards Ouagadougou. The noise was deafening. Once they passed we brushed the dust off ourselves and Malcolm opened the gates for us.

"Who were they?" I asked Malcolm.

Malcolm fumbled to close the gate behind us. I looked at the large fluorescent light that stood above Anna's kitchen and lit a path towards their house. My house was completely dark, I had not thought to turn on an outside light.

"Probably convoys of illegal arms or mercenaries traveling late at night. They service any rebel group or government willing to pay them," the gravel crunched under our feet towards their house. "The problem is they travel at night on unlit roads much too fast and end up killing themselves or other people. The roads are littered with burned out shells of trucks—there is nothing left of them—but the government has no money or mechanism to dispose of them. It's all very secretive."

Malcolm stopped supposedly to drop me off at my house. It looked gray and spooky in the night. Anna didn't miss a beat, "Would you like me to walk you to your house?"

"Would you?" I asked. "Thank you."

"Goodnight, Katherine," Malcolm hurried on. "I need to do a little work in the office and then I'll be in, Mother."

"Goodnight," I called to Malcolm.

I followed Anna to my gate and up onto the stoop. I fumbled to find the key in my pocket. "It's bringing back a lot of memories having you here," she said. "When we arrived we had to build the houses—no one had come before us—and there was no electricity—it was much harder than it is now."

"I'm sure I seem like a complete wimp to you," I finally got the padlock opened and pulled open the tin door. We stepped inside to the dark pantry and Anna turned on the light for me.

"No, it's not you. It just puts the lack of progress here into relief. Change is very slow here, and things at home are moving forward all

Chapter 2

the time. I'm not sure which one is better, but it's fascinating to me." Anna turned on the light in the kitchen. "Here's the outdoor light, too," she showed me.

"Was Miriam serious about her house god tonight?" I asked Anna.

Anna searched my face and then stopped at my eyes. I could almost see her wondering how much to tell me. "This is a very spiritual place and I mean all kinds of spirits.

"Legend credits this area as the birthplace of Voodoo which was exported with the slaves to the Caribbean. The witch doctors in the villages still wield extraordinary powers over the tribes," she nodded as she spoke. I leaned against the counter and she did, too. I was glad she was staying. "This is a very spiritual place, it's good to be aware of that. But, don't dwell on it. Always remember that God is stronger and in control."

I looked at her, "Now you have me spooked."

She waved her hand, "Don't be spooked. Just remember where your strength comes from if you need it." She headed towards the door. "Lock up behind me. We'll see you in the morning."

I pulled the tin door closed and then let the screened door shut. I stood at the kitchen window and watched her flashlight bob across the compound and disappear around the corner of her house. I changed into my sweats and a t-shirt and pulled the sides of the net down before crawling into bed. I moved around the entire bed meticulously tucking in every inch of netting. I watched all manner of insects land on the net but I was secure in my pink cocoon, until I rolled over and realized that I had left the lights on.

3
Drive Me to Mahadaga

"Have you ever driven manual before, dear?" Fiona asked me in her Glaswegian accent from the passenger's seat.
    I looked at her, "You mean stick?"
    To which she brought her hands to her mouth like a small mouse and giggled behind them, "Stick?"
    "This," I wiggled the gear shift, "is a stick."
    "Oh, of course, dear," she giggled. I rolled my eyes and shook my head.
    Malcolm walked across the driveway towards our car that was parked under the Flamboyant tree. I rolled down the window. It was overcast and extremely humid.
    "Are you all ready?" he asked.
    "I'm ready." I said. He leaned down and looked passed me to Fiona.
    "Fiona?"
    "Oh, I'm fine dear. I'm just a wee passenger."
    "Now, you do have your International driver's license?"
    "Yes." I was mystified by the importance he placed on this $5 jobbie I had picked up at the Triple A. I bought it because it was on the list the mission agency sent me, but it seemed a bit of a joke with my passport picture stapled haphazardly on the inside of the flimsy green tri-fold. I pulled it out. "You do mean this, right?"
    "Ah, yes. Please keep it with your passport at all times." He pulled two letters out of his shirt pocket and handed them to me. I immediately recognized the sprawling writing and my face reddened. "And, these arrived for you this morning."

Chapter 3

I looked at the postmark and realized John had mailed them two weeks before I left! I tucked them under my leg. "Thanks." Fiona and Malcolm glanced at one another.

"Well, just follow me then," Malcolm continued. "I'm worried that it might rain and wash out some of the roads or bridges closer to Mahadaga. But, if we don't take it now it will be three months before we can reach them again."

"Why?" I asked.

"Because once rainy season really sets in none of the roads near Mahadaga will be passable until they dry up." He tapped on the roof of Janet's Toyota Corolla. "Plus, they need these supplies to finish the construction before the rains set in."

We watched Anna close the padlock on her kitchen door and lug an oversized picnic basket to the passenger's side of the truck. She turned and waved at us before crawling in. We waved back.

"Anna is so lovely," Fiona murmured to herself.

"Let's get going then," Malcolm gave a final tap on the roof and jogged to his truck. He tightened the ropes holding a tarp in place across the flatbed and climbed in behind the wheel.

I pulled the Corolla out of the compound's gated entrance behind the white pick-up truck. Danjou waved us through and closed the compound gate behind us. I stalled and quickly restarted the Corolla's engine and lurched forward to catch up with Malcolm on the Fada Road. I glanced at Fiona who quickly pulled her seat belt on. She caught my eye.

"Nothing personal, dear," she clicked her belt into place and neatly rearranged her skirt. She cracked her window allowing some much-needed breeze into the stuffy car. The wind lifted wispy white curls on top of her head and gently laid them down. She breathed in deeply and out again.

"Oh, the smell of Africa," she explained, "I have missed it."

I cracked my window and sniffed. "All I smell is pee with a dying campfire thrown in."

"You'll smell it soon enough, dear," she gazed out the window. "And it will stay with you forever."

Drive Me to Mahadaga

Black clouds rose up from the horizon as if God were filling up a cup of coffee. We were eventually drowned in darkness when the sky opened and dumped rain and hail with such force I struggled to see the taillights of Malcolm's truck.

The windshield fogged. Fiona produced a monogrammed hankie from her shirt and wiped the windshield for me.

"Thank you," I said.

"I think he's pulling over, dear." Fiona wiped the screen again.

I shifted down and pumped the brakes as a seasoned veteran of icy D.C. winters. I stopped the car behind Malcolm's truck off to the right side of the road. Malcolm shielded his face as he ran towards our car. I rolled the window down further. Rain pounded my arm and face but it felt good.

"We're going to sit this one out," he had to yell over the rain and pelting hail.

"Okay!" I yelled back.

"Keep the engine running and your lights on," he instructed.

"Fine, will do," I rolled the window back up and then down again an inch. I pulled up the emergency brake and moved the stick into neutral.

Fiona sat with her hands primly resting on her wool skirt and her legs crossed. Two little pink pom-poms peeked out over the heels of her bleached white Keds.

"So, Katherine?" Fiona asked, "How long will you be in Burkina?"

"For a year."

"Oh, that's a good amount of time."

I stomped my Doc Marten boots on the floor mats to keep my feet from falling asleep. "It already seems like I've been here longer than three days though," I laughed. "Anna said you served as a nurse when you lived out here?"

"Yes, for ten years," she wiped the windshield again, "I delivered hundreds of babies—too many to count."

Fiona's glasses magnified her eyes making them look like two plump blueberries. I turned on the wipers and let them swish twice and turned them off again. "So what do you do back in Scotland?"

Chapter 3

"I am a nurse at Glasgow Memorial."
"Are you married?"
"No."
"Really?"
"I came close a few times but it just never happened."
"Oh, so, you don't have any children?"
She looked at me and shook her head, "No."
"Do you regret that? I mean, are you okay with that?"
"Why, I think so, yes, dear," she was amused.
"I just thought that everyone wanted a family."
"I have lots of family," she assured me.
  I watched Fiona's petite hands adjust her Peter Pan collar and gently push a stray curl from her forehead. She seemed so nice. Certainly someone would've wanted to marry her?
  She rolled her window down further. The rain was letting up.
  I rolled down my window, too. I watched Malcolm step out of his truck. He adjusted the straps of the tarp again. He tightened the last strap and approached our car.
  "The rain is letting up so I want to push on," he took out his handkerchief and wiped his forehead and stuffed it back in his shirt pocket. "We will be pulling off the paved road in a few miles to head south to Mahadaga. I'm hoping the road isn't washed out, but we'll see."
  "Will we take another route if it's washed out?"
  Malcolm laughed, "No, Katherine. Like I said, there is only one road to Mahadaga. If we can't travel on it we'll have to wait until after the rainy season is over."
  "When will that be?"
  "About three months from now—late September or so."
  "Oh, right," I smiled, trying not to seem a complete ignoramus. "Well, I'll stick close behind."
  I started up the car again and set off behind Malcolm.
  "So, are you from Glasgow?"
  "Actually my family is from the area around Loch Ness, which might be familiar to you. But, I have lived in Glasgow most of my adult life."

Drive Me to Mahadaga

"So, what's the real truth about the Loch Ness monster?" I wondered.

She brought her hands to her mouth and giggled, "Oh, dear, Katherine, you Americans are so lovely."

"I mean, is it all made up?"

"Of course it is dear," she giggled. "Although some people have made a lot of money getting Americans to come and visit Loch Ness."

"C'mon, not just Americans?"

"I'm afraid so, dear," she wiped the windshield again. "Well, and maybe a few Irish."

I shifted up to fourth gear. "But what about the videos?" I looked at her.

She shook her head, "No."

"The eyewitnesses?"

"No."

Malcolm signaled right and we turned south onto the mud road towards Mahadaga. The dirt road was primitive: Pot-holed and uneven. We zigzagged back and forth across the width of the road picking our way through the surest spots. It was painstaking. Some holes had filled with water and others were muddy lagoons. I shifted the Corolla up and back between second and third gear. Fiona kept the windshield clear of steam for me. I opened my window all the way. The air was like pea soup.

Beads of sweat trickled down my forehead and nose. I swiped my nose to knock a bead off and grabbed the steering wheel again.

After more than two hours Malcolm signaled right and pulled over to the side of the mud road. I followed and stopped the car and turned off the engine. Malcolm and Anna got out so we did the same.

"I'm going to run ahead and see if the bridge is washed out," Malcolm announced. "I'll be back soon."

"I need to go to the bathroom." I announced to Fiona and Anna. "Any suggestions?"

"Sure." Anna opened the back door of the four-door cab and leaned inside. She pulled out a roll of toilet paper and handed it to me.

"Thanks," I took the roll. "Do either of you need to go?"

"Fiona?" Anna asked.

Chapter 3

"No."

"You're on your own," Anna smiled. "You'll be fine."

I went behind the Corolla and squatted. I would rather be seen by some passerby than have a snake bite my rear-end. I finished peeing and returned to the Corolla to pick up my letters. I tucked them in the pocket of my skirt and walked over to the truck to find all four doors open to the cab and Anna sitting in the passenger's seat in front and Fiona in the back.

"Donut?" Anna proffered a Tupperware brimming with homemade donuts. Some were plain and others had sprinkles.

I wiped my hands on my skirt and took one, "Thanks." I sat down on the edge of the back seat near Fiona.

"Tea?" Anna handed me a plastic teacup and saucer.

"Oh, thanks," I accepted the cup and saucer and took a sip. "Are we planning on camping here or something?"

Anna shrugged. "It depends on what Malcolm finds down at the river."

I took a bite of my donut. "Okay, I was joking when I said that. Is that really a possibility?"

"Sure, if the bridge is gone and the roads are flooded we won't be able to go anywhere. But, let's wait to hear what Malcolm finds." Anna turned to Fiona and resumed the conversation I had interrupted. "So, I told Mary that if she wanted to send the kids to the Missionary School in Niamey, maybe she should consider home schooling Zack this year so both boys can attend together next year."

"Yes, it's much better if the boys can go together," Fiona agreed and nibbled on her donut.

I set my tea down on the floor and pulled out both letters. I decided to read one now and slipped the other one back in my pocket to read later. I looked for a moment at the handwriting and felt mixed emotions. I took a deep breath and opened the letter. It was only front and back of a loose-leaf page. John had an amazing ability to fill up paper and yet say nothing. The one note of substance was that he had already talked to PMI about a two-week mini-mission over Christmas and had already begun raising funds. At the bottom he signed it, "I can't wait for our wedding night!" and underlined it three times. My

Drive Me to Mahadaga

heart sank and my stomach felt queasy. I crumpled up the letter and stuffed it back into my pocket.

I looked up to find both Fiona and Anna watching me.

"Bad news?" Anna asked.

"No."

"You seem upset."

"No, I'm okay."

"Who was that from?"

"My fiancé."

Fiona and Anna looked at one another. "What!" Anna was stunned. "You're engaged?"

"But, you're so young!" Fiona gushed.

"You haven't even mentioned him!" Anna added.

I sighed, "I know."

"What's his name?"

"John Gruber."

"Do you have an engagement ring?" Anna asked.

"Yes, it's in my cosmetic case."

Anna cocked her head to the side, "Why?"

"I don't know—I guess I just needed some time to think."

Fiona and Anna looked at one another again.

"So, when is this celebration to take place?" Fiona asked.

"When I get back."

"Oh." They both said.

"He wants to visit for two weeks over Christmas."

"Here?"

"Yeah."

"Oh, well, we need to talk to Malcolm about it but I'm sure that would be fine."

I nodded.

"You don't seem too excited about all this," Anna continued. "I mean, you haven't even mentioned him."

"I know." I tried to explain, "I have so many voices telling me what to do."

"Marriage is a big decision, even if you're confident about it." Anna agreed.

Chapter 3

Fiona was smiling at me. "What?" I asked her.

"How old are you, dear?"

"I'm twenty-three, but I'll be twenty-four before the wedding." She brought her hands up and giggled behind them. "But, that's still so young, dear."

"You sound like my Mother." I said and looked up to see Malcolm approach the truck. I stood up and asked him, "What's the deal?"

He slid in behind the wheel of the truck. "The bridge is washed out."

"Donut?" Anna offered him the Tupperware.

"Oh, thanks, Mother," he took a donut. Anna poured a cup of coffee from his special thermos and handed it to him. "Now that's a good cup of coffee." He slurped again.

"Excuse me, but didn't you just say," I started to ask him but Anna interrupted me.

"Katherine has some interesting news for us." Anna smiled. I sat back down.

He turned in his seat to look at me. "Oh, yeah? What's that?"

But before I could say it Anna blurted out, "She's engaged and her fiancé wants to come and visit over Christmas for two weeks."

Malcolm raised his eyebrows, "Really?"

"I'm sorry I didn't mention it earlier. I've just needed some time to think about things on my own."

"And, what is this young gentleman's name?"

"John. But, he's not so young."

All three raised their collective eyebrows.

"He's thirty-five."

They nodded their heads slowly. "Really?"

"Yes, but didn't you just say that the bridge was washed out?" I was ready to change the subject.

Malcolm was still looking at me, "Yes, yes it is."

"So, shouldn't we be doing something?" Anna and Fiona looked at me. "You know, proactivity and all that?"

"Is this his first marriage?" Anna couldn't leave it alone.

"No."

"Does he have children?"

— 69 —

"No."

"Oh, well, that's good." Anna nodded to herself.

"What about the bridge, folks?" I didn't want to discuss John any longer.

Malcolm dropped his head back and looked at me through his bifocals. Fiona and Anna shot glances to one another.

"The bridge?"

"Oh right, well, it's washed out, Katherine."

"You mentioned that. But, it does seem that we could be doing more than just sitting here eating donuts!"

They shook their heads in dismay as if I was being unreasonable! "What?" I demanded. "Look, the bridge is washed out and we don't know how long we're going to be here unless you've got some supplies in the truck and we're supposed to rebuild the stupid thing! It's going to be dark soon and I'm not looking forward to bunking down in the Corolla in the middle of nowhere. But you all seem perfectly content to sit here and have a tea party!"

Their looks were blank for an instant and then they erupted into hysterics. I threw my hands up in frustration.

Malcolm calmed himself, "Katherine, we just have to wait."

"For what?"

"For help, for the water to go down. I don't know yet," he shrugged.

I looked at the mass of untamed foliage outside the truck. I glanced back to find them all still looking at me.

"I'm sorry. I'm just dying to know," Anna asked conspiratorially, "Is there a wedding being planned in your absence?"

"Yes." I sighed. "But, I really don't want to talk about this anymore."

"Okay," Anna held up her hands in surrender. "Mum's the word."

Anna and Fiona picked up their conversation where they left off about the challenge of schooling teens in the bush. This spilled into the revolution of 1983 when Upper Volta became Burkina Faso, culminating in the high cost of paper napkins in Ouaga. I nodded off for a while and woke up in time to hear the conclusion: cloth was better anyway. I swallowed the last of my cold tea and glanced at my

Chapter 3

watch. We had been sitting there three hours. Malcolm got out of the truck and headed back down the road without a word. I looked at Anna but she seemed unconcerned so I watched him disappear around the bend.

"Where's that roll of toilet paper, dear?" Fiona asked me.

I handed it to her and she slipped out of the truck and disappeared into the bush.

I looked at Anna and blurted out, "Fiona is single."

Anna raised her eyebrows, "So?"

"I just don't think I've ever met an older person who chose to be single. Normally they are widows or divorced or something."

Anna nodded her head; "Fiona's special. Most of us couldn't handle the loneliness, especially out here."

"I guess so."

She took another donut, examined it and popped it into her mouth. "That's what happened with Gritty and Stan, you know?" She spit little crumbs on the back of the seat and wiped them off. "I bet you had they both been back in the States they never would've married."

Fiona returned to the truck and slid inside. I watched her rearrange her skirt and dab her nose with her monogrammed hankie.

I glanced at my watch as Malcolm reappeared with a group of young African men. He had been gone about forty minutes. They came to the truck and circled around it while Malcolm spoke to them in Gourmantché. I looked again to Anna for my cue but she seemed completely non-plussed. I sat and watched.

The group left and Malcolm slid behind the wheel of the truck. "Ready, Mother?"

"Sure," she screwed the cap on both thermoses and sealed the Tupperware.

"Uh, what's going on?" I asked Malcolm from the backseat.

Malcolm looked at me in the rear view mirror and smiled. "Well, we're going to drive to the river and that group of men is going to carry this truck and the Corolla across the river."

"Oh, I see." I nodded. "And, you just happened to come across this group of men who volunteered to do this?"

"They were waiting near the river."

Drive Me to Mahadaga

I nodded my head slowly, "So, you're telling me groups of men wait near washed out bridges to carry cars across the river?"

"Something like that. It's their way of making some money during rainy season."

I nodded and looked around seemingly the only one phased by the course of events. "I suppose this is something State Farm recommends when you can't get in touch with a regular tow?"

"Who?" Malcolm asked.

"Never mind." I waved my hand. "So, where will we be during this adventure?"

"In the car."

"And what do you recommend if they drop the car, with us in it, into the river?"

Malcolm looked at me in the rear view mirror again, "I would roll down the window and get out as quickly as I could."

"Thank you, that is very helpful."

"We have a saying here, Katherine: 'That's Africa', and it covers a multitude of things." Anna lifted both hands to prove her point. "That's Africa."

I got out of the truck and headed back to the Corolla. Fiona joined me in the passenger's seat.

"I suppose this is old hat to you, huh?" I asked her.

"Well, dear." She buckled her seatbelt.

I started up the car and followed Malcolm around the bend and down toward the river. If there had been a bridge there was no sign of it now. The water was moving fast carrying a lot of debris but it wasn't very wide. Our carriers casually stood around smoking waiting for us to approach.

Malcolm stopped his truck and got out again. He spoke with one of the men who wore a ski hat with a large rainbow colored pom-pom on top, as if to identify him as chief negotiator. Malcolm motioned to me so I got out and joined him.

"Keep the engine off and the steering wheel straight," Malcolm explained, "once they set the car down on the opposite bank I want you to give a few moments for the water to run off and then start up the car."

Chapter 3

"Okay," I looked at the motley crew. One smiled at me. I smiled back.

"Êtes-vous Americaines?"

"Oui." I answered and they all laughed. I looked at Malcolm, "Is that funny?"

"I think the embroidered Giraffe on your shirt gave you away."

I rolled my eyes, "Would you leave me alone about the clothes?"

He smiled reassuringly. "Let's get going. I think they're eager to spend the cash on some more beer."

I hurried back to the Toyota.

"Is everything okay dear?" Fiona asked as I settled back in to the driver's seat and buckled my seat belt.

I started the engine, "Malcolm just wants to get going before the guys drink anymore."

I followed Malcolm another 20 feet to the bank of the gushing river. We watched as twelve men surrounded the truck, bent their knees and with a collective heave lifted the truck onto their shoulders. Most of the men were barefoot but those that did have shoes wore flimsy boardwalk flip-flops. The pom-pommed one hollered and they took slow baby steps together into the river. The river was chest high on the shortest man and about 15 feet wide. The truck looked as though it was skimming across the gushing water. Once they arrived on the opposite bank they let the front of the truck down with a "clump" and then scurried around to the back and pushed the truck up the bank until it was on solid ground. They turned and ran back into the river whooping and splashing.

I looked at Fiona, "Are you ready?"

"Oh, yes, dear."

I released the emergency brake and double-checked we were in neutral. The Corolla was much lighter. I rolled the car down as close to the bank as possible. The rainbow pom-pommed man held up his hand and the group surrounded the Corolla. It was a strange sensation seeing the tops of the men's heads and the water rushing below. The men walked the car up the bank and placed us down behind Malcolm's truck with a thud. Malcolm walked over and leaned in the window.

Drive Me to Mahadaga

"Are you alright?!"
"I'm fine, Fiona?"
"Oh, yes. I'm fine, thank you."
"Go ahead and start up the car."
I did as instructed and the car started right up. "Great." Malcolm exclaimed, clearly relieved. He haggled with the crew for a while and finally settled on a payment. We were on our way.

The last leg of our trip to Mahadaga led us south out of the dense bush and into arid countryside. Scrub brush rolled past thorny trees and a few hills dotted the horizon. Young boy shepherds shooed their herds of miniature goats and sheep off the road to let us pass and then stood and waved at us as we zoomed by. Every few miles we passed by groups of women walking with bundles of firewood on their heads and babies strapped to their backs. They nonchalantly stepped off the side of the road to let us pass and gracefully bowed their heads to greet us.

"Where are they getting the firewood?" I wondered out loud. "I've seen about 5 trees in the past 20 miles and they're huge Flamboyant trees, they're far too big to cut down!"

"Oh, the women work very hard. They walk for miles a day to collect firewood and then the next day for water. It's an extraordinary amount of work to live off this land," Fiona waved and smiled to everyone we passed.

Malcolm slowed in front of me so I followed suit. We came to a stop in front of a rusted gate that blocked a portion of the road. Just off to the right side of the road was a small mud hut with a thatched roof. Malcolm honked his horn. Eventually a gendarmie in fatigues walked around the side of the hut and approached Malcolm's window. They talked. And talked.

"Do you think there is a problem?" I asked. They had been chatting for more than five minutes.

Fiona chuckled, "I imagine it can be very lonely sitting in that hut waiting for traffic. He's probably enjoying a wee chat, Katherine."

Finally we pulled away and the guard waved us past. I glanced at my watch, it was almost 4:30 p.m., and we had been at the guard gate for almost 20 minutes.

Chapter 3

"You might want to consider storing your watch, Katherine." Fiona spoke over the engine noise.

"Why?" I glanced at her and continued roughly two paces behind Malcolm's truck.

"The African's say, 'Westerners have the watches, but we have the time.' You will save yourself some frustration by packing away your watch, or at least ignoring it," Fiona looked at me expectantly with her two blueberries. "You will miss the lessons of Africa if you are constantly frustrated with her ways."

I glanced at her again and nodded. She rubbed her hands on her skirt and smiled again. The moment had passed. "Now, if I remember correctly, Mahadaga is in that clump of mountains," Fiona pointed through the windshield. "It's one of the last outposts in Burkina."

We pulled into the mission compound at dusk. I followed Malcolm's truck through the gates and up the drive to park in the middle of several mud-brick homes surrounded by Acacia trees. No sooner had we turned off our engines then families streamed out of all the homes to greet us. There were hugs and greetings and introductions all around.

Malcolm and Anna's daughter-in-law, Mary, was the compound's very pregnant hostess and her three young children helped Fiona and me unload our bags from the trunk of the Corolla.

"Let me show you all to your room," Mary said and heaved my duffel bag off the ground and slung it over her back.

"I can carry that, Mary," I tried to take it from her but she wouldn't let me.

"I hope it's okay if you two share a room?" she looked at Fiona and me.

"That's fine with me. Katherine?" Fiona looked at me.

"Sure, that's no problem." I followed Mary and the kids and Fiona up the path to the compound's Guest House. It was a typical bush house: mud brick with a corrugated tin roof, screened windows with thief proofing and a tin door with a padlock.

"It's simple, but clean." Mary explained after showing us into the room. "And, there is a bathroom inside." The kids scrambled onto one of the beds and bounced.

Drive Me to Mahadaga

"This is lovely, Mary," Fiona set down her bag. "Thank you."
"Yes," I chimed in. I was searching the room for mosquito nets but did not see one.
"Would you prefer a mosquito net, Katherine?" Mary asked.
"If it's not too much trouble."
"Not at all, the hooks are already on the ceiling so I'll have Daniel put it up later."
"Thank you."
Mary looked around the room. "The only other thing is our generator shuts off at 8:00 p.m. So it's candles and flashlights after that."
I looked at my watch: 6:55 p.m.
"Now, I don't want to scare you or anything, but we do have snakes. So, be sure to keep your flashlight with you, okay?"
Thousands of tiny pins tickled the back of my kneecaps. I put my hand on the back of the rickety wooden chair to balance myself.
Fiona giggled, "Oh, Katherine, snakes don't like people."
"Well, kids, why don't we let Fiona and Katherine settle in?" She looked at us, "When you're ready come on over to our house for a spaghetti dinner?"
"That sounds lovely," Fiona smiled and patted the kids on the head.
"Thank you." I added.
I threw my duffel bag on to the bed and sat down. I watched Fiona open her bag and place all her clothes in neat piles on top of a table next to her bed. I took out my flashlight and waited for her to finish.

We sat in a large circle of cobalt blue and Kelly green woven chairs in Daniel and Mary's sitting room, the cement floors were covered with Muslim prayer mats and the walls with family photos. We balanced our plates of spaghetti on our laps and watched the kids make their rounds receiving hugs and kisses from everyone in the house.
"So, the Yanks have given Saddam an ultimatum?" Malcolm put down his plate and crossed his right leg over the left and rubbed his ankle.

Chapter 3

Daniel quickly swallowed, "They are already piling up their troops in Saudi Arabia." He shook his head, "They think they rule the world." To which many in the circle nodded in agreement and rested their eyes on me.

I surrendered my hands. "President Bush hasn't phoned me asking my opinion on this matter."

"Has there been much response from the Muslim community here in Mahadaga?" Malcolm looked to the others.

"Not really," Daniel responded. "But, things may change if a war is started."

"Why?" I asked.

Daniel looked at me, "Because Western, or American aggression, is seen as Christian aggression and a threat to all of Islam."

"The Muslims have done a better job than the Christians in many ways of creating a sense of solidarity amongst their followers. The Christians in the Sudan have been persecuted for years by the Muslim government but the rest of the Christian world has not felt themselves threatened by that action as a Muslim would," Malcolm added.

Daniel nodded in agreement. "That's right. So, when the Yanks show up in Saudi Arabia to fight the Iraqis who knows what kind of reaction we will see from the Muslim community throughout the Middle East and in Africa."

"But, Saddam kills his own people. He is no man of faith," Francoise, a French nurse, added.

"The only reason the US is in Kuwait is to protect their oil. Anyone who believes that US foreign policy has humanitarian considerations is fooling themselves. It just makes good rhetoric," Daniel was overheated.

"I think that's a little harsh, Daniel. The truth must be somewhere in the middle," I felt I had to add something, but I was shocked by his vociferousness. I thought everyone liked Americans, the friendly folks who brought the world the Big Mac.

"Look, the US is the bully of the world playground. They get away with a lot of bad policy because countries depend on their financial support and are greedy for the income potential from doing business with the US," Daniel was emphatic.

Drive Me to Mahadaga

"There is something to be said for the existence of a benevolent superpower," Fiona commented. "I'll never forget after the War when America paid for Europe to get back on its feet. I have a fond memory of visiting England in the late 40's and the US soldiers always gave us bubble gum," she smiled. "I am of a different generation. I wouldn't want to live there, but I have very warm feelings towards the Americans."

Irmgard, an elderly German nurse, snorted, "Don't get me started on American occupation and country building. Although," she lifted her index finger, "my sister did marry a Yank and he vas wery nice. He took her to Disney World for their vedding anniversary last year."

I had never pondered my "American-ness" before and looked around at the Canadians, Germans, Swiss and French assembled and felt excited to be a part of an international group but the initial feelings weren't mutual. The discussion continued around the construction of a new addition to the overcrowded dispensary. Malcolm explained that Mahadaga was so deep in the bush it provided primary health care for people in at least a 30 mile radius.

"The dispensary has beds for the very ill but it does not serve food. So, the entire family makes the journey to the dispensary and sets up their fires for cooking and sleeps outside. Because the rainy season is upon us many people come to see us now before the roads are impassable. We had a line of around 250 people stretched down the road to see us today alone," Daniel explained to Fiona and me. He seemed more relaxed now that the subject had moved away from American Imperialism.

"Oh, and some Fulani women arrived today," Francoise added.

"Really?" Malcolm perked up. He turned to me, "The Fulani are a very small but elite tribe. In fact, they are the only tribe I know of where the women don't do any domestic labor. So, they have what are called 'black Fulani'' which basically means they take slaves from lesser tribes, like the Gourmas."

"Yes," Daniel added. "You can often tell a Fulani woman as well because she wears gold coins around her head. People say some coins date back to the Roman Empire via Arab traders—they are passed down from mother to daughter." He held out his hands, "But, as

Chapter 3

fascinating as they are, it sometimes causes trouble because they feel they should be automatically put at the front of the line. It can be very tricky."

The screened door opened and a stately woman walked in, "Janet!" Anna hopped up from her chair and hugged her. Her white hair was pulled into a neat bun and tied behind her head with a blue scarf.

Janet spotted Fiona, "Dear old friend," she walked towards her with open arms. "It's so good to see you again," she kissed her.

"Oh, and you as well," Fiona beamed.

"And, this is Katherine," Malcolm introduced us, "She's our new short-termer in Fada and the one who safely brought your car to Mahadaga."

I stood up with my plate in my left hand and held out my right to shake hers. But, she grabbed my outstretched hand and pulled me towards her for the Euro double-cheek kiss. I looked at her quick brown eyes.

"I have been desperate for an automobile. Thank you terribly for bringing it here," she said in her British accent. She looked at me closely.

"You're welcome."

"Katherine is also engaged and her fiancé will be visiting us in Fada for Christmas." Malcolm added.

Everyone in the circle looked at me. "Oh," many of them said.

"Do you have a ring?" Mary asked. Everyone looked at my hand.

"It's in her suitcase." Fiona and Anna jinxed.

"Why don't you wear it?" Mary wondered.

I was uncomfortable sharing my feelings in front of a group of complete strangers. Luckily, Anna was happy to fill in for me.

"She's thinking about things," she stage whispered and waved everyone off.

Thankfully Janet continued her way around the circle and the group forgot about me.

People slowly finished and took their plates to the kitchen and piled them in the sink. I looked at my watch: 7:45 p.m. I looked at Fiona, "Are you tired?"

Drive Me to Mahadaga

"No, dear, why?"
"Well, I'm tired. I think I'll go back to the room."
"It's awfully early, dear."
"I know." I thanked Mary and said goodnight to everyone. I clicked on my flashlight and made my way up the path to the Guest House. I heard footsteps behind me and turned to find Daniel running up with a bundle in his arms.
"Mary said you might want this?" he handed me the mosquito net.
"Thanks," I was hoping he would offer to put it up for me but he didn't.
"Goodnight!" he called over his shoulder as he jogged back down the path.

I entered the room and turned on the bright overhead light. I stood on the rickety wooden chair and hung the mosquito net from the existing hooks. The bed was on rollers in the center of a nook and didn't touch any walls.

I quickly changed into a sweatshirt and sweatpants and put fresh socks on and slid under the mosquito net with my flashlight and John's second letter. I moved my way slowly around the mattress tucking the mosquito net underneath to make sure no creepy-crawlies would have an opportunity for a midnight visit. I looked at my watch: 7:58 p.m. I had made it. Like clockwork, the generator shut down two minutes later leaving me blinking into the blackness of the room. There was no moon that night and never had I known such complete darkness. I held my hand up in front of my face but I could not see it—no shadows, no silhouette, nothing.

Now that the generator was off I could clearly hear the folks enjoying themselves back at Daniel and Mary's. I clicked on my flashlight and opened John's letter. Again, it filled both sides of a loose-leaf paper and updated me on his family and the weather in North Carolina. He also wrote two prayer points: 'Your spiritual maturity', underlined three times, and 'Our wedding night', underlined four times. "P.S. You haven't left yet, but I wanted some mail to greet you!"

I lay there thinking about John. It was an escape to the familiar. I was overwhelmed by all these new feelings and revelations about

Chapter 3

who I was and what it meant to be an American. It was all too much for me. I closed my eyes and pictured him. I felt his arms around me, his touch; his desire for me. "God, I need you," he breathed into my ear. I caressed my stomach.

I dozed off but was easily roused by the crunch of footsteps nearing the door.

"Do you think she's asleep?" I heard Fiona ask.

"I don't know," Anna answered. "We'll find out!"

I sat up underneath the mosquito net. "I'm awake," I called. They both entered. Anna shined her flashlight on me and they giggled. Anna shined the flashlight on the candlestick so that Fiona could light it. The candlelight gave a warm glow to the room.

"Do you have everything you need, Fiona?" Anna asked.

"Oh, yes, dear, thank you." We watched as she slipped off her shoes and pulled two slippers out of her bag. They had bunny heads on the toes.

"Aren't those fun!" Anna laughed.

"Oh, one of my colleagues gave me those for my birthday."

I rolled my eyes from under the net. Geek. Fiona picked up the candlestick from the table and headed into the bathroom with her nightie in her hand.

Anna looked at me, "So, did you make it under your net in time?"

"In time for what?" I asked.

"For the generator to go off?"

I heard Fiona burst into her giggle from the bathroom. "Well, I was tired. But, yes, I did manage to make it under the net with two minutes to spare."

Fiona re-emerged from the bathroom with a long cotton nightgown on with lacey bits across the chest and up around her neck. Her bunny heads poked out underneath as she walked by my bed with the candlestick. "I think Katherine is chicken, don't you Anna?"

Fiona put down her candlestick and proceeded to imitate a chicken in the middle of the room. Her arms bent and flapping and knees wiggling back and forth, "Bock, bock, bock, bock," she danced around the room, her bunnies even joined in the fun. Anna burst into a fit of laughter while I sat in my dark corner.

Drive Me to Mahadaga

"Hey!" I protested. "I'm new here! Give me a break!" Fiona extended her neck back and forth adding to the chicken imitation. Malcolm heard the commotion from their room next door. "Mother?" he asked from outside. "Is everything okay in there?" "Oh, yes," she managed. "Fiona says Katherine is a chicken." Malcolm burst into laughter outside the door. "And, Fiona is doing a startlingly good imitation of a chicken!"
They were all laughing and couldn't stop. I sat there bundled under my net being laughed at by the geriatric crew but could say nothing. It was true. America's suburbia had done nothing to prepare me for African bush living with these Canadian farmers and Highland women.
"Oh, I think we've hurt your feelings, dear?" Fiona sat down on her bed and dabbed her forehead with her hankie. Malcolm and Anna said goodnight and left in a whirl of giggles. "You know we're just havin' some fun, Katherine?"
"I know." I said from under my dome.
I laid my head on my pillow and watched Fiona kneel beside her bed to pray. She rested her curly gray head on her folded hands while her nightgown fell regally around her on the floor. I dozed off and opened my eyes again. A small flame flickered on a weary lump of wax but Fiona was still on her knees. I rolled over onto my other side and fell into a peaceful sleep.

"Katherine!" I heard my Mother call my name. "Katherine!" I blinked into the darkness and looked around trying to remember where I was. "Katherine?" I recognized Fiona's voice.
"What?"
"Are you alright?
"I was fine until you woke me up!"
"That's not you, then?"
"What?"
"Listen."
Someone was wheezing. Loudly. It sounded as though they had serious congestion.
"Maybe it's Malcolm or Anna?" I offered.

Chapter 3

"No, it's definitely in the room."

Fiona fumbled on her nightstand and then clicked on her flashlight. I blinked adjusting my eyes to the light. She slid on her bunny slippers and bent down to shine the flashlight around the floor into each corner of the room. She stopped in the corner behind my bed.

"Oh my," she said and shined the flashlight up into my face.

"What?" I said.

"You have a visitor."

"A visitor?"

"Just hold on there, Katherine," she headed for the bathroom. "Don't get out of your bed."

She re-entered the room wielding the large wooden rod that Mary had installed to hang the shower curtain.

"Fiona! What are you doing?" I exclaimed.

"Shh! There's a snake coiled behind your bed," she laid her flashlight down on her bed and gripped the rod with both hands and lifted it over her head. "If I can whack it over the head while it's sleeping I can stun it and then we'll have a better chance of killing it."

"Are you out of your mind?" I gasped. Fiona shuffled her bunnies around my bed in ready stance—there was a good two feet between my bed and the wall. She swung the rod over her head and slammed it down. It sounded like she pounded a stuffed duffel bag. She turned around and lunged onto her bed. The wheezing had stopped.

She picked up her flashlight and shined it under my bed. "Oh my," she said.

"What now?" I snapped.

"I think I need to take another whack at it, dear."

I watched Fiona step off the bed and lift the wooden pole over her head again. Her bunnies poked out from underneath the nightgown as she took deliberate steps back to the corner. With all her might she slammed the pole down.

"Bam!" It sounded like she had hit a piñata. Fiona took a step back. She picked up her flashlight again and shined it into the corner. "Well, that should do it for now," she dropped the pole onto her bed.

Drive Me to Mahadaga

"Fiona?" It was Malcolm outside the door. "Is everything alright in there?"

Fiona pulled open the door. "Oh, everything is fine now, dear, we just had a little excitement."

"Excitement?"

"There was a wee snake near Katherine's bed so I gave it a good whack."

"Fiona Keys!" Malcolm exclaimed. "Are you okay?"

"I'm fine now but I think we need to take care of it before it wakes up."

Malcolm shined his flashlight under my bed. "Oh, my." He then shined it into my net. "How are you, Katherine?"

I was speechless. I sat on my haunches staring at Fiona.

Daniel and a guard arrived and bagged the beast in a burlap sack and took it outside.

"The guard chopped his head right off." Fiona reported to me from the door.

I eyeballed Fiona from across the breakfast table the following morning. She sat innocently sipping her tea and nibbling a baguette neatly spread with butter and marmalade, but I was no longer fooled by her Peter Pan appearance. Here sat the most fearless woman in the world dressed in Grandma's clothing. She caught my eye and smiled at me.

"How are you this morning, dear?"

"Fine." I ignored the snickers from around the table and sipped my tea. Everyone had heard about Fiona's heroics of the previous night and of course my contrasting paralysis.

"Well, you've only been in the country a few days, Katherine," Malcolm mused, "and I dare say it will be hard to beat the excitement of last night. Cobras normally like to sleep in seclusion, the guard thought he might have been sick."

The controlled silence erupted into laughter and I smiled, "Thank you," I nodded, acknowledging everyone's attention. "Thanks," I swallowed my tea. "I guess I missed the session during missionary training on how to stun a snake with a curtain rod."

Chapter 3

"That's right," Malcolm laughed, "maybe you should write them and tell them to include it for future training sessions."

"I'll remember to do that."

"And, maybe they should include a session especially for the Yanks on baggage limits!"

"I will certainly make that recommendation." I assured him, but he couldn't hear me over the laughter.

4
Home in Fada N'Gourma

I watched Anna bustle around her kitchen from a stool wedged in between the refrigerator and the cabinets.

"Try this," she leaned across the bar and handed me a chocolate, gooey blob of her latest creation. I popped it into my mouth without hesitation. I had learned that Anna's cooking was legendary amongst the missionary population of Burkina Faso. After 30 years in the bush her Bible and the *Joy of Cooking* were both duck taped, yellowed remains.

"Why don't you buy a new cookbook?" I asked her as she tried to flatten the wrinkled page to make out a recipe.

"Why would I do that?" she shook her head.

Once we returned from Mahadaga I enjoyed the privilege of dining every night at Anna's table because Fiona was still with us. But, when Fiona took her leave back to Scotland and I was kindly asked to start cooking for myself, my complete ineptitude in the kitchen was discovered and Anna initiated cooking lessons. This week's lesson was yogurt. Anna had even cobbled together a handwritten cookbook for me featuring specialized dishes one could make with the limited ingredients found in the Fada market. If it weren't for her generosity I would have starved since my arrival two months ago.

"Oh!" I had almost forgotten to tell her. "I heard someone trying to break into my house last night!"

"What exactly did you hear?" she was typically non-plussed.

"I heard someone outside the front door—it sounded like they were trying to break in." I explained.

"Oh, near your front door?"

Chapter 4

"Yeah."

"They're just after your rats," Anna waved her hand.

"What rats?"

"You have a rat's nest under your house—it's under your front stoop—it's been there for ages. Someone was just looking for dinner, so don't flatter yourself." Anna lifted the cover off a saucepan, stuck in her wooden spoon, swirled it around, transferred a taste to a teaspoon and licked it.

"Flatter myself?"

"I mean they're only after your rats, so don't worry."

"Thanks, that's such a relief," and she laughed.

I started coming to sit with Anna during my morning break from the office shortly after our return from Mahadaga. She had a treat and a Fanta waiting for me on the counter next to my stool. It only took me a week to learn that as long as I stayed planted on the stool I was welcome in her kitchen. Gritty had lived on the compound 200 yards away from Anna for 30 years and still hadn't realized there was a stool in Anna's kitchen for a reason.

"Did I tell you the LaFargue's are coming to stay at the Guest House tonight?"

"No," I licked the chocolate off my fingers. "Who are the LaFargue's?"

"They are a missionary family stationed in Diapaga, a couple hours northeast of Fada."

"Oh, I remember seeing their name on some mail."

Anna maintained that the compound's Guest House was like running a busy Bed & Breakfast. It was there for colleague missionaries traveling back and forth to bush outposts but Anna and Malcolm opened their doors to everyone, whether they were associated with the mission agency or not.

"Well, they phoned Malcolm last night and said that Beverly is having some contractions. So, they're going to drive her into the American hospital in Ouaga but break up the trip by staying with us tonight."

"How far along is she?"

"She's around 35 weeks so they don't want to take any chances."

Home in Fada N'Gourma

"Do you need any help?" I always offered but she rarely accepted my help. The kitchen and hospitality were her coveted domain and she didn't appreciate interference.

"I'll be busy preparing dinner for all of us," she said to herself and then looked at me. "Maybe later you can set the table on the porch for dinner?"

"Great!" I smiled thinking of how silly it was that I should be so excited to set a table. But, it was an important sign of acceptance, and maybe even friendship? I got up from my stool to head back to the office before she changed her mind. "Thanks for the snack."

"Of course," she went back to her work.

I walked out the kitchen door and up the cement ramp to my office. The screen door clapped closed behind me as I sat down at my desk. The familiar gong of the London Tower signifying the BBC's World Service News at the top of the hour rang out of Malcolm's prized short-wave radio. NATO had set the January 15th deadline for Saddam Hussein to get his troops out of Kuwait and the world was buzzing with war talk. Even deep in the bush people talked about the war and many believed it was really a war between Christians and Muslims; not land and oil. It was September 15th and the World Service was our reliable link to the great countdown.

Malcolm and Philippe stood next to my desk listening intently to the news update. Philippe, the President of the protestant church in Fada, was a tall, regal man with silver hair. I had met his family my first night in Fada when we dined at their home. He and Malcolm were trusted confidantes and I had become accustomed to their daily meetings spoken in hushed Gourma.

The mission had set up its post in Burkina after the French handed control of the country back to the nationals in the 1960's. The country was then known as Upper Volta before a revolution in 1983 that changed the name to Burkina Faso, "land of the upright men." Philippe was one of the young people that Malcolm discipled when he and Anna first arrived. They had seen the church in Fada grow under their steady leadership and now the mission was in the process of handing all control over to the local church.

Chapter 4

"We're working ourselves out of a job," Malcolm explained to me one morning when I asked him what he had been doing the past 30 years in Fada. Every morning I sat down in the little chair in front of his desk to ask for instruction in the office that day. "Just tackle the correspondence." He always said. And then he would share with me his thoughts, his concerns for the community or a particular family in need. I began to see Fada through Malcolm's eyes, and perhaps even life through Malcolm's eyes, and it captured me. He was tireless in his concern and dedication to the people around him.

Malcolm also managed the other missionaries dotted around the country and the money that was donated to the work of the mission from around North America and Europe came through our office. It was my task to try and organize the office files, many yellowed and moth eaten, and respond to correspondence that in some cases were dated four years prior.

"It's been so long! What if they're dead?" I had initially challenged Malcolm.

"Just write the thank you note, please," he was not amused.

The news ended and Malcolm flipped off the radio. He looked at Philippe and then at me.

"Are you okay?" I asked.

"Yes. I'm just concerned how the Muslim community here in Fada will respond if there is a war." Malcolm looked his colleague. "What do you think, Philippe?"

Philippe rubbed his gray bearded chin and nodded his head slowly. "I will have to think about this, dear friend." He glanced at me and back to Malcolm. "Let me think before I speak."

Malcolm nodded as Philippe spoke, appreciating his words. I looked back and forth to both of them. I felt giddy about the war and the buzz. America was pulling out all its finest new toys that even the reporters on the BBC had to admit were "impressive." And, I had a terrible habit of laughing when I was nervous which gave the impression I was insensitive. I knew Malcolm would never trust me to share one of his conversations with Philippe again if I burst into laughter, so took a deep breath and looked away.

— 89 —

Home in Fada N'Gourma

"Katherine?" Malcolm sounded concerned. "It's very scary, but don't worry. We always have to remember that God is in control." He comforted me. He and Philippe retreated into his office.

I finished typing a stack of letters and headed back to my house just after noon for rest hour. I walked across the dusty compound to my mud brick house that sat near the entrance gates along the Fada Road. I unlocked the padlock, opened the corrugated tin door and pushed through the screen door. I latched the screen door behind me and went to stand at my window above the kitchen sink.

From my kitchen window I had a birds eye view of the whole compound. The burgundy gate entrance was to my right. Straight ahead was Malcolm and Anna's one story mud brick house, painted white, with thief proofing on the windows and a covered porch facing my house. Large elephant ear plants shaded the porch making it feel breezy and secluded even during the most intense heat of the day.

To the left of Malcolm and Anna's was the Guest House. It was a long narrow building of three bedrooms, each with a door and a window facing me with the kitchen to my farthest left. A cement path led from Malcolm and Anna's kitchen past the office and across the front of the Guest House. The path continued up a slight incline past various storage sheds with corrugated tin roofs to end at the front door of Stan and Gritty Wauken, the other permanent missionary couple. Stan's homemade business cards read "Wauken for the Lord". He handed them out at every meeting we had and to every guest that came through, much to Anna's annoyance.

I watched Gritty whiz in through the gates on her orange moped. Dust kicked up behind her and the guinea fowl scattered in all directions. Her linen dress was hiked up over her knees revealing two generous white legs. A chicken dangled upside down from her left handlebar, tied on by its feet, and her large floppy bag dangled from the right. Besides helping in the pharmacy, Gritty was a nurse and spent her time wheeling around town and bush villages administering immunizations and helping women give birth. She returned to the compound everyday for rest hour with dinner strapped onto some portion of her moped.

Chapter 4

    The church was to my left further down the compound wall and had its own gate onto the busy road to encourage visitors inside. And beyond the church there were several clusters of mud huts with thatched roofs where various Gourma families lived that contributed to the life of the church.

    The dirt driveway widened in front of Malcolm and Anna's house and circled around the majestic Flamboyant tree that stood in front of the Guest House. The shade the tree offered served as a parking lot and as a waiting room for people who came to meet with Malcolm. When the meat man came he rested his rickety wheelbarrow on its trunk and artisans who passed through set up their displays under the tree's expansive arms.

    I watched the guinea fowl wander around the Flamboyant tree. They seemed to lose and then rediscover one another, never tiring of the game. Standing at my kitchen window watching the comings and goings of life on the compound gave me a sense of peace, and belonging.

    Danjou caught my eye as he appeared from behind Anna's house and headed down the path towards the gate. I could hear his bare feet pad along the drive and see tufts of dust swirl behind him. I quickly ate a baguette and a piece of cheese for lunch confident I would be well fed that night at Anna's.

    Cooking took so long that I often ate canned tuna fish and baguette in between meals at Anna's, to which I was frequently invited. My friend was the super-sized bottle of Pepto Bismal that I brought from home and kept in my refrigerator door. I was way past needing a spoon. I took a swig and slipped under my mosquito net for a nap.

    I lay down and immediately the closets of my mind opened and I was naked with John. I had invited the memories when I first arrived as a comfort but they were becoming a drain on me—they seemed to take over. Oddly, my desire for John had increased palpably since our separation as our physical relationship had moved to a new level of intimacy. My imagination was happy to embellish upon the awkward, embarrassed interludes that were the hallmark of our limited physical contact.

Home in Fada N'Gourma

I rolled over and looked through my room and out the kitchen window. I shook my head and smiled remembering the John I knew versus the one that my mind had created. "I need to start reading or something," I got up and walked down to the bookshelf in the sitting room. Above the shelf of Louis Lamour novels was a selection of Penguin Classics. I pulled out *Anna Karenina* by Tolstoy and took it back to my bed with me.

The white Land Rover roared into the drive attacking the silence of rest hour. I had just woken up and stood at my kitchen window swigging Pepto. Danjou chased the truck whooping and waving his machete. Having visitors was always a celebration in the bush.

A man, who I figured must be Jim LaFargue, hopped out of the driver's side and scooted around to the passenger's side. He opened the door and helped Beverly out of the truck. I watched from the safety of my window as she stood and rubbed her bump with both hands and then bent backwards and stretched. I had never really been around anyone pregnant before and I was struck at once by a feeling of unease. *That would've been you.* I shook away the thought as I had done many times before. It was one thing to remember my *mistake* and another to consider that many months later I would've had a child. Becoming pregnant was such a fear for sexually active young women that the notion that someone would purposely try to become pregnant had rarely crossed my mind. I watched Jim take Bev's hand and then rub her bump for her and I felt jealous of their intimacy.

Jim then aided two small LaFargue's who tumbled out of the truck and joined the guinea fowl in their game. I had thought that if I were married the three-hour respite in the middle of the day would be a perfect time for lovemaking. Apparently I was right.

Anna exited her house with Malcolm close behind to greet them. There were hugs all around. Even Gritty and Stan straggled down the cement path from their house to join in the greeting. Danjou and his wife, Amina, and their children added to the growing crowd and soon many of the families from the compound had gathered under the Flamboyant tree to welcome the Lafarge's to Fada. Should I join them too? I wasn't sure I was a part of the team yet. I saw Anna point

Chapter 4

in my direction. Could they see me at my window? All heads turned towards me.

"Katherine!" Malcolm hollered, "Come on out and join us!"

"Okay!" I quickly left my house and joined the group. Malcolm introduced me to the LaFargue's and their two sons Zach and Matthew. Bev and I smiled at one another, she had dark hair and striking green eyes. Matthew squinted into the sun to look at me, "Mommy, she has a pink mustache!"

Everyone looked at my upper lip and smiled. I quickly licked them and tasted the leftover Pepto.

"Katherine," Malcolm shook his head, "You are priceless."

After I set the table on Anna's porch that evening I sat on my stool in her kitchen to await further instructions.

"Beverly is resting," Anna explained as she managed three bubbling pots on the stove and meat in the oven.

"How is she feeling?"

"She says she's okay but I don't know, she looks very tired to me," Anna stopped short when the kitchen door opened. It was Gritty.

"Oh. Hi," Anna said. "Can I help you?"

Gritty shuffled into the kitchen and leaned against the stove. "No," she said lazily. She picked up Anna's wooden spoon and dipped it into one of the pots. "Whatcha cookin'?"

Anna snatched the spoon from Gritty's hand. "You'll have to wait for dinner to see!"

"Well, aren't we a little protective?" Gritty looked at me but I avoided her eyes by rearranging my skirt. After all, she didn't feed me.

"Yes, I am protective of my space. This kitchen is my space."

"Well, I guess if all you do is cook you would feel that way, wouldn't you?"

"I do not have to defend my ministry to you, Gritty!" It was an old battle between them but the scars were fresh.

"Ministry? Ha!" Gritty headed towards the door. "I cook as well as all my other responsibilities."

— 93 —

Home in Fada N'Gourma

"Oh, really? Like that rabbit you tried to pass off as chicken last Easter—you call that cooking? Because you're too cheap to serve chicken unless you happen to run over one!" Anna clapped her hands over her mouth; stunned the words had escaped.

"Rabbit?" Gritty demanded. She looked indignant and then embarrassed as if she'd just been caught. She looked at me and then Anna and left. The kitchen door gently clapped shut behind her.

"Excuse me," Anna whispered over her shoulder as she left the kitchen. I heard her bathroom door shut and latch.

"Just like home," I mused to myself and wondered if I dare touch Anna's pots.

"Hello? Anna, are you in there?"

I slid off my stool and opened the screen door, "Hi, Jim," I explained, "Anna is in the other room, can I help you with something?"

"Uh, well, I think we're going to need some help. Bev's water broke and she's having some strong contractions."

"Oh, my," I managed to say.

"Oh, yes," he rubbed his stubble with both hands.

"Malcolm is in his office. Why don't you let him know and I'll tell Anna."

"Tell me what?" Anna walked back into the kitchen composed and went directly to her pots.

"Bev's in labor," Jim explained.

"Oh dear! Well, you go get Malcolm and we'll meet you in your room." Anna turned off the oven and the gaslights on the stove. She hung up her apron, went to the freezer and removed a tray of ice, put it in a recycled plastic bag and began beating it with a rolling pin.

"Thirsty?" I asked.

"Oh, no," she smiled. "Each time I was in labor I craved ice so I'm just crushing a little for Bev to suck on."

"Oh." I had no clue about childbirth, and to be honest, I wasn't really all that interested in finding out more.

I followed Anna with her bag of ice chips to Bev's room in the Guest House. The boys were playing soccer around the Flamboyant tree with Danjou's kids. Jim and Malcolm were already inside. Bev

Chapter 4

was covered in sweat, lying on top of her sheets. She looked at us and smiled.

"Sorry, Anna," she struggled to sit up, "I know it's going beyond the call of duty having to help me give birth!"

"Don't be silly, Bev. The baby doesn't know you haven't arrived at the hospital yet." Anna walked over, handed her the bag of ice and took an extra pillow from the other bed and put it under her feet.

"Oh, thanks! You're terrific," Bev popped ice chips into her mouth. I stood near the door watching Bev in amazed silence. I thought women in labor were thrashing and screaming.

"Has anyone let Gritty know?" Malcolm asked.

"No," Anna stated.

"Why don't you go and tell her, Mother?" Malcolm asked, "Bev will need her help most of all."

"Of course. I'll go and get her now," Anna headed for the door and I followed her outside.

"Anna, I'll go get Gritty," I volunteered. I didn't want to stay there with Bev.

She looked relieved; "Do you mind?"

"Not at all."

"Thanks, I'll go and get some more supplies," she headed down the beaten path towards her kitchen.

I walked up the incline to Gritty's house. I clapped outside their door and waited. And waited. I walked around the back of the house to find them sitting on their porch sipping drinks. Gritty was reading a *Time* magazine with Ronald Reagan on the cover in a presidential pose.

"Gritty!" I stepped up onto their cement porch; "Bev is in labor."

She looked at me over her reading glasses, "Oh, yeah?"

"Yeah."

"What do you know about it?"

"Labor?"

"Yeah."

"Nothing!"

"Well, you won't say that tomorrow," she said with a mischievous smile. "Will she, Stan?"

Home in Fada N'Gourma

"No sir-EE," Stan shook his head and both of them cackled. "Or, I guess I should say, 'no ma'am-EE', huh Grit?" Which sent him into a fit of laughter climaxing in a snorting session. My face must have betrayed my disgust because Gritty abruptly lost her cackle and announced:

"I will be there in four minutes." After which Stan fell silent and they resumed reading.

I hotfooted it back to Bev's room. I knocked on the door and called, "Anna?"

"Yes, just come on in," Anna answered. Bev was leaning on the headboard while Jim rubbed her lower back.

"Gritty's on her way," I announced.

"Thanks," Anna arranged the table full of supplies.

"Four minutes," I added with a smile. Anna shook her head and muttered something under her breath. "Should I just go back to my house and you can call if you need me?" I hoped.

Anna looked at me, "Absolutely not! We need you here."

Gritty ventured in with her floppy medical bag three minutes later. "So, that little LaFargue isn't going to wait for the hospital, huh?"

"Thanks for helping us out, Gritty" Jim said. Bev smiled at Gritty.

"How close are the contractions?" Gritty was all business.

"They're roughly six minutes apart at this point," Bev explained over her shoulder. Jim stopped rubbing her back and she sat down on the bed. "But my water broke earlier and I can feel her head hanging real low."

"Her?" Gritty and Anna jinxed.

"Well, here's hoping," Bev nodded toward the two boys running around outside.

"I'll need to check and see how dilated you are," Gritty explained as she pulled on surgical gloves. "Lay down and pull your knees up for me." Bev did as instructed. I looked out the window.

"You're getting there," Gritty was pulling the sheet back down over Bev's legs when I looked back, I felt nauseous. "The cervix is very soft and I think I'm feeling the top of the head." Gritty looked at Anna; "Can you get me two buckets of water and some soap?"

— 96 —

Chapter 4

"Sure," Anna disappeared out of the door. I heard the familiar clap of the Guest House kitchen door shut behind her.

I walked outside and sat down on the cement path. Jim followed me out and herded the boys into their room next door. The sun had dropped behind the Guest House casting long shadows across the compound from the Flamboyant tree. I could smell the open fires from the families cooking on the compound.

It was the summer of 1986 and Madonna's *Poppa Don't Preach* was popular. It was beyond ironic that Madonna should sing about keeping her baby and I hadn't even considered it. I went to a clinic less than 100 yards from my mom's office in Fairfax, she had no idea I was there. I sat in a waiting room with six other women and couldn't help but think of a poem I had read somewhere about death being a leveler of men. Well, abortion was a leveler of women. A group of us gathered in a little office waiting to be briefed by a nurse. Two of us wore college sweatshirts and looked suburban, three others looked like high school students and there were two older women that looked wasted by life. But, how could I look down on them? We were all there for the same reason. A nurse finally arrived and showed us the procedure in detail when I turned my head from her in disgust. My stomach sank to my knees and I thought *My god, what am I doing?* But, what was my alternative? Tell my parents and move home where I would be the resident disappointment? Drop out of school and live in an apartment somewhere to begin life as a single mother? The options scared me to the core. I was supposed to *be* something, I was from a *good* family. And when it was over I was relieved, relieved not to have to make any of those choices and avoid the complicated results of my actions.

But, it never went away. I tried to make it a new beginning but I didn't count on the sadness. I drank more. It was always a shadow in the corner of my eye, like my broken foot that pains me when it rains, our bones and bodies have memories like our souls. I knew it was a boy because my eyes popped open the moment of conception, it was a whisper but I heard it.

Anna emerged from the Guest House kitchen with two large buckets of sloshing water. I scrambled up to assist her.

Home in Fada N'Gourma

"There's another box of stuff on the table in there—would you bring it to the room please?"

"Sure," I went into the kitchen and picked up the box. There were soaps and a variety of sponges, fresh bath and hand towels and scissors. I carried it back to the room and stopped. I knocked. Anna opened the door.

"Why are you knocking?"

"I didn't want to interrupt or anything." I lied. I did not want to see the birth.

Anna looked at me for a moment and stepped outside letting the door close behind her. "What's the matter, Katherine?"

I didn't know what to say. "I guess I just feel a little nervous. I mean, I don't have any experience with birth and I just feel like I'll be in the way."

I thought she would be mad at me, or snap at me and tell me to grow up, but she didn't. Somehow, she always answered with compassion. "That's the difference being out here, you know? Everyone is needed. There aren't lots of other people around to fill a specific role. We have to do everything: help with birth, bury our dead, marry our loved ones—everything." Her eyes lingered on me.

I dropped my head under her gaze. She rubbed my shoulder.

"Now," she whispered, "understand that we *need* you here. And, try to appreciate that and not be afraid of it." She took the box out of my arms and walked back inside. I followed her. She put it on the table next to Bev's bed. Gritty rummaged through it.

"Ooh, here comes another one, get Jim, someone get Jim!" Bev demanded. "He's putting the boys to bed!" I darted out the door to get Jim. He was already on the path. I held the door open for him and he stepped inside.

"Breath through it, baby, c'mon now," Jim didn't miss a beat. Gritty was timing the contraction on her watch. Bev's face reddened and she tucked it into her chest. She tightened her face. "Breath, baby, c'mon now, don't push yet! It'll pass!" And it did.

Bev wiped the sweaty hair off her forehead and looked around. "Whew! We're getting there!" she laughed. "I'm ready for this baby to be in my arms!"

Chapter 4

"Well, don't overdo it, Bev, save your strength," Gritty told her, "I think we should wait a little longer before you start pushing."

Malcolm opened the door and stuck his head in, "What can I do, Mother?" he asked Anna.

"Maybe you could finish putting the boys to bed? I think Jim is going to be tied up for a while."

"Thanks, Anna, that's a great idea," Jim nodded at her and looked at Malcolm, "That would be a big help."

"It's not very often I get to play Grandpa, it will be my pleasure." We heard the boys squeal with delight when Malcolm stepped into their room. We smiled at one another.

Jim picked Bev's hairbrush up off the nightstand and sat down on the bed next to her. "Thank you," she beamed at him, anticipating the pleasure of that gesture. He pulled up sections of her long hair and slowly brushed from the roots down to the ends. It was so tender she closed her eyes and leaned into him. He kissed the top of her sweaty head.

I caught myself smiling at seeing this display of intimacy. But then I felt sad when I thought of John, we never treated one another which such gentleness. I walked back outside to get some fresh air. Anna and Gritty joined me.

"Remember when Sarah was born, Anna?" Gritty looked up at the stars.

"Oh, how could I forget?" she smiled to herself and then looked at me. "Gritty helped me give birth to two of my children—both of my girls. Sarah, the younger one, was born during rainy season so we were stuck here. The roads were completely washed out."

"Yeah, it was just me and the tribe's old mid-wife to help and boy did Anna rip. Ooh!" Gritty chuckled. "She couldn't sit down for weeks."

Anna shrugged her shoulders, "What can you do?" she laughed. I smoothed the back of my skirt. "Yes, and what about your Timothy?" Anna asked Gritty.

"Yeah, I bled for days after Timmy was born. Finally Stan took me into the American hospital to get me fixed up." Gritty explained nonchalantly. "The doctor asked me why missionaries kept having

— 99 —

Home in Fada N'Gourma

babies in the bush and would I tell everyone to please come into the hospital for deliveries." Both women laughed heartily.

"Why didn't you go to the hospital?" I wondered.

"Women have been giving birth long before hospitals were around, you know?" Anna explained.

"Yeah, and died a lot more frequently, too," I countered.

"Well, I think it's more that as missionaries we're supposed to be tough, at least back then we were," Gritty eyeballed me and continued, "and not go fleeing to the city when things get uncomfortable when none of the Africans have that luxury."

I shrugged my shoulders; "I don't see how taking care of your health is being elitist." Both Anna and Gritty looked at me but didn't respond. Their missionary bravado seemed misplaced to me at times.

As if on cue, Jim leaned out the door. "C'mon ladies, we've got a baby to deliver," Jim held the door open for Gritty and Anna and I followed her into the room.

"Lay back so I can check the head, hon," Gritty instructed Bev. She pulled a new pair of surgical gloves on, lifted the sheet and stuck her hand between Bev's legs. Bev squirmed. "Relax." She continued her examination. "The head is right there—let's start pushing on the next contraction."

The counting and the breathing seemed endless. Bev was alternately panting and breathing and then eerily silent, exhausted.

"Another one's coming!" She gasped.

"PUSH!" Gritty yelled and Bev squeezed with all her might. Our faces scrunched up, trying to push with her.

Jim coached, "Now breath, two-three-four. And PUSH!" he and Gritty yelled in unison.

"I see the head! Oh! C'mon Bev just keep pushin', it's comin' Bev."

"Ahh! I can't! I can't!" Bev screamed and shook her head.

"C'mon baby!" Jim yelled.

The head came: Dark, matted, hair spotted with blood and wet with mucus. Gritty cupped the delicate head and neck in her meaty hand. "One last push, Bev." She maneuvered the shoulders and in one fell swoop the rest of the body oozed out with a gush of mucus. Gritty

Chapter 4

pulled the baby up and Anna clamped the umbilical chord. "A big, healthy boy," Gritty said while she wrapped him up in a blanket and showed him to his mother. And then he coughed and then screamed; a loud throaty cry that made us all smile because it was the sound of life. Gritty placed him in Bev's outstretched arms and he quieted.

"Another boy," Jim whispered.

"Hello, beautiful," Bev said to him as they both admired this new creation.

I was unabashedly staring. I was amazed by what I had seen. "That was a miracle," I said to Anna.

"It sure is," she smiled, too, and then gently lifted the baby from Bev. "I'm just going to clean him up and then you can try to nurse him."

Gritty nudged me; "Get me some more towels and the plastic sheeting to put on the floor for the afterbirth." I did as I was told and armed myself with several towels and took one of Anna's buckets of soapy water and put it on the floor next to me. "I'll need you to wrap it up immediately, it will attract too many animals if we don't take care of it right away."

Gritty delivered the afterbirth onto the floor. I knelt down and gathered the deep black, red, and grey mass up in the plastic sheet when in a moment of unprovoked clarity I saw that because I had chosen to end the little life of my son did not mean his life had ended. I knew that moment that someday I would know him again, that because of me he had been denied this life and leapfrogged straight into the arms of God. Tears overwhelmed my eyes and streamed down my cheeks. *My God, how can you ever forgive me?*

I dunked the towels in the water and scrubbed the floor. I dunked and scrubbed again and scrubbed again until I wiped every drop of blood and mucus off the floor. I wiped my runny nose with the back of my shirtsleeve and kept going, and then snorted back the snot ungracefully when it kept coming. I gathered the mass up in the tarp and sat back on my haunches with it in my lap. Gritty had been tending to Bev and glanced at me and I felt ashamed, I sensed she could see through me.

Home in Fada N'Gourma

"Birth is messy," I could feel my eyes were red and puffy and looked away from her.

She returned her attention to Bev. "Life is messy," she agreed after thinking about it. She finished sewing Bev some minutes later.

"Bev, you and the baby rest and we'll switch you to another bed after we get something to eat," Anna instructed.

Thankfully Anna either didn't notice me, the blubbering idiot on the floor, or she was too exhausted to ask. Her tentative way relieved me. I walked out with the soiled towels and sheeting piled in my arms back to Anna's kitchen. Gritty and Anna followed. Danjou was standing near the door, he asked Anna for the news. Anna told him in Gourmantché that a boy was born. He smiled and said he would share the good news. Anna asked him to take the waste to the compound's dump. I dropped my armload into Danjou's wheelbarrow.

I washed my hands again in Anna's sink and sat down on my stool. I glanced at Anna's kitchen clock, it was 11.30 p.m. It had been a long day and I was tired. Gritty washed her hands, too, and while she dried them she regarded me with a softness in her eyes I had not seen before.

I met her gaze but said nothing. Anna returned from her bathroom.

"Stay out of my pots, Gritty," Anna chided.

"It's probably done cooking by now, wouldn'tcha think?" Gritty picked up a wooden spoon, but Anna moved in between Gritty and the stove before she could reach a pot.

"I'll feed you if you want to eat, just go sit on the porch-"

"I'm going home," I interrupted their game. They stopped and looked at me.

"Don't you want anything to eat?" Anna was surprised.

"No, I can fix myself something," I got up from the stool and headed for the door. "Goodnight."

"I think she earned her keep today, don't you Anna?" I heard Gritty ask Anna as the door clapped shut behind me.

"Yes, I think she'll do." Anna agreed.

I put the kettle on and looked out my kitchen window across the moonlit compound. I watched Gritty take a seat with Stan and Malcolm at the table on Anna's porch while Anna flurried around

Chapter 4

them serving her postponed dinner. I saw the light on in Bev's room across the way and smelled the dwindling fires from the families nearby. There was a sadness inside me that I accepted as a scar of life, I could never undo what I had done. *Lord, forgive me.*

Dirt crunched under the wheels of Danjou's heavy-laden wheelbarrow as he pushed it down the drive towards the gate.

Into the night I called, "Bonsoir, Danjou."

It was too dark to see his face, but I thought I saw a flash of his white teeth. I smiled back.

"Bonsoir, Mademoiselle," he whispered back and continued on his way.

5
Picnic at Fada Mountain

I quickly dressed and scribbled a note: "I'm going to the Post Office. I'll be back soon." I walked out of my house and handed it to Danjou who was pumping water up into my drum.

"Pour Malcolm, s'il vous plait?"

"Oui," he clicked the back of his throat and nodded. He was my friend now.

I slipped out of the gates, turned left and walked with the rest of the Fada morning rush hour on foot headed to the market. Women balanced oversized woven baskets on their heads brimming with tomatoes, okra, and yams. I nodded and smiled at them but hurried along. I was on a mission. I had visited the post office everyday for the past month and they kept telling me the mail truck had broken down and they didn't know when the mail would next be delivered. It was driving me mad not to have any mail. I felt isolated and starved.

"You realize going down there isn't going to change anything?" Malcolm shook his head in amusement yet again at my impatience.

"I readily acknowledge that it just makes me feel like I'm doing something," I told him in the office yesterday.

I stepped up to the post office window but I could only see the top of the man's head sitting inside because his stool was so low. I leaned over the sill. "Post?" I asked.

He shook his head, "Non, Madame."

"Are you sure?"

He smiled, "Yes, I am sure."

"Isn't there someone you can call? I mean, am I the only one in town who has missed receiving any word from the outside world for the past *month*? We haven't had mail since September 20th!"

Chapter 5

He shrugged his shoulders, "They said they would be here when the truck is fixed."

I asked through my clinched teeth, "Isn't there more than one truck?"

"Non, Madame." And laughed as if that was the most ridiculous notion he had ever heard.

I turned around and stomped down the stairs of the post office and muttered under my breath about the ineptitude of the government of Burkina Faso. I passed two elderly women whose breasts were so long that they swung lazily across their stomachs. I shook my head in disbelief and continued on. I marched through the dusty compound and into the office and slumped in my chair.

Malcolm's chuckled from his office. "I take it you weren't successful, Katherine?"

"No, I was not." I was irritated. How could I possibly continue my dysfunctional relationship if I couldn't have contact with the outside world? "Malcolm, this country is in severe shortage of two things."

"Oh, Katherine? And, what are those?"

"A decent postal system and under wire." I knew he wouldn't laugh but I did.

Anna opened the screen door to the office and leaned her head inside, "The mail has arrived!"

I hopped up from my chair. "But, I was just down there."

Anna headed back into her house with me close behind. She explained over her shoulder, "They said they were worried about the crazy white woman who kept bothering them so they delivered it to us right when it arrived!" she laughed heartily.

"Great," I shook my head. "Heaven forbid anyone should expect any efficiency around here."

I followed her through her kitchen and into the sitting room. Mail was spread all over the dining table.

"Wow!" I couldn't contain my excitement. The proverb says 'Like cold water when you're thirsty so is good news from far away': the arrival of mail had become a definitive celebration in my missionary life. I picked up a stack and began sorting it into piles. The familiar sprawling handwriting of John and my Grandma's shaky cursive were

Picnic at Fada Mountain

dependable standbys. In the sea of white airmail paper I spotted a pink envelope and pulled it from the bottom of a stack. The loopy handwriting of my Mom greeted me—she rarely wrote so I quickly opened it.

"If you're still ready to throw your life away on that hick please write and let me know what color you want the napkins to be at the reception," she wrote. "Just kidding." But I knew she wasn't joking. John was not the dream husband she had for me and, to be honest, he wasn't the dream I had for myself. But, her letter hurt and offended me. I grabbed my stack of mail and left Anna's house without a word. I marched across the compound to my house, unlocked the padlock, pushed opened the screen, and burst into tears in my little pantry. I walked through my kitchen and into my sitting room. I looked at the couch and pretended my Mom was sitting right there.

"How dare you write this to me!" I yelled. "How dare you treat me like a child. You don't respect me or my decisions!" Anger overwhelmed me and all I could do was scream. "Ahhhhhhhh!" I threw myself onto the nearest couch. "Lord! What should I do?" I pounded the couch. "Why don't you answer me!!" I pounded again. "Why is this so *difficult*!?" I pounded my arms and legs until it hurt. I fell limp and pressed my face into the rough wool of the blanket and sobbed.

"Katherine?" I heard. I lifted my head, "Katherine, are you okay?"

It was Anna. I got up from my couch and walked through my kitchen to the screened door. My eyes were red and puffy and my hair static fright. I looked at Anna through the screen door. She was holding a little cake shaped like a bunny. It was covered in white fondant and had two raisins for eyes. She looked at me and she smiled her gentle smile. I hadn't even tried to compose myself, I was too exhausted.

"Are you okay?" she asked through the screen door.

"I don't know," I managed as a new floodgate of tears opened. She pulled the screen door open and stepped inside and held me. I laid my head on her shoulder and let myself be held.

Chapter 5

Finally I stepped away from her and tried to pull myself together. "I'm sorry." I explained but she waved her hand. I continued anyway. "My Mom isn't thrilled about John."

She nodded. "Well, if you were confident in your feelings it wouldn't matter so much." Her words stung. I waited for a qualifier but none came.

"My Mom just called my fiancé a hick, shouldn't that bother me?"

She shrugged, "Do you think he's a hick?"

"Well, no." I sounded unconvinced. She raised her eyebrows. "I mean, he's just very Southern and they aren't used to him."

"Are you comfortable with him?"

I dropped my head. "I'm just so confused, Anna. I respect him and in many ways I wouldn't have made it to Burkina without him."

She shifted her weight, "Luckily, you have some time away from each other to think and pray."

"I have been praying—pleading, really—but God doesn't seem to have anything to say to me about this."

She smiled. "He will."

Her confidence unnerved me. "When?"

"Maybe it's you that needs to make a decision," she said and held out the little bunny cake. "I made this for you." I took it from her.

"It looks too cute to eat," my cheeks cracked when I smiled. I inspected it more closely. The little body of the bunny had ridges "Did you cook this in a soup can?"

"Uh huh." She scrutinized her handiwork and then looked at me, "I thought we could all use a break from the compound."

"Oh yeah?" I perked up. She had a beautiful way of moving forward.

"I'm going to make a picnic dinner and we'll take it to Fada Mountain."

"That sounds great."

She nodded, "It's a full moon tonight so we can sit out there and enjoy the stars." She backed out the door. "I think I'll even invite the Waukens." She winked at me and left.

I watched her hurry back across the compound. I looked down at the bunny. Somehow she had managed to attach its little ears with

— 107 —

Picnic at Fada Mountain

fondant as well. It seemed inhumane to rip off its head and stuff it in my mouth. I set it on a plate and put it on top of the refrigerator near my yogurt starters.

I walked into my living room and read my other mail. John informed me his flight schedule for the Christmas holiday; he would be here from December 20th through January 3$^{rd.}$ He explained that he was raising money for his own "mini-mission" and that he would be building church benches while he was here for the new mission church on the outskirts of Fada. The weather in Beauville was cooling off and the leaves were turning. Football season was underway and he was looking forward to an upcoming family reunion for Thanksgiving. I re-read his letter. His simple life used to annoy me but now I was vaguely jealous of his routine, his complete assurance of whom he was in that little corner of the world.

I picked up Kate Chopin's *The Awakening* and opened it to my marked page and laid down on one of the beds that served as a couch. I had finished *Anna Karenina* and cried when she threw herself in front of the train. I closed *The Awakening* a few hours later and mused over yet another woman who felt she had no choice but to commit suicide, this one swimming out into the Gulf of Mexico. Both women had married young and eventually fell in love with other men but societal restraints kept them from being together. Women lived harder lives, I decided, thinking of my own mom. She had four kids but when she went back to work she still did the majority of the parenting and house care. Other friend's mothers who divorced ended up in town houses while the men bought sports cars and dated their young secretaries. The books on Elinor's shelf had become unexpected friends, and I was always encouraged to know that I was certainly not the first conflicted woman to walk the Earth. I closed my eyes and fell asleep.

"Katherine?" I opened my eyes and looked around. It was dark. "Are you in there?" Malcolm was at my screened door.

I cleared my throat and answered, "Yes."

"C'mon, we're leaving now for our picnic."

"Okay." I got up and fumbled for the light switch. I heard a Gecko lizard scurry away.

Chapter 5

"We're all waiting for you in the truck."
    I darted to the bathroom and quickly brushed my teeth and ran a brush through my hair. I grabbed my blue cardigan sweater from my closet and my keys and flashlight from where I had left them on the kitchen counter and pulled my door shut and locked the padlock. I hurried across the compound to Malcolm's truck underneath the Flamboyant tree and hopped in the opened back door.
    "Sorry, folks," I said as I got in the back seat next to Gritty and pulled the door closed. Stan was squished against the window on the other side of Gritty and Malcolm and Anna were in the front seat.
    Gritty looked at me, "So, what's wrong with you?"
    "What do you mean?"
    "What do you mean 'what do you mean'?" she blurted out. "The whole compound heard you lose it this afternoon." She didn't pause for me to respond, " I figured your fiancé was here already but I guess not, huh?"
    Stan guffawed, "Yeah, Grit, right, her fiancé." He shook his head, "We sure do know how newlyweds are, don't we, Grit?" He elbowed her in the side and she punched him in the arm.
    "Ow!" he rubbed his arm and looked out the window.
    Malcolm started up the truck and pulled out of the compound. Gritty ignored Stan and stared me down.
    "What?" I demanded.
    "What's wrong with you?"
    "Nothing I really want to talk about right now." Did I really need to explain that? It annoyed me that I seemed so transparent to her.
    "It's John isn't it?" I said nothing. "You're having second thoughts, aren't you?"
    At that Anna turned around in her seat, "Gritty, leave the poor girl alone."
    Gritty stared at me but I ignored her. Eventually she looked away and I felt able to breathe again.
    Fada Mountain, which was actually an old dump that had sprouted green life, was about a mile outside of Fada. The moon was full and as we approached we could clearly see the hill bathed in soft focus

from the moon's gentle rays. Anna hopped out first and pulled her trusty picnic basket out of the flatbed.
"Can I help you with that, Anna?" I asked already knowing the answer.
"No, I'm fine." I followed her hobbling across the brush towards the mountain, her small frame weighted down by the basket she insisted on filling and carrying everywhere. "I was caught once without food out here and that was enough—I learned my lesson," she had explained to me a few weeks ago. She never leaves the compound without food and water and then some to share. Malcolm caught up with us with several lawn chairs that he set up in a circle.
"It seems like we should have a bon fire or something," I commented.
"We would be here for hours trying to find wood to burn," Malcolm explained. I should've learned by now that no joking was appreciated, no matter how innocent, when it came to the hardships of life the majority of Africans endured, particularly the women. "That's a full time job for many women."
I nodded and regretted my comment. I thought of the women that I see walk by the compound everyday with branches balanced on their heads. I sat down in a chair. Gritty sat next to me and I quickly thought about moving but where would I go?
Anna opened her basket and handed out napkins and utensils. I leaned my head back and looked up at the night sky. Layer upon layer of twinkling lights and far away places; I had thought the sky only looked like this in fairy tales.
"There's the Southern Cross." Stan pointed to the horizon.
The night sky looked like an Olympic stadium filled with thousands of waving flashlights.
"Katherine?" I looked at Anna and took the plate she offered. It was piled high with a hamburger and potato salad.
"Thank you." I had eaten Anna's hamburger's many times now. The meat was mealy and she handmade her own buns, mayonnaise, and catsup so it all tasted different from what you would expect, but it was tasty.

Chapter 5

Anna handed out plates of food to the rest of the group and then made herself one and sat in the chair on the other side of me.

"Let me ask the Lord's blessing." Malcolm stated. We all bowed our heads.

"We thank you Lord for your abundant grace, your creation, your provision and for your Son."

I looked up but everyone else's heads were still bowed. After several months I still couldn't figure out their timing!

"Amen." Malcolm said at last and we all looked up.

We ate in silence, occasionally looking around when we heard various animals.

"There are mountain lions around here," Stan stated.

"Yes, and we've seen porcupines, too." Malcolm added.

"Really?" I had only seen animals at the zoo.

Stan finished first and stood up, "Where do you want my plate, Annie?"

I saw her face tighten. She hated when Stan called her that. She pulled up the basket cover, "Just put it in there, please."

Stan did as he was told and stood for a moment. "Hey, Malcolm, I'm going to walk around the mountain to see if I can spot any animals." He burped. "Oh, excuse me ladies," he wiped his mouth with the back of his shirtsleeve. "Do you want to join me?"

Malcolm stood up and put his plate in the basket. "Sure." The two men set off towards the mountain. The three of us sat in silence. It was Gritty who spoke first.

"Katherine," she said to the sky. "I wasn't trying to pry when I wondered if you were having second thoughts about your marriage."

I looked at her but she gazed up into the night sky. She rested the back of her neck on the lawn chair. She sighed. "It's just that—I can't believe I'm going to say this, but it doesn't matter anyway—I just wish I had thought more about my marriage before I did it."

I caught Anna's eye and we both looked at Gritty.

"I mean, two kids and thirty years later I'm in for the long haul, don't get me wrong, I take my commitment seriously. It's just I was lonely and I felt that if I didn't take him there wouldn't be anyone else," she shrugged. "I lived alone in a bush outpost delivering lots of babies for four years. And, let me tell you, for a 28 year old woman, that's for the birds." She snorted. "I knew Stan was the other single male from the mission stationed in Burkina but I had never met him. Then, one day he showed up in my compound on an evangelistic tour and that was it," she laughed, remembering. But then, she remembered more and fell silent. She sighed.

"He's from the polluted side of Milwaukee and I'm from Upstate New York, the most beautiful country God ever made. But you get tired of speaking French and when he showed up that day speaking English with an American accent, it was like music to my ears. Of course, that turned out to be the only thing we had in common," she guffawed.

After a while Anna whispered, "You have two wonderful children."

"And they're God's blessing to us. I know that." I saw the moon reflect in Gritty's watery eyes when she looked at Anna. "But, I wasn't passionately in love with Stan. I was passionately in love with being married and having a family." Gritty wiped away the tear stepping tentatively down her cheek. "Stan just happened to be the only other single male missionary in the country. If I had the chance to do it again, I would ask myself if it was really the man I wanted or if I was just afraid to be alone."

We searched the night sky as if it had answers for us. I looked back at Gritty and felt warm to her for the first time.

"I've been reading these books from Elinor's library like *Anna Karenina* and *The Awakening* where all the women commit suicide, it's kind of disturbing," I stated to no one in particular.

Gritty laughed, "Believe me, there have been plenty of times I have thought about throwing myself in front of a train but the bush trains are just too damn slow and there isn't a body of water in West Africa deep enough to drown in!"

"Gritty!" Anna laughed in spite of herself. "Oh, Katherine, life is hard for women. Even today we have more freedom, but society still has different expectations for women than for men."

"Why?" I asked.

Chapter 5

    Gritty shrugged, "Some would say it has to do with original sin, where after the Fall one curse on women, besides pain in childbirth, was that we would desire our husbands. Or, to put it differently, women would find their fulfillment in men."
    I didn't like what she said, but I could hardly deny the familiar theme in the books I had been reading and in my own life, whether I was prepared to admit it or not.
    "But," Anna chimed in, "we can overcome that through a personal relationship with a loving God. It is a daily struggle, but I try to remind myself everyday that I am valued because God loved me first and try not to lean on Malcolm too much for what only God can give me," she nodded to herself as she spoke.
    Gritty looked at me, "Why do you want to marry John?"
    "Well," I glanced at Anna who looked at me with equal curiosity. I looked back at Gritty. "I ask myself that everyday."
    "Do you love him?" Gritty asked.
    "Yes, I do. And I guess because John was a part of all the changes I went through this past year it's as if he's wrapped up with my faith in God."
    "God loves you and John whether you're together or not." Gritty said. "Sometimes God uses other people as vehicles for us to see God or hear Him in a way that we wouldn't otherwise. And then our emotions run amuck and we end up strapped to them for life," she leaned her head back on her chair.
    "Gritty!" Anna chastised again.
    "Let me ask you this, if he never changed from who he is today would you still love him and accept him?" Gritty asked me.
    I glanced at Anna. "No," I admitted. "And, I think there is a lot more baggage from his divorce than he lets on, you know? It seems hard for him to trust anyone, especially women."
    "How long ago was the divorce?" Gritty asked.
    "About five years now."
    "So, why do you want to spend your life with someone you're not comfortable with and who doesn't trust you?"
    "You make it sound easy! But, it's not. My mother asks me the same questions."

Picnic at Fada Mountain

Gritty snorted, "Well, she's looking over her shoulder, isn't she? She sees things that you can't yet."

My warm feelings evaporated. "It drives me crazy when middle-aged women say things like that, it's like they have this secret language or something -"

"Yeah, it's called hindsight," Gritty snapped at me. "She's trying to save you from some misery. She's not the one who will have to sleep with him every night and wake up with the same face every morning. You're the one who needs to believe that he's the best friend you've ever had and that together you can face whatever life throws at you."

We searched each other's eyes. The moon's rays softened her lines making her look younger, more vulnerable. I caught a glimpse of her in my mind's eye as a young, courageous woman who sailed off to Africa on her own full of dreams. But then life became so disappointing that she stopped dreaming and lost hope. Gritty gazed back up at the stars.

"It seems to me he was a really important part of your conversion," Anna's words stepped gently in between us. "He was there during very important changes in your life, and certainly God had a hand in that."

I nodded at her, "Yes, I believe that."

"But, maybe for a season, not a lifetime?" she ventured.

I considered her words and felt some relief. "Yes, maybe."

"Hey, Grit," it was Stan with Malcolm a few steps behind. "They are preparing for a sacrifice on the other side of the mountain."

I looked at Malcolm who explained, "There is a hut with fresh thatching on top of it and a table underneath."

Anna looked at Malcolm. "Maybe we should head back to the compound, eh?"

Malcolm shrugged. "They won't be out until later."

"Its just animals, anyway," Stan chimed in, "They wouldn't want to eat you, Annie."

Anna dropped her plate into her basket and stood up. "I think I'm about ready to go anyway."

Chapter 5

Malcolm held out his hand, "C'mon, Mother," Anna took his hand and he pulled her towards him. "It's a beautiful night, let's take a quick walk around the mountain before we go."

"You all can come, too," Malcolm said to the rest of us so we followed. Malcolm shined his flashlight on the ground, "Look at the porcupine needles."

I picked one up. I could hear animals scurry away. We walked half way around the mountain when Malcolm shined his flashlight up towards a crude hut. Two tree limbs held it up and thatched roofing covered the top. A makeshift table made with a hodge-podge of wooden pieces stood in the middle. As we moved closer the stench overwhelmed me. My mouth got hot and I dry heaved. I turned around and covered my mouth.

"Take a deep breath, Katherine," Malcolm said to my back. "It's a pile of carcasses, move quickly by."

I did as I was told and scurried to catch up with Anna. We continued our journey around the mountain but stopped short. An old woman stood in front of us. She was hunched over and a long cloth was draped over her head and down to the ground.

"We should go." It was Malcolm. He greeted her in Gourma but she didn't respond. We hurried past her and around the mountain back towards the truck. Perhaps it was my imagination, but I felt like I was being chased. I picked up the lawn chair I had been sitting in and quickly folded it and hurried to the truck. I turned to see Gritty, Stan, Malcolm and Anna hurriedly fold their chairs and join me.

"Did you know her?" I asked Malcolm.

"Well, I don't know her. But, suffice it to say that the hut was hers and we were in her territory."

"What was that smell?" I asked Malcolm.

"Blood and rotting animal carcasses," Malcolm moved around to the driver's side of the truck. "When blood is baked in sun it smells horrible."

We piled into the safety of the truck. Malcolm drove across the brush and onto the paved road to head home.

I couldn't get the picture of the woman out of my mind. I rolled down my window and enjoyed the fresh air.

Picnic at Fada Mountain

"I think there is a funeral tonight," Gritty announced.
"Is there, Gritty?" Malcolm answered over his shoulder. "Philippe didn't mention anything to me."
"It's not one of the Christian or Muslim families," Gritty explained. "I heard someone talking about it at the pharmacy today."
"Oh," Malcolm nodded.
I looked at Gritty, "Whose funeral?"
"I don't know who it is but it means we won't get much sleep tonight."
"Why?"
"Because the family carries the dead body from place to place at night trying to hide its final resting place from the evil spirits," she explained in her unaffected way. "It's an animist tradition, but you'll find even the Christian and Muslim families still seek the Medicine Man for healing, regardless of their religion."
I nodded and leaned my head out the window to get some more air.
Anna looked over her seat, "You'll hear a lot of cackling and hysterics; it's their way of mourning."
"What are you thinking about, Katherine?" Gritty was so close I could feel her hot breath on my cheek as she spoke. I leaned my head out the window further.
"Miriam's house god. When I first arrived we had dinner there and she mentioned their house god."
"Oh yeah, there are gods for everything," Gritty explained. "That's why when I tell people about the God of Jesus they say 'we know about the good God we just worry about the bad gods.'"
"What do they mean by bad gods?" I asked.
Gritty leaned closer to my face, "The gods that take away their babies during birth, their crops, their rain." She hissed the words and spat on my cheek.
Stan leaned around her and added, "Grit has had to bury a lot of wee little babies."
"I'll bet," I could barely contain the disgusted look on my face, "Could you maybe back up a little? I'm almost falling out of the window."

Chapter 5

Gritty and Stan scooted away a few inches. Thankfully we pulled up to the familiar burgundy gates and Danjou popped his head through to see who it was before pulling both gates open wide for the truck.

Malcolm parked the truck underneath the Flamboyant Tree. I opened my door and hopped out before he had pulled up the emergency brake. "Do you need any help, Anna?"

"No, thanks, Malcolm can help me," Anna winked at me. "Go get some sleep. You've had a long day."

"Goodnight, everyone," I turned on my flashlight and hustled across the compound to my house. I flipped on the kitchen light and stood at my window watching everyone unload the truck and head to their houses. I turned to put the kettle on to boil when I noticed something moving on the floor. I scrambled up to sit on the counter from a safe vantage point before looking more closely: hundreds of baby spiders were crawling all over one another in the form of a circle on my kitchen floor. I sat and watched them for a moment. What do I do with hundreds of baby spiders? Do I stomp all over them? Do I scoop them up and throw them outside? Do I let them roam my house so that the Gecko lizards have something to eat?

I spotted a much larger, hairier version of the spider on my wall. I then looked up to my ceiling and noticed three Geckos watching the floor.

"Okay," I told the lizards, "you guys take care of this one." I slid off the counter and quickly made my tea. I stepped over the baby spiders and flipped off the kitchen light and went into my bedroom. I changed into my sweats and a T-shirt for bed, brushed my teeth and, out of curiosity, went back into the kitchen and flipped on the light. The baby spiders, the hairy spider and the lizards were nowhere to be seen. "Who needs Raid?" I turned off the kitchen light and crawled under my mosquito net with my journal, Bible, flashlight and my latest selection from Elinor's shelf called *Shepherd of the Hills* by Harold Bell Wright.

I wrote in my journal for a while but I felt edgy. I opened the book but I was too distracted to read. I slid my journal, the book and my Bible under the net and onto the floor. I flipped off my flashlight and lay on my back. I tried to pray but I couldn't concentrate long enough. My room was quite light from the full moon. I don't know if it was my talk with Gritty or the woman we had seen, but I felt unsettled.

My nighttime musings had begun innocently enough remembering times alone with my fiancé to feel close to him, to feel needed. But these grew into something unrecognizable so I endeavored to push them away. That void was then filled by memories of other lovers, other souls that had touched mine briefly and yet had stayed with me. I relived the abortion and other humiliating times like when strangers pulled me from a bush where I had passed out walking home from a bar during college in the dead hours of the morning. Each experience rose and confronted me one after another and I felt raw shame.

I had a recurring dream where I was scrambling to crawl out of a ditch but the dirt was loose so I couldn't make it to the top. I kept grasping at the dark soil but only dug myself in deeper and it eventually suffocated me. I would wake myself up panting, clinging to my pillow, and wet with sweat.

I rolled over and looked out at the night sky through my kitchen window. The window offered me as much solace during the night as it did during the day.

"Lord, forgive me," I whispered. I licked a bead of sweat off my lip.

I could hear the Mullah call his people to prayer, it pirouetted across the lake that lay on the other side of the Fada Road from our compound. Now that the rainy season was over the lake had begun drying up, but it was still a large body of water. That night there seemed to be more activity, it sounded like a hysterical party. I eventually dozed off...

I opened my eyes and saw him. He was on all fours straddled on top of me. I blinked to focus my sleepy eyes but he was still there. His face was painted and draped over his head he wore a cloth like the old woman. He had deep scars on his cheeks; I recognized them as tribal markings. His arms were strong and his legs straddled mine.

I opened my mouth but no words came out. I shut it again. He was vibrant, alive. To this day I can recall his image without effort; the Gourma Man has stayed with me. He breathed in deeply.

Chapter 5

"Gour-Ma," he leaned in to my face. "Gour-*Ma*," he threatened. I turned my head away and braced for an attack.

I looked back at him but he hadn't moved. He stared at me. His large, dark eyes penetrated me with the whites behind them glowing like two full moons.

He leaned into my face again, "Gour-ma," he said but never touched me.

A bead of sweat trickled down my forehead. I thought it dropped from him, but it was mine. I swallowed but had no saliva. "Help me, Lord," I whispered from my gut. "Help me, Jesus." I said out loud.

I turned my head to the left, and looked through to the kitchen and out of my familiar window. The moon was still there. And somewhere from far away, or was it from within? A voice barely audible whispered, "Do not fear, Katherine." The words so simple and clear had I not been listening I would've missed them. It was a message not to my ear, but to my soul.

I looked back at the Gourma man.

"Gour-Ma," he said again but this time with effort; defeated. He wavered and then pixilated into thousands of dots, and was gone.

I sat bolt upright in my bed. I was drenched in sweat; my hair stuck to the back of my neck. I pulled it up into a ponytail and held it there for a moment. I thought about changing my wet clothes but didn't dare leave my bed. I touched my cheek: it was hot. I felt my forehead and wiped the last beads of sweat away with my hand. I lay back on my pillow and stared up into my mosquito net. I lifted my T-shirt and massaged my stomach lightly as I often did before falling asleep.

"Forgive me, Lord," Thinking again about all the exhausting dreams and memories that filled my nights.

"I have. Forgive yourself," came the response.

At once I realized that the relief from guilt and shame for which I sought was granted but I had been unwilling to accept it. I rolled over onto my side strangely comforted. A peace descended on me and I was buoyed by a silent confidence; an assurance that I was set free by forgiveness and was truly not alone.

Danjou pumped the water into my drum as he did every morning at dawn. But this morning was different; I was seated at Elinor's writing desk and watched him walk past the window across my back porch towards the well. I had always wondered why she would want to sit at her desk and stare at the compound wall, but when the sun rose the desk was bathed in a ballet pink glow and it was if God himself announced, "Good morning, Katherine, and welcome to a new day."

I responded out loud, "Good morning, Lord!" and basked in the gentle warmth of the first sun. Minutes later it became the stronger, orange morning light and set about to the business of the day. I stood up and made myself a cup of tea and brought my journal and Bible to the writing table. I decided that I didn't like the tablecloth Anna had covered it with so I pulled it off and tossed it on one of the nearby beds.

What a treasure I had uncovered! Elinor had carved almost every inch of the wooden table with words. Across the top was etched, 'I rise before dawn and cry for help; I have put my hope in your word. Ps 119:147.' And next to that she had carved, 'May I seek you in the morning and learn to walk in your ways.' Other words I recognized as Gourma with English etched below them: peace, holiness, and names like Israel and Samaria. I surmised they were words she regularly used in her translation work. It was a glimpse of Elinor and I felt as if I'd been invited to discover her sacred place.

I wrote in my journal and thought for a long time about the night before. I saw the face of the Gourma man in my mind's eye. I sensed that I stuck my big toe into an ice cold bath and pulled it out in time to know not to get in. I wrote, "Do not fear, Katherine," in my journal. I thought about John and all the same fears of breaking up with him came to the surface of my mind so I wrote it again, "Do not fear, Katherine." I remembered my son and wrote, "Hold him safe, Lord, because I would not."

I considered my own mission and realized I had barely even been off the compound since I had arrived five months ago. I had been so focused on my own issues that I hadn't really involved myself in Fada outside the compound walls. I changed into my khaki skirt and pink polo shirt with the Ostrich on the breast and looked in the mirror.

Chapter 5

"That's the next thing I'm going to do," I told my reflection. "Bush clothes."

I walked across the compound into my office and through to Malcolm's. My step felt lighter and I caught myself humming. Malcolm looked at me and then at his watch. He had never seen me before eight in the morning and it was barely seven. His hair was still wet from his 'a.m. icer', as he called it, and his Bible lay open on his desk.

"Am I disturbing you?" I asked.

"No, please," he waved his hand. "Please sit down."

"Is there someone who can help me in the market? Maybe someone who can help me have some clothes made?"

"Well, Anna is very busy…"

"No, I wouldn't ask anything more of Anna." I interrupted him; "I meant one of the girls from the compound."

Malcolm regarded me for a moment and smiled. "I don't think that will be any problem." He took off his glasses and laid them down. "I'll talk to Philippe about it today."

"Thanks." I looked around his office.

"Are you okay, Katherine?"

"I'm fine."

"I mean, it's awfully early and you seem awfully alert. You were even humming, which I dare say is a first."

I smiled. "I had a dream last night."

Malcolm nodded slowly, knowingly.

"And, I also realized that I've been too focused on what's been going on back home and not here, you know?"

"It's hard not to think about the people we love, especially when they're so far away."

We sat in silence for a moment, not an awkward silence but a peaceful silence.

"This is a very spiritual place. This area, in particular, is supposed to be the birthplace of Voodoo before it was exported with the slaves to the Caribbean." He rubbed his hands together. "Our dream life has had its exciting moments as well," he assured me.

"Oh, yeah?" I smiled, eager for some details.

Picnic at Fada Mountain

"Yes." He said with finality, not giving any. "The spirit world is alive and active. But, don't dwell too much on that," he waved his hand. "Dwell on God and let Him take care of the rest."

"Yes, I'm gathering that is our lifelong challenge," I smiled and he nodded.

He put his glasses back on which meant I was dismissed. "I'll see what I can do to find you some help."

"Thanks." I headed out. I stopped and turned around to tell him about the Gourma Man and he was still looking at me. He nodded and smiled as if to say, "You're okay," and I realized I didn't need to tell him. I left and walked back across the compound to my house. I waved to the meat man leaning against his wheelbarrow underneath the Flamboyant tree.

"Bonjour, Madame!" He took off his cap and bowed deeply, as he had always done to Anna.

"Bonjour," I said to the rest of the group of elderly women sitting under the Flamboyant tree waving flies away. I guessed they were all waiting to see Malcolm. To be honest, I had never noticed them before.

6
Sarai & Rachel

Powder blue, ballet pink, lemon yellow, pistachio green and perhaps a teddy bear brown. It was hard to tell as the little birds moved so quickly! Anna thought they were African Rollers, little finch like birds that swirled in groups together, and she had suggested I put some sugar water in a pie pan to attract them.

I had just finished my morning time at Elinor's desk when something caught my eye. I had strategically placed my pie pan a few feet from my desk window so what a delight it was to look up and see the rainbow of birds jostling for position around the rim of the pie plate! They jumped and splashed and pecked at the water. Suddenly in a swoosh of color they were gone. But they had just lined up on the compound wall. And suddenly they were back! One by one they landed on the pie plate and then like dominoes they flew off again. My fun was over. I sighed and wondered what to do with myself that Saturday in early November.

Clap, Clap. I heard outside my door. The Burkinabé clapped instead of knocked I assumed because most of them lived in mud huts and didn't have doors. It was a courtesy.

I pushed open the screened door to find a young woman clutching a green plastic bag that billowed when a breeze caught it. Her glasses were uneven which magnified one eyeball leaving the other to enjoy its natural state. I had learned that many charities sent used prescription eyeglasses to developing countries so when one needed corrective lens' they simply tried on eyeglasses until they found a pair that seemed to better their vision. Being an imperfect correction, many people adjusted one lens or the other on their face so, from my personal observation, crooked glasses were the norm.

"Oui?" I smiled.

"I am Sarai," she told me in French. "Philippe sent me here to help you."

"Oh!" I held the door open wide for her, "Please, come on in."

She slid off her orange plastic flip-flops and left them on my cement block stoop and I followed her inside. Sarai was tall and muscular. She kept her hair cropped to her head without any ornamentation. She wore a faded Dallas Cowboys T-shirt and a swath of African fabric wrapped around her into a long sarong: teenage bush chic.

We stood in the kitchen and I explained to her, in French, why she was there. Because my French was questionable she kept shaking her head in confusion so I repeated myself several times and often referred to my French dictionary throughout our discussion. At long last, she held up her green plastic bag, made a clicking sound in the back of her throat and declared, "Let's go to the marché."

I padlocked the door and off we went.

Sarai introduced me to areas of the market I had not known existed. She bartered for me in Gourma, to the consternation of her peers, which meant I had better fruit and vegetables than anyone else on the compound! She introduced me to a tailor and once he waved his measuring tape around me we presented him with fabric I had chosen from another market stall to make three new African dresses for me. We returned to the compound heavy laden with plastic bags.

Sarai took out the flour I had purchased and dumped it all over a dilapidated metal table that stood next to my front stoop.

"What are you doing?" I asked her.

She ignored me and continued her work. I watched as she smoothed the flour with her hand like butter cream frosting evenly over the table. She looked at me and pointed to the small black bugs that began to make their way up to the surface of the flour.

"Weevils?" she asked.

I looked closer.

"Weevils." She pointed again to the bugs. "This table is for cleaning your flour," she instructed me.

Chapter 6

I inspected the bugs more closely. "It's there so that the weevils can crawl out and die?" I marveled at the outrageousness of the whole affair!

"Oui," Sarai clicked the back of her throat and nodded. "The sun will kill them. Then sift your flour clean of them in the evening."

Sarai took out my trash, which until this day, I had lugged across the compound to Anna's compost and dump heaps. She picked up my sealed container and walked out of my house and around to the side yard. "Burn your trash in here," she instructed again. She tossed everything in the metal drum buried halfway into the ground, struck a match and it exploded with flames and quickly died down. I followed her back into the house.

She swept, she dusted, and she hummed to the "Tracy Chapman" cassette I had brought from home and I followed her around enjoying the company of someone in my house.

I pulled two bottled drinks out of my refrigerator. "Fanta or Coke?" I asked her.

"Fan-ta."

We stood and sipped our cold drinks for a moment. "Would you like to come back next Saturday?" I asked her.

"Oui," she looked away from me and smiled.

I had put a frying pan on the stove with some hot oil in it to cook some potatoes and had forgotten about it. I drenched a towel under the kitchen faucet to do some cleaning in my room and inadvertently a corner of the wet towel draped over the frying pan and flames leapt to the ceiling! I screamed and dove for cover on the floor.

The flames dissipated and I looked up to see Sarai nonchalantly turn off the gaslight and move the pan to the back burner. I regarded her from the floor.

"That was scary!" I got up off the floor and wiped off my skirt. Sarai tried to keep a straight face but she turned her head away and burst into laughter. She was so overcome she bent herself in half laughing and I couldn't help but laugh along with her. We laughed together for a long time.

From that point on, Sarai showed up every Saturday morning and clapped outside my door. I grabbed my collection of empty plastic grocery bags and money belt and padlocked the door behind us. As we meandered down the Fada Road toward the market it seemed that Sarai always had a question for me she must've spent time thinking about during the week.

"Is it true in America that money comes out of walls?" she asked me in French.

I was confused but it quickly dawned on me, "Oh, you mean a cash station?" I smiled. "Yes, it does come out of the wall of a bank but you have to put money into the bank first."

Another day she asked me, "Is it true in your country that people go on diets because they're so fat?"

"Yes."

"Why don't they just stop eating?"

How could I explain to Sarai that we had so much of everything that we simply couldn't control ourselves? How does one explain excess to someone that considers one meal a day the norm and frequently spends all day long preparing for that one meal?

"Our lives are over complicated, Sarai."

She nodded and clicked the back of her throat. "Oui, like the movie *The God's Must Be Crazy*."

"Yes," I smiled. Talking with me seemed to confirm the truth she saw in that movie.

"That is my favorite movie."

"I know." She had only ever seen that and *Purple Rain* on the crumbling mud brick wall of the local Fada cinema.

In late November, Sarai and I were cutting behind stalls and mud alleys to the Fada Road after another successful market day. I had picked up my new dresses from the tailor and was hunting for more material. The rains had been poor so fresh vegetables were scarce but I had discovered some 'Hits', a cookie sandwich with a thin layer of chocolate, in one of the larger stalls and amused the shopkeeper by purchasing ten packages. I knew that just because they appeared one week did not mean they would be there again. Chocolate was extremely difficult to come by, so I didn't take any chances. I inhaled my third one and looked at Sarai.

"Are you sure you don't want one?"

Chapter 6

She scrunched up her face and waved her hand. "I don't like them."

I shrugged and took another before dropping the remaining package into one of my bags. I looked up and caught Stan's eye. Oddly, he was standing in a market stall and looked to be selling something. I walked over to him.

"Hi Stan, what are you selling today?" I teased, I didn't think he was really selling anything. But, he waved his hand across the table.

"Well, today I've got some fine cuts of meat. And, hey, Christmas is comin' up and I've got just the thing for you. Hold on!" He turned around and rummaged through some old boxes. I glanced at Sarai who was inspecting the meat. "Ah!" he returned triumphant with the saddest looking three foot artificial Christmas tree I had ever seen.

"It looks like its been through a war!" I laughed.

He took off his cap and gave it a few swipes. "Aw, it's fine. I'll give it to you for 20,000 CFA."

"What?" I did a quick calculation in my head. "That's almost thirty dollars!"

"These are extremely difficult to come by in these Muslim parts of the world."

"No doubt, Stan. But, I'm not buying it." He shrugged and tossed it over his shoulder.

"How about some meat then, sweetie?" He waved the flies away and lifted up a bloody slab of something on brown paper.

"Well, sweetie, it doesn't have a red band on it. Aren't you supposed to run it by the inspector?"

He didn't like being called sweetie any more than I did. "Naw, I don't need the inspector. I've been doin' this a long time. I know my meat is healthy."

I looked at him for a moment. He wore a Hawaiian shirt with old black polyester pants. His grey hair was slicked back. It hit me: he should've been a used car salesman. His breast pocket bulged with pencils and pens.

"Do you need a new pen? I'll give you three for 1,000CFA."

"That's okay, Stan. I've done enough buying for today."

"Well, don't come cryin' to me if you run out of pens. They're hard to find out here."

"I don't think you need to worry about that." I assured him. I looked around for Sarai.

"Hey, how about some canned tomatoes then?" he pushed. "The rains have been poor," he wiggled his eyebrows.

"Stan, I think you missed your calling, you should've sold used cars."

Stan pulled himself up straight and wagged his finger at me. "I've been out here servin' the Lord for thirty-one years. Everything I do is for His glory. This little market stall has helped a lot of people afford things they wouldn't normally be able to." Another customer walked up so he quickly forgot his indignation and went to wait on them.

Sarai rejoined me and we left. "Did you know that Stan had a market stall?" I asked Sarai.

"No," she said but she looked away from me and smiled. Sarai and I headed home.

Downtown Fada N'Gourma consisted mainly of rambling rows of corrugated tin roofed stalls that made up the market. Fada was considered a larger town because you could shop in the market everyday, whereas in small villages market days might be only once or twice a week. There were bars, restaurants and hotels on the outskirts of the market with names like 'Café Noir', but they were hard to distinguish with the untrained eye, they all looked the same to me, mud brick with thief-proofing on the occasional window. The bakery sat on the corner of the market in a mud brick house where I always stopped and bought five or six baguettes on the way home. Anna taught me to freeze them until you need them and then to quickly run them under water before heating them in the oven.

Past the bakery there was a large circle, or roundabout, at the city's center. Dotted around the circle were various government administrative mud brick buildings all painted Pistachio green. In the center of the circle stood a cement pedestal where the flag of Burkina Faso proudly waved. This center also served as a focal point for the town, when there was a parade or celebration it took place around the circle.

Chapter 6

In most cities in Burkina there were army checkpoints where the gendarmerie would ask to see passport, car papers, and inquire into your plans. A little extra cash seemed to smooth the passage. The Fada checkpoint was at the circle so there were always army men standing around talking and smoking waiting for a car or truck to stop.

"Bonjour, Madame," one of the army men greeted me.

"Bonjour." I waved and they all chuckled.

"Why do they always laugh, Sarai?"

She either didn't hear me or didn't want to answer. She was one of the few young women who could attend school on a regular basis so she was generally privileged within the Fada community. She may have been as uncomfortable as I.

After the brief interruption of the circle, the Fada Road resumed to two lanes lined with Mahogany trees. They were planted by the French and gave the otherwise brown countryside a splash of oldie worldliness. We crossed the bridge over the shrinking lake, which was well used by women bent over washing clothes by hand and naked children running in and out of the murky water. The familiar burgundy gates greeted us on the right after crossing the bridge.

We returned from the market and I changed into one of my new dresses. The material was English Wax, which was a stiff cotton material with a sheen. The background was black with red and yellow geometric shapes in the fore ground. I had also purchased a pair of sandals in the market that were black with gold designs. Sarai nodded in approval when I showed her my new outfit.

"Trés jolie!" she exclaimed.

I stood spreading my flour on the metal table while Sarai tackled the inside. Even though it was officially the "cool season" it only seemed cool at night. The afternoon was lovely and warm so my new dresses afforded me room to get a little sun on my arms and chest. "We have a visitor coming tonight," I told Sarai. She clicked the back of her throat and nodded.

The Guest House was filled to capacity so Anna had asked if I would mind sharing my house with a young woman named Rachel Staples. She was Canadian and was passing through on her way to

Niamey, the capital of Niger, where she would be stationed. "Would I mind?" I laughed when Anna asked. "Of course not!"

From my table I watched Anna exit her kitchen with a young woman following behind. She was dressed in a long cotton skirt and a polo shirt, much like I had worn when I first arrived. She had short blond hair and patted it into place like Anna did as she walked along. I met them at my gate. "Hi!" I exclaimed. "I'm Katherine."

"Hi." Rachel smiled. "I'm Rachel."

"Well, I guess I don't need to make any introductions." Anna smiled. "Please join us for dinner around six, okay?"

"Sure, Anna." I was so excited to have a new friend the thought of feasting on Anna's food didn't even hold the same appeal.

"Oh," Anna handed me a letter, "This arrived for you this morning."

"Thanks," I immediately recognized the oversized scrawl and my heart sank, it was from John. It was the first letter I had received since writing him to say that I didn't think I was ready to marry him. "C'mon in and I'll show you around." I said to Rachel. Anna squeezed my shoulder and headed back to her kitchen. Rachel followed me inside.

Sarai stood in the kitchen sipping a Fanta with a rag tossed over her shoulder. I introduced them to one another and showed Rachel into my sitting room, which would now be her bedroom. Rachel stood and looked around for a moment. She looked from the lizards scampering across the walls back to Sarai sipping her drink. She looked at my writing desk stacked with airmail paper next to a weary candle and then up to the volumes of Penguin Classics piled on top of Louis Lamour on the bookshelves. Finally her eyes rested on my African dress and me and scaled down to my gold and black sandals and finally she looked up and met my eyes.

"How long have you been here?"

"Me? Since July."

"Of this year?"

"Yeah!" I laughed. "Why?"

"It looks like you've been here a lot longer. You seem really settled in."

Chapter 6

"I do? Well, that's nice of you to say. But, I would bet Malcolm and Anna might think otherwise."

She slumped down on one of the beds. "I just feel so overwhelmed."

I was relieved that I wasn't the only one who struggled. I knelt down next to her, "Listen, Rachel." She looked exhausted. "I promise, it gets easier."

I sat Sarai and Rachel down at my table. I served them mint tea and short bread cookies that I had spent hours making the previous night. I couldn't help but snicker to myself thinking of what my Friday evenings used to entail. Making shortbread cookies was decidedly healthier. I verily danced around the kitchen. Guests! I joined them at the table.

Sarai nibbled a cookie, scrunched up her face and gagged. "You don't have to eat it, Sarai." She looked relieved and went back to her Fanta. "Sarai is suspect of eating anything that hasn't boiled for hours over an open fire." I explained to Rachel.

"I think they're good." Rachel said.

"Thanks." I helped myself to one. "Anna gave me a special bush cookbook that she wrote herself."

"Really?"

I took a bite. "So, what will you be doing in Niamey?"

"I'll be teaching in the missionary academy."

"What subject?"

"English, to seventh and eighth graders."

"That's great." I sipped my tea.

"What do you do here?"

Sarai caught my eye and smiled. "Well, I help Malcolm in the office and Anna with the Guest House." I looked at Rachel. "And, generally survive."

She laughed. Her eyes were as brown as mine were blue. "It seems like you're surviving pretty well," she said.

"Well, thanks," I said. "If you'll excuse me for just a second, I need to read this letter."

"Sure," she said and took another cookie.

— 131 —

I walked into the kitchen and opened the letter. "I refuse to believe you don't want to marry me. And anyway, I have already raised my funds for my mini-mission so I'm still coming. I recommend you pray about this more before my arrival in December. I love you anyway, Love, John." I joined them again at the table.

"Bad news?" Rachel asked.

"I guess it depends on your perspective," I mused. "It's John, my fiancé, he wrote to say he is still coming to visit over Christmas."

"And this is a bad thing?" she was confused. "I would think that would be very romantic."

I sipped my tea. "I am dreading his visit." Suddenly my cheeks flushed and the tears streamed from my eyes. I dropped my head into my hands. Sarai got up from the table and hurried back to my room with her towel in hand. Rachel sat and sipped her tea.

"I'm sorry." I snorted ungracefully. "I know I sound awful but I just want him to go away! But, now he's coming for two weeks and I'm going to have to break up with him face to face and I'm afraid of his reaction."

"What, like he'll hurt you?"

"No, just that he won't take 'no' for an answer."

She raised her eyebrows in response, "Do you not love him?"

"I'm sure I do love him, but I don't want to spend the rest of my life with him. " I added, "John told me that he believed God had put us together and I have really struggled with the weight of those words. I've finally come to peace with the notion that, yes, God did bring us into each other's lives, but not for a lifetime."

"Well, the man is supposed to be spiritual head of the household."

I looked at her. "Do you really believe that John should make a lifelong decision *for* me even if I don't feel the same way?"

"No, I'm just saying that sometimes we need to allow the man to lead." She sipped her tea. "I mean, women are different—with our hormones and physically—we're not really created for leadership."

I scoffed at her words! "How can you say that with a straight face? Do you hear what you're saying?"

"Yes. I'm saying women are different."

Chapter 6

"Of course we're different, but that doesn't mean one is superior to the other."

"It's an issue of obedience and authority," she stated.

"Whose authority?"

"The Bible's."

"My Bible says that male and female were created in God's image and without one or the other that image is incomplete."

Rachel shrugged. "We disagree."

We sat in uncomfortable silence. Why did I assume this was going to be an easy, automatic friendship?

"How many serious relationships have you had?" I wondered.

"Well, none really."

I looked at her with different goggles. "You have never dated?"

"I have dated. But, I haven't really had a serious relationship." She bit into another cookie. "I mean—I have been kissed," she waved her hand to set the record straight.

"Kissed?" I was stunned.

"Don't think bad of me," she giggled.

"For being kissed?" I sighed. "I don't think bad of you." The torrid trail of past relationships shuffled across my memory like a chain gang. I had been in one serious relationship after another since I was seventeen. Was I afraid to be on my own? Did men give me a feeling of purpose and self-worth? And here was Rachel, willing to hand complete authority over to anyone of the male species and yet her life had been refreshingly unencumbered by the complications of a penile presence.

Rachel seemed buoyed by food and drink. She ate my last shortbread cookie.

"The problem I've always had is that people think I'm perfect." She swallowed hard and continued. "I've been a committed Christian since I was four so I've always understood the need to save myself for marriage."

I nodded and swallowed the last of my tea. Clearly I had missed this message.

"And, I've always known I would be a missionary. I'm a fourth generation missionary. My family has always enjoyed a special call to spread the Gospel to God's unreached people." She explained quite matter of factly. "So, I was always looking for someone who had a heart for missions and respected my desire to keep my virginity."

So, here I sat with missionary royalty. "Great." I said at last. "Let me go check on Sarai." I left Rachel sitting at the table.

We were the same age in the same spot in the world at the same time and yet our paths leading there could not have been more different. Rachel arrived with a sense of privilege, a journey that had been laid out for her from a young age and never challenged. The world for her was black and white: saved and unsaved. In contrast, no one could have predicted that I, a sorority girl with a burlap sack of wild oats to sow, would've been called as a missionary. I arrived on the mission field with a keen sense of my brokenness. I struggled each night with a feeling of unworthiness that God truly loved me. I had come to recognize that Jesus quite literally saved me from myself.

Sarai was in my room shaking out my mosquito net. "Do you really use this?" She asked. I had gotten used to her state of bemusement when it came to my living practices.

I took my purse out of the bottom drawer and paid Sarai a 500 CFA note. Normally she took the bill and split but today she lingered. "Is something wrong?" I asked her.

"Non." She shook her head and fixed her eyes on the ceiling. "May I have more money, please?" she asked in English. "The choir is having new dresses made for Christmas and I can not pay."

"How much do you need?" I asked her.

"One more 500 CFA."

I pulled another bill out of my purse and handed it to her.

"Merci beaucoup," she looked relieved. She clicked the back of her throat and left. Anna had advised me to pay her the 500 CFA as that was the compounds' standard rate, but I was pleased to help Sarai buy a new dress for Christmas. I mused over the universality of our lives and rejoined Rachel at the table.

"Is everything okay?" she asked me.

"Oh, fine, Sarai just wanted a little extra to have a new dress made for the choir's Christmas performances."

Chapter 6

"That's sweet."
"Would you like something more to eat?"
"No, I'm fine."
"So, you'll have to find someone out here?"
"Yeah, but I hear the pickings are slim," Rachel said.
"You might want to talk to Gritty about that."
"Who?"
"The Wauken's. They will be at dinner tonight."
"Oh." Rachel looked around. "What about you?"
"What about me?"
"How did you end up on the mission field?"
"I felt called."
"Do you have any family in missions?"
"No, lots of lawyers but no missionaries," I smiled.
"Do you come from a mission-minded church?"
"Not particularly."
"Have you lived overseas before?"
"No."
"Have you traveled overseas?"
"No," I giggled. "I guess it's good that none of those questions were on the application, huh?"
She seemed put out. "Who's supporting you?"
"The Episcopal church I grew up in outside D.C.."
"Episcopalian?" she scrunched up her face.
"Why, what's wrong with that?"
"Nothing, I guess. I'm just surprised they supported you. I mean, do they even believe in the Resurrection?"
"The Resurrection? You mean that died and rose again three days later thingy?" I razzed her. "Well, the laity certainly does—the priests are coming along at their own pace." I smiled. "Is there something wrong?"
"No, you just don't seem like the missionary type. I mean, don't take this the wrong way, but you don't fit the missionary mold."
I burst into laughter, "Well, thank God for small mercies!" My months in Burkina had buoyed my confidence and I knew that I had been called regardless of my lack of missionary pedigree.

We sat in uncomfortable silence. "Anna is a great cook." I changed the subject. "We'll have a good dinner tonight."
"How old is John?" Rachel asked.
"He's thirty-five."
"Really?" Rachel nodded. "Is this his second marriage?"
"Yes, but he doesn't have any children."
"Why are you still engaged to him?"
I looked down. "I wrote and shared with him that I was having doubts but he won't listen to me. He has raised money to come to Burkina on his own 'mini-mission' to build benches for the new church, so he is excited for the opportunity. I guess I want to see him one last time, I want to see his face and know that I'm making the right decision. It's hard to let go of someone who loves you."
"I know I would only become engaged to someone who I felt passionate about physically and emotionally and spiritually."
"Is that really possible?" I asked with my hands, "I'm beginning to think our expectations are out of whack."
Rachel shook her head vehemently. "No. I refuse to believe that God has asked me to save myself for anything less than the perfect person for me."
"Perfect?"
"Yes."
"I think you might be waiting a long time."
She dismissed my words with a shrug, "Then I'll wait."
That evening Rachel and I presented ourselves to assist Anna. She was feeding dinner on her porch to all the visitors on the compound which numbered sixteen. The rains had been poor and there wasn't a lot of food in the market.
"What are you feeding everyone?" I asked from my stool.
"Well, I found ten pumpkins in the market. I filled them with ground beef, some tomatoes and onions, lots of seasoning and I'll hope for the best!"
Anna's sheer ingenuity astounded me.
"Plus, I've made fresh bread and some donuts for dessert."
Rachel shook her head. "I'll eat better here than I do at home!"

Chapter 6

Rachel and I helped set up the porch for dinner. I settled into cobalt blue woven chair and watched in delight as the variety of nationalities gathered on the porch for dinner. Gritty struggled up onto the porch with Stan in tow.

I introduced Gritty to Rachel.

"I was telling Rachel how you met Stan out here," I explained to Gritty.

"Are you a career missionary?" She asked Rachel.

"Yes, this is my first term."

"What's your last name?"

"Staples."

"Oh, your Grandfather was Erwin, he set up the station in Liberia?"

"Yes."

"Oh, right, well, it's great to have you here." I wouldn't have thought Gritty capable of 'perking' but she perked. She and Rachel and Stan began the "Do you know?" game.

"Excuse me," I mumbled and headed to the kitchen to help Anna carry pumpkins to the porch. "Do you need some help carrying those?" I asked Anna in her kitchen.

"Oh, thanks." She handed me a platter. We walked through her living room towards the porch.

"I saw Stan in the market today," I said to her.

"Oh yeah? What was he selling this time?"

I chuckled. "He tried to sell me his little Christmas tree for thirty dollars!"

She shook her head. "Honestly. He's been trying to sell that thing since their kids left home years ago." We stopped in front of the porch door.

"He didn't like it when I told him he should've been a used car salesman."

She smiled, "Well, I know how you feel. But, the Lord calls people, we don't."

I felt like she had slapped my wrist. I moved to open the door for her.

"Listen, Katherine, I say that because I have to tell myself that everyday. I've asked the Lord so many times of all the missionary families in the country why we have to live with them. But, I've stopped asking because I've realized that the Lord is still working on me after all these years. He's still refining me. And, that makes me feel good."

Anna turned and backed out of the screened door with her platter of pumpkins.

I helped her set the pumpkins down on the table and sat down. Malcolm quieted everyone.

"Anna and I would like to welcome you to Fada," he smiled and made eye contact with everyone. "In our house we pray before dinner. So, I invite you to please bow your heads with me as we thank the Lord for his provision."

Everyone did as they were told. "Lord, we do thank you for your provision, your love and the reminder that there are never any chance meetings. In your Son's name we pray. Amen."

I looked up with everyone else, but Malcolm still had his head bowed. We sat quietly waiting for Malcolm to finish his silent prayer.

Once he opened his eyes Anna hopped up and began serving generous slices of pumpkin loaded with the ground beef mixture. Malcolm went around the circle asking people in French and English where they were from and how they came to be in Fada.

"We are Swiss-French," the first man explained as he pointed to the pretty blond woman next to him. "We ferry cars across the Mediterranean on a barge and then caravan them across the desert. We sell them in Ouagadougou."

Malcolm looked at the rest of us. "The Swiss have extremely high regulations for cars because their roads are so mountainous and snowy."

"Yes, that's correct. So, each year we bring a load down to Burkina Faso and sell them for a profit. They are in perfectly good condition." He looked at his companion. "But, this time we got caught in a sand storm and Francoise rear-ended me. She is not so well."

"I'm sorry to hear that. Will you see a doctor in Ouagadougou?"

Chapter 6

"Yes, we will," he patted his companion's hand.

Malcolm looked at the next woman. She was short with thick gray hair and wore a suit, which looked out of place. She had a quick eye and strong hands, belying her petite stature. "And your name?" he asked.

"My name is Elisabeth Luder," she stated in English with a heavy French accent. "I am Belgian by birth, Canadian by choice."

Malcolm smiled, "Elisabeth, your reputation proceeds you, I recognize your name."

"The ex-pat world is small, is it not?"

"It is. But, I must add that there aren't many who would choose to be Canadian, and I speak as a proud Canadian."

"I escaped with my family to Canada during the War and chose to become a Canadian citizen." She lifted her fork and stuffed it unceremoniously into her mouth.

Malcolm looked to the African man sitting next to Elisabeth. "And you, Monsieur?"

He slightly bowed his head. "Ah. I am from Sierra Leone. I am seeking political asylum in this country to escape those who would like to hurt me in mine."

"We understand the civil war is getting worse?" Malcolm asked.

"Yes. Yes, it is." The Sierra Leone man shook his head. "Forgive me for not being at liberty to give my name."

"Of course, we respect your privacy," Malcolm looked to the next group of six.

A big, burly man with a heavy German accent explained. "I am Erich Mueller and these are my colleagues. We support several projects in this area through our pharmaceutical company and came to see the work in practice. I have corresponded several times with Stan, so it is good to see where our money goes," he nodded in Stan's direction. "We have also visited the game park, yes?" He nodded and looked around the circle. "We fly out of Ouagadougou tomorrow."

"Oh." Malcolm said. I knew very well how he felt about gaming. The government put a price tag on each big game and it was a very lucrative business for them. "Did you kill anything?"

"Yes, I've got a lion."

— 139 —

"Where is it?"

"In a duffel bag in the room. I skinned it."

"Whoa!" Stan enthused. "I'll bet that cost you a pretty penny, huh?"

The man smiled, "It wasn't cheap, yes?"

Malcolm introduced the Waukens' and me and Rachel. "And, of course, my wife, Anna."

"So," Elisabeth Luder unbuttoned the top button of her jacket. "A war rages in Liberia and the world is only interested the American's countdown to destroy Iraq, yes?"

"The world is interested in the powerful," Malcolm nodded in agreement.

"A generation of parents has died of AIDS leaving ten year old boys to fight a war." She shook her head in despair.

"Have you just come from Liberia?" Gritty asked.

"Yes. I remained there as long as I could but the troops entered our village at night and set fires and looted. I left on foot. God be praised, I was welcomed at a Catholic hospital and I fled with two of the sisters in their car to Ouagadougou."

"The Lord was with you," Malcolm said.

"Oui," Elisabeth agreed. "I wish He would show himself in Liberia."

"Where are you going?" Malcolm asked her.

"Niamey."

"Oh, that's where I'm going." Rachel piped up.

"This one is a Staples," Gritty said to Elisabeth and motioned towards Rachel with her thumb.

Elisabeth put her head back and regarded Rachel through her bifocals. "Erwin Staples' daughter?"

"Granddaughter."

"Ah, bon. Well, we will journey together to Niamey."

"So, tell me," Erich put his plate down on the ground next to him and settled back into his weaved chair. He crossed his arms over his chest. "Vat is it you do here exactly?" he asked Malcolm.

Malcolm put his fork down and sat back in his chair. "I am the director of a mission agency. We established this station in the 1960's

Chapter 6

after the French left and have been here ever since. Now that the nationals run the church, and have started their own seminary and mission churches we are really here in an administrative and counseling capacity."

"Ah, the French leave and you begin a new form of colonizing with your religion, yes?"

Malcolm slightly smiled. "Well, one could see it that way. But, we have brought a perfect message, although delivered in our human hands."

Erich shrugged. "But I look around and see poverty all around me, what difference has Christianity made to these people?"

Malcolm nodded. "We are here as practical agents of change, no doubt. We believe that the key to poverty is education and we have sponsored literacy classes for years and have offered those classes through the church. We have also translated the New Testament into Gourma so that the church members could begin to read and teach in their own language."

Malcolm nodded towards Gritty, "Gertrude has been teaching pre-natal classes and serving as a mid-wife for almost thirty years. And, thanks to your company's contributions, she and Stan were able to open the pharmacy on the other side of the compound which offers immunizations and basic primary medical supplies to the whole community."

Gritty and Stan both nodded in agreement but made no move to speak. I wondered if they might be as keen as I was to hear the thoughts of this mostly quiet and private man.

"These are outward markers that seem to tell us there is growth, the seminary is recruiting and the church pews are full. But, I am privy to different stories that tell me the message of the Gospel is truly taking hold."

Malcolm straightened up in his seat, "When we first arrived it was standard belief that if a woman gave birth to twins it was because she must've been unfaithful with either another man or a god. It was not believed that one man could produce more than one baby."

Malcolm glanced at Gritty. "I became aware of a practice by mid-wives at that time to snap the necks of the newborns and bury them in the bush before anyone in the tribe heard about it because the mother would be thrown out of the tribe into the bush to eventually starve. It is through basic pre-natal education that twins are allowed to survive and, thankfully, the practice of throwing women out of the tribe to die is now largely unacceptable."

I shifted in my seat uncomfortably. I couldn't help but glance at Gritty and then at Stan. I had assumed that because I found them weird that their ministry was ineffective. I looked at Gritty's haggard profile. She caught my eye and we smiled at one another.

Erich, along with everyone else on the porch, nodded respectfully as they considered Malcolm's words. Encouraged by a rapt audience he continued.

"There are other 'traditions' such as female genital mutilation and forced isolation during a woman's menstrual cycle that have been addressed in the past generation through basic education and the women's lives are improving because of it." Malcolm shifted in his chair, "The women do the majority of the work in these small agrarian communities as well as give birth every two to three years throughout their reproductive years, the men are beginning to appreciate that keeping the women healthy is in their best interest as well. But, there is a long way to go."

"Oui," Elisabeth nodded her head and repeated, "There is a long way to go."

"So, Erich, to answer your question, we will probably never know how effective we have been in our service in Fada. I can only trust in my belief that if the message of the Gospel is heard then it results in changed lives and eventually that has an impact on the community at large."

Malcolm looked around and smiled self-consciously, "But, I've been preaching and I'm no preacher."

"I have always found it difficult to believe in a God that allows such pain and injustice in a world that He supposedly loves," Erich said thoughtfully. "If I ever see God, I vill have many questions."

"It is a fallen and imperfect world in which we exist. But the Lord has given us the ultimate freedom, which is to live and love and enjoy His creation without ever acknowledging Him." Malcolm responded.

Chapter 6

"Believe me, sir," Elisabeth turned to Erich, "I have chosen to believe in Him and I have many more questions for His inaction than you ever will."

Erich was taken aback and we all looked at her. "What do you mean, Elisabeth?" Malcolm asked her.

"Just what I said," she shrugged at Malcolm and then turned back to Erich. "I have put my faith in God, and I believe that He can act. But I have just come from Liberia where the faithful were shot on their knees praying for His deliverance," tears welled in her eyes but she sniffed them away and straightened her shoulders. "They *believed* that God would act on their behalf and He did not. You don't feel a need for God right now and you can enjoy the luxury of debating His existence in your mind," she tapped her temple. "I have no such luxury. I am locked in a battle with Him right now because I know He's there, I know He can act and He does not," she took a breath to calm herself. "I, sir, will have the better questions."

The man from Sierre Leone nodded in response to Elisabeth, "Yes, I believe you will," he said to her.

Erich nodded thoughtfully, respectfully at her words.

The Swiss couple stood up. "Thank you for dinner," they nodded. "Best of luck with your good work. Bon soir," they stepped off the porch hand in hand and crunched across the gravel towards the Guest House.

"Bon soir," the remainder of the group called after them.

Erich stood up with his entourage. "Vell, thank you for good food and interesting talk. I enjoyed it very much," he held out his hand for Malcolm. Malcolm stood and shook his hand vigorously. "You have your work cut out for you here, yes?" Erich then turned to Elisabeth and kissed her on either cheek. She gave him a quick nod in response.

"Thank you for taking an interest," Malcolm shook hands with the other Germans. The rest of us stood up and said good night as they stepped off the porch into the night.

Elisabeth, Rachel, the man from Sierre Leone and the rest of us from the compound remained on the porch. Malcolm looked at Elisabeth. "I would really like all of us to pray together before we leave."

We all agreed and pulled our chairs into a tighter circle and held hands. Mine were sweaty. We nodded at Malcolm to begin.

"Lord," Malcolm began. "We come to you tonight reminded of our own brokenness. Of the world we live in which is full of evil and hate. We pray for the people who have been killed that they are safely with you now, out of harm's reach. We pray for Elisabeth, who has been hurt by what she has seen and heard. We pray that you will restore her. Show yourself to her again. Let her feel your presence. Give her courage and strength."

Our heads were bowed, but the unmistakable voice of the man from Sierre Leone spoke up after Malcolm in his heavy French accent, "Dear Father in heaven, let us never forget that you are the beginning and the end. You promise that the church will endure until Christ's return. We do not pretend to know or understand your plans, but have mercy on those of us who seek to know that which is unknowable. Help us to pray when we don't understand. Help us to forgive the unforgivable for our own freedom."

I couldn't help but glance up at his poignant words and saw that I was not the only one. We all watched as Elisabeth and the man from Sierre Leone bowed more deeply and clutched one another's hands more tightly as they prayed their silent prayers.

"I'll close," Anna whispered and we bowed our heads again.

"Lord, be with each one of us this night. Give us each the strength and courage to do the things you ask us to do."

"Amen," we all said together.

We all stood up and helped Anna carry the dishes back into the kitchen.

"Bon soir," Elisabeth called and stepped off the porch into the night.

"Bon soir," we all called after her.

"Merci," she called over the crunch of her footsteps towards the Guest House.

Rachel and I finished clearing off the dishes and walked back to my house together. We were both silent. I was tired.

Chapter 6

Rachel came out of the bathroom and stood in my room looking around. She was dressed in the most frou-frou nightgown I had ever seen.

"That was quite a night, huh?" I asked her.

"Yeah. I'm really tired," she lingered in the doorway.

"Are you okay?" Our relationship had started out on an awkward foot earlier.

"I guess so."

"Malcolm has mentioned a decent restaurant in downtown Fada, would you like to go to it tomorrow night?" I asked her. I had been curious to go but had no one to go with!

"What kind of restaurant?"

"I don't know, but as long as we order cooked items we should be okay."

"That sounds good," she giggled.

"I think I'm going to get ready for bed myself," I pulled my sweats and t-shirt from the bottom drawer of my dresser.

"Good night," she said.

"Good night," I watched her walk down the hall into the living room.

I washed my face and brushed my teeth and crawled under my mosquito net. I flipped off my light and listened to the Mullah call the Muslims to their late night prayer. It had become so familiar now it comforted me like the distant sound of a train's whistle as it chugged through a sleeping town. I thought about Elisabeth and how she and the man from Sierre Leone, who had been unwilling to share his story with us, understood one another most clearly. It humbled me to think of how myopic my life had been.

I rolled over and looked through my bedroom and out of the kitchen window. Even though I had heard stories tonight of brutality and death I had never felt so alive and energized. I felt like I had tapped into the heart of life, stripped of any pretenses. In suburbia Washington, D.C., there seemed a relentless pursuit of perfection: the perfect children, looks, car, home, and job. But, perfection is unattainable. People have that peculiar habit of being human and imperfect.

The 80's were a curious time to have spent my formative years. The *Me* generation continued their perpetual quest for gratification and decided that marriage and family life was not compatible with an existence dedicated wholly to *self*. Many of my friends' parents divorced, regardless if they were churchgoers, and most parties degraded into rage or tear sessions. I'll never forget one night in 10th grade when several of us were spending the night with a friend, Sue, whose parents had recently divorced and she was now living in a townhouse with her mother. We were all drinking beer and we weren't used to drinking and at some point Sue disappeared from the group. We searched the house and found her in the upstairs hall bathtub full of pink water having slit her wrists and then tried to drown herself. We pulled her out of the tub and dressed her superficial wounds in gauze and wrapped her in a towel and sat in the hallway with her until dawn. She didn't want to kill herself, she was desperate for love that her hurt and distracted mother could not give. But, we were only sixteen and secretly relieved to leave Sue the next morning in the misery we couldn't begin to understand.

My senior year Sue was the friend I called when I had a vicious fight with my mom and had to get out of the house. I phoned and asked her to pick me up, knowing that she had no curfew or concerned parent to contend with. She pulled up to my house in her black Mustang, a gift from her guilty dad, and asked me if I was sure I didn't want to go back inside, that it would be better for me and my mom to work things out.

"Are you joking?" I asked her.

"You just don't understand," she said. "None of you do." She was referring to the rest of our group whose parents were present and we could rebel and pound against a wall of unconditional love knowing it would still be standing the next day.

Sue grew up quickly. She made adults nervous because she seemed too street smart for a seventeen year old. Her security blanket had been yanked out from underneath her and she perceived that she was alone in the world. She started with beer but quickly slid into harder drugs and landed in rehab by the age of twenty-one. By

Chapter 6

twenty-three she was in recovery and began her new sober life all over again.

"Bottled water and baby steps," she wrote me in a letter last year, fulfilling one of her 12 Steps by sharing with me her recovery process. "I hope you'll find the freedom of recovery someday, too."

Here in Burkina life was hard. No one expected it to be easy. And maybe that was where our cultures diverged, in our expectations. Westerners with money can hide the uncomfortable realities of life, like death, with pretty flowers and a piece of green turf. But there was no padding here. When you live with death as a daily shadow you don't expect a trouble-free life of "perfection."

But, my thoughts tired me out. When my mind quieted I could hear Rachel's rhythmic breathing in the other room. It was a comfort to have someone in the house. I prayed again and finally dozed off.

The next morning I woke before dawn but I couldn't go sit at the writing desk because Rachel was asleep in the living room. I snuck in and retrieved my Bible and journal off the desk and returned to my bed and wrote. I pulled the curtain open in my room, which I normally left closed because it was too close to my bed, and watched the sunrise. Danjou walked past the window a few minutes later, he had become used to seeing my face in the living room window. He looked into my bedroom window and I waved good morning from my bed. He nodded and went about his business of pumping water up into the drum that sat on top of my house.

I prepared us some toasted baguette and sliced mango for breakfast. Rachel buttoned her frilly nightgown up to the neck and sat down waiting to be served. I joined her at the table.

"Did you sleep okay?" I asked her.

"Yes, did you?"

"I think so," I smiled. "It's always a good sign when I can't remember my dreams because some of them have been pretty intense."

"Really?" she buttered her baguette.

"Hello? Are you in there?" I left Rachel at the table and walked through the kitchen to find Gritty at my screened door. She had her floppy hat on.

"Good morning," I unlatched the door.

"Is Rachel here?" She walked past me and headed towards the living room. The last time she visited my house she picked up all my cards I had standing on my desk from John and read them! I was so angered I taped them all down by their spines after she left. It wasn't that they were so private, normally the weather in Beauville, I just didn't like her in my space. I followed her into the living room.

"Hi Rachel," she said and leaned down to give her a hug.

A hug? Gritty? I walked back into the kitchen to make another pot of tea. While I filled up my kettle at the kitchen sink I watched Anna hurry down the path to the Guest House kitchen with a large tray of cinnamon buns held out in front of her. I heard the screen door to the Guest House kitchen clap shut behind her. She was busy feeding all the guests breakfast before they set off. She always worked.

I leaned down to turn on the gaslight when I heard Gritty ask, "I came by to see if you'd like to visit the pharmacy that Stan and I run on the other side of the compound to get a feel for our work?"

"Oh, I'd like to see that," Rachel said.

"It's so good to meet a young woman dedicating her life to the Lord's work, you remind me of me my first term."

I walked back in and sat down at the table. "Would you like some tea, Gritty?"

"No," she said absently. She went to pick up one of my cards but it was secured to the desk. She tugged at it but gave up. I stuffed a baguette into my mouth to muffle my laugh.

"I'm excited but a little nervous, I've done a short-term assignment," Rachel waved at me, in reference to my status as a "short-termer", code word for second-class missionary. "But I've felt certain of my call since I was four."

"I did, too!" Gritty enthused over another shared characteristic and sat down at the table next to Rachel. "My first term was exciting but very lonely. I met Stan my fourth year in Burkina."

"I'm praying I'll meet my soul mate out here, too. Someone with the same heart for missions."

"Well, you'll be in Niamey, it's a big city. You won't be lonely," Gritty waved her hand dismissively. "I was alone in the bush."

Chapter 6

"I'm still praying about being married." Rachel glanced at me.

"Don't worry about being married, there's so much of the Lord's work to do!"

"I know. I love teaching. But I'm very eager to be married."

Gritty snorted and rolled her eyes to heaven. "You've got plenty of time."

Rachel's face flushed. I took another bite and looked back to Gritty. This was getting interesting.

"I'm not going to rush anything, but I've saved myself and I expect to meet the perfect husband that God has in store for me."

Gritty pinched off a crumb of baguette and rolled it between her fingers into a ball. "I thought that, too."

"Thought what?" Rachel furrowed her eyebrows.

"That because I was a virgin I was sinless and that I deserved a perfect marriage." She waved the chunk of baguette at Rachel, "Didn't turn out that way, ma dear." Gritty addressed people as "ma dear" when she was irritated.

Rachel adjusted her lacy bits again, clearly unused to being challenged in this way. "I know that we all have sinned and fallen short of the glory of God," she rattled off the Bible verse. "But, I believe God rewards us for saving ourselves and being obedient." She glanced at me and back to Gritty.

"If there is some reward, I can't tell you what it is," Gritty stuffed the chunk into her mouth and tackled it with some difficulty.

I watched Gritty gnaw on her baguette and thought it was sad that her marriage had been so difficult she couldn't see the "good" in any of it. I debated in my mind whether to share my thoughts and sighed out loud after deciding that I had nothing to lose. "It's not about the sex, really." I ventured. They both looked at me. "I've been thinking about this a lot and I think it's about complications."

Gritty stopped chewing. Rachel's eyes widened, "What do you mean?"

"I mean that sex complicates relationships. It's a boundary that is crossed whether you want to admit it or not. It's not so much the physical act but the emotions that come with it, the vulnerabilities."

Rachel didn't quite know what to say. Gritty regarded me with something like surprise mixed with respect. She swallowed the last of the baguette in a clump.

"Do you hurt?" Gritty asked me with such tenderness that tears filled my eyes before I could say anything.

"I feel shame. And, it's not that all my relationships were bad or that I regret all of them. But, I regret not respecting myself more, you know?"

"I saw you crying when you were helping with Bev's labor," she held up her hand. "I don't want to know what that was about, but you do know that nothing is beyond God's forgiveness?" Gritty assured me.

"I know that God has forgiven me. And I'm working on forgiving myself." I took a bite of mango. "So, you should be thankful you don't have such complications."

"We have others." Gritty waved her hand and stood up from the table. She tossed her floppy hat over her head. "Thanks for being honest when you didn't have to be," she squeezed me on the shoulder with her meaty hand. "It's the hypocrisy of our faith: the longer we're faithful and the closer we are perceived by others to walk with God the less and less honest we're willing to be about our weaknesses." She shook her head, "Like somehow we're supposed to become perfect, but we never do," she added quietly and left.

"I'm going to make that cup of tea and then get dressed and go on over to the office," I stood up feeling surprisingly unburdened. "Malcolm is going to wonder about me."

"You go ahead, I'll clean up for you," Rachel watched me.

Anna fed me my morning snack on the stool in her kitchen.

"I'm so glad Elisabeth stopped to see us last night. It was so good to pray for her before she leaves for Niamey," she dropped a blob of cookie dough onto a baking sheet.

"Yeah, I keep thinking about everything she said," I agreed.

"You know, Rachel is from a great missionary family," Anna enthused and spooned another blob. She was impressed.

"So I've heard."

Chapter 6

Anna looked up at me. "She seems like a lovely girl."

"She is." It was a strange comfort to realize that hierarchies existed even in the mission world. That no sector, no matter how holy, could separate itself from the human condition. "We're going to walk down to the Fada restaurant for dinner tonight."

"Oh, good for you," she nodded her head as if satisfied that I was treating her properly and went back to her cookies. "There's not a lot in the market right now so I don't know what they'll be serving. Just make sure it's cooked."

Later that evening Rachel and I double-checked our directions with Malcolm before slipping out of the compound gate and onto the Fada Road. It was cloudy so we couldn't see the moon even if there was one. It was dark. We flipped on our flashlights.

The road into the market was just as busy as it was during the day. People greeted one another and carried on about their business as if it were early morning. But, to be honest, I seriously could not see anyone until they were directly in front of me when the whites of their eyes reflected in the beams of my flashlight. It was surreal.

We skirted around the west side of the market looking for the promised white "Restaurante Fada" sign. The market stalls were illuminated by torches or by a lonely light bulb, but Fada nightlife was bustling and energetic.

A waitress met us at the gate to the outdoor restaurant. "Deux?" she asked. She weaved us through several empty tables and finally chose one closest to the kitchen. There was no one else in the courtyard. We sat down and she handed us two menus. "I will return after you make your selection," she said in French.

We looked at the menu with our flashlights. "I don't think it will take us long to deliberate," I chuckled. Basically it was either a 1/4, 1/2 or whole chicken with fries and our choice of either Coke or Fanta to drink. The waitress returned and we ordered two helpings of fries, two Cokes, and a whole chicken to share.

"The chickens are skinny," Rachel reminded me.

The waitress returned promptly with our Cokes and disappeared into the kitchen.

We sat and watched the activity on the street outside the restaurant. People laughed and called to one another. Some noticed us sitting in the restaurant and called, "Bonsoir Mesdames!" as they peddled past on their bikes. We waved. There were little white lights decorating the trees above our heads and a small candle on our table. It was all very festive.

We had been sitting for about twenty minutes before either of us spoke. We had both finished our Cokes.

"Do you want another Coke?" Rachel asked me.

"Have you seen the waitress?"

"No," she giggled. "I have a sneaking suspicion she's in the back cooking our chicken."

"You're probably right." I said when we both heard the unmistakable shriek of a chicken and the hyper flapping of wings when out ran a chicken from behind the kitchen with our waitress in hot pursuit. They ran past our table, across the front of the kitchen, and back behind the kitchen again.

I looked at Rachel and she at me when we both heard a loud chop and the final shriek of the feisty chicken.

We both burst into laughter realizing we had just lived out the classic "poor service" cliché at home. We needed no words. It was just the funniest thing I had ever heard.

Our waitress appeared fifteen minutes later looking surprisingly composed for someone who had been in the back wrestling, killing and de-feathering a chicken. "How is everything?" she asked us.

"We haven't eaten anything yet!" I laughed. "Could we each have another Coke and at least some *pommes de frites*?"

"Okay," she shrugged and returned to the kitchen.

Rachel and I looked at one another again and burst out in laughter. It felt really good to laugh.

Our waitress eventually returned with our Cokes and a plate of cold fries. We were so hungry by that time it really didn't matter that they were cold. "I suppose catsup is out of the question," I said to Rachel. She nodded. We happily polished off the plate of fries together.

Chapter 6

"You know," Rachel licked her fingers as we had no napkins, "I've been thinking a lot about what you said this morning. And, sometimes I wish I knew what it felt like not to know God."

I looked at her. "What do you mean?"

"Ever since I can remember I have been praying, reading the Bible and been surrounded by people who do the same. Sometimes I wonder if I really do know Him or if I have assumed a tradition," she paused. "You have a real sense of God's grace and I envy that."

As I listened I mused again over how different we were. I sipped my Coke.

"I also think that I have a fear that by becoming a career missionary I'll never be married."

I nodded, "I understand. My fear is that I'll keep picking the wrong person."

She smiled at my comment and continued, "I knew so many single missionaries from our church and very few of them were at peace about being single. Every time they were home on furlough we worried for any single men in the church. I guess I have a fear that I'll be the same."

"At this point in my life I don't think it's such a bad thing being single and living in a mud house somewhere south of Timbuktu," I said.

"Easy for you to say! You're engaged!"

"Well, maybe in name, but I won't be after he visits for Christmas," I admitted but felt a pit in my stomach contemplating the task in front of me.

"Do you feel called to be a career missionary? With the real potential that you might never date again, much less marry?" she asked me.

A smile answered the question before I had a chance to think about it. "I like to think of myself as independent soul, which I am, but I would be lying to myself if I thought I could live a celibate life. History is on my side."

"Yes," she raised her eyebrows, "I guess so."

"It may be that you will be single for a time, but it may not be for a lifetime," I repeated some of Anna's wisdom to Rachel.

She nodded in response.

"Personally, I am looking forward to a season of singleness," I said.

Our waitress reappeared with our skinny chicken dinner. We had been sitting there for almost two hours! It was nine p.m. We pulled and picked at the chicken but there wasn't a lot of meat, it reminded me of eating a crab. We paid the bill and walked around the lit market and onto the dark Fada Road towards home.

"Are you hungry?" I asked Rachel after we got inside my house.

"Starving!"

I pulled out a pack of Hits cookies and we ate them together over a cup of tea before bed.

Two days later we stood in the shade of the Flamboyant tree watching Elisabeth and Rachel load their bags into Malcolm's flatbed. Malcolm was driving them to meet the Bush Taxi in Fada's city center.

Rachel hugged me, "It was great to meet you. God's blessings in your mission."

"Thank you. Yours, too." I said.

"And, I'll be praying for you during John's visit," she added.

"Please do," I said. "I'll need it."

Elisabeth double-cheek kissed Anna and then me. "Thank you for some much needed rest, edible food and prayer," she said to Anna.

"You are welcome anytime," Anna waved her hand without hesitation.

"Bon, I will return. Au revoir!" She climbed in the front seat of the truck.

"Be back soon, Mother!" Malcolm hollered to Anna and climbed in the driver's side.

Danjou pulled open the gates and the truck turned left onto the Fada road in a swirl of dust.

"Well," Anna clapped her hands together.

"Well?"

"Back to the kitchen."

"What are you making?" I asked.

"Oh, dinner mints for Christmas."

Chapter 6

"Those little pastel colored ones?"
She nodded, "Yes, those."
"Can you actually make those?"
"Of course!"
I shook my head. "I thought they just appeared from a factory somewhere."
"Nonsense! Come and I'll show you," she nudged me towards her kitchen. "It's really very easy."

7
The Visit

I saw John before he saw me. His face had the obligatory flush and he looked confused as he made his way through the airport crowd towards the door. I looked over my shoulder to Malcolm and Anna who sat on the edge of their bench. Their smiles reassured me and boosted my confidence. I took a deep breath and wiped my sweaty palms on my skirt.

John caught my eye. I could tell he was nervous because he smiled like a salesman: teethy.

"Hi, welcome to Burkina," I said as he came through the door.

"Thanks," he leaned down and we hugged. He took a step back and surveyed me. "You look different."

"How so?"

"I don't know. I guess you look like a real missionary now."

"Oh, thanks!" Tact was never his strong suit. I waved Malcolm and Anna over and introduced them to John. The setting sun cast an orange glow across the parking lot as we walked to the truck, I wrapped my sweater tighter around my waist and got in the back seat behind Anna. It was a cool evening, but it wasn't cold. It was only five days away from Christmas but it didn't feel at all "Christmassy"; that might have had something to do with the fact that I was living in a sub-Saharan Muslim country.

Anna played tour guide and introduced John to all the sites of Ouaga during our journey back to the Guest House. I regarded John from my side of the truck. It seemed like no time had passed since I had seen him last. He nodded and listened politely to Anna. When she turned away to point to something outside the truck he looked at me. We regarded one another and then I felt uncomfortable under his gaze

Chapter 7

and looked away. He lifted my left hand and squeezed it. I looked back at him. He tapped my empty ring finger and raised his eyebrows in question. I had not worn the ring in so long I had forgotten about it. I pulled my hand away and he looked out of his window. I could tell he was mad. I couldn't help but notice that his bald spot had gotten bigger.

We unloaded John's bags and Ellen showed him to his room next to mine in the Guest House.

"We'll eat dinner in twenty minutes, okay?"

"Thanks, Ellen." I said as she pulled the door closed behind her. I sat on the bed and watched John arrange his luggage.

"So, what do you think?" I asked him.

"Of what?"

"Of Ouaga, Africa, the Guest House…everything."

He looked around the room as if he had just noticed it. "It's fine." He sat down on the bed next to me. "What I'm more interested in is why you aren't wearin' my ring?"

I sighed and looked at my empty finger, "I don't know, I guess I didn't want anything to happen to it." I lied and then I felt bad about lying. "And, I told you that I needed a little space and time to think," I admitted.

His neck, face and ears all flushed in a cherry red. He took a breath and looked down at the floor. "Pastor Jay says that doubt is okay. He says that marriage is one of the biggest decisions we'll make and that it's normal to be afraid."

"I'm not having doubts about marrying Pastor Jay, I'm having doubts about marrying *you*."

"I know that, Katherine. I'm just tellin' you what he told me."

"Have you been talking with Pastor Jay about us?"

"Well, after I got your letter I went to see him and he read the letter and reassured me that I should still come. So, -"

"You *what*?" I interrupted him. "Why did you show Pastor Jay my letter?"

"Because I was hurt. I was confused. I needed someone to talk to. I wanted to just cancel the trip and the engagement an' just call the whole thing off but Pastor Jay said I should have faith, that

The Visit

relationships are difficult and that I couldn't bail out just because you were having doubts."

I shook my head and looked away.

"So, here I am. I came because I believe that God has put us together an', an' that we can work it out. I want to try to work things out. I love you," he put his head in his hands. "I do." He cried.

I put my hand on his shoulder and moved closer to him. My stomach ached from the pit inside. My head hurt from all of my thinking and praying. "Please don't cry," I said but tears welled in my eyes. "I love you, too," I said and I did. He turned and held me and cried on my shoulder.

He pulled me close. It felt weird to be touched after so many months alone. His hands were strong on my back. I let myself be held for a minute and then I pulled away. We looked at one another's tear stained cheeks and chuckled.

"We're quite a pair," he wiped his eyes. I thought I knew what I wanted to do but now I was confused.

He stood up and went into the bathroom and returned with a long piece of toilet paper. He pulled off some and handed it to me. We both blew our noses and composed ourselves. He unzipped his duffel bag and pulled out a pair of leather slippers. "Mama gave me these as an early Christmas present."

"That was nice."

He dropped his on the floor and pulled out another pair of ladies leather slippers. "A pair for you, too." He handed them to me.

"Oh," I looked at the tag: size 5 1/2. "That was so sweet!" I pulled off my shoes and tried them on. They were lovely and soft. And suddenly I glimpsed a snowy Christmas with our matching slippers on in front of our cozy fire and wondered what in the world was wrong with me.

"Do they fit?" he asked.

"They're great." I straightened out my legs and admired them. "Remind me to write thank you notes for you to hand deliver."

"Yeah, this is the first Christmas I've missed wif my family."

"With."

Chapter 7

"You correctin' my speech again?" He shook his head. "I haven't missed that."

I smiled. "Sorry."

"Well, actually, me n' Mary were in Florida for one Christmas when we were first married. But, that's the only one."

"Yeah, this is my first Christmas away from my family, too."

"Do you think I have time for a shower before supper?"

"Sure," I stood up and walked to the bathroom. "Let me show you how to work the shower. The water will be cold tonight, but the best advice I can give you is to shower in the afternoon once we arrive in Fada."

He followed me into the tiled room and looked around. I pulled the curtain around the rod to create a shower over the area that dipped down in the middle of the floor.

A lizard scurried by on the wall next to his head. He jerked away and almost knocked me over.

"Sorry, did you see that?"

"The lizard?"

"Yeah!"

"It's just a Gecko lizard, it won't bother you."

"Glory! That was an ugly thing."

I giggled. "They are all over the place. I have them all over my house in Fada. I guess I've gotten used to them."

He smiled. "It's nice to hear you laugh."

He put his arm around me and pulled me towards him. I turned and gave him a warm hug. He kissed my cheek. I left John to shower and change and we joined the group for dinner on Ellen's porch.

John went to bed after dinner completely wiped out by the trip. I lay in my bed in my now familiar room at the Guest House and stared up at the ceiling. I couldn't believe John was snoring away in the room next door. The person who had occupied a lot of my thoughts and prayers from an ocean away was now less than 20 feet from my bed. I didn't expect him to be struggling, too. I didn't expect us to cry together. I didn't expect to feel that scary pit inside when things are falling apart.

The Visit

Am I a fool to not want to marry him? What if I never meet anyone else who wants to marry me?

I rolled on my side and looked out the barred window. The question is: Do I want to spend my life with John? I sighed and rolled on my back. The ceiling offered nothing but its dependable existence. *The cursed animosity of inanimate objects,* I recalled the phrase from a Madeleine L'Engle book quoting Ruskin I had recently read.

"I know you're there, Lord. Give me courage," I whispered.

The next morning we left John in the Guest House to rest while we went shopping. We returned to the Guest House with the flatbed filled with supplies, including some for the Mahadaga dispensary. The four of us ate lunch in the Guest House kitchen.

"We'll leave for Fada after rest hour," Malcolm announced and excused himself. Anna tidied the sink and countertops.

John looked at me, "Rest hour?"

"Yes, it's actually three hours long, do you have a book or something to read?"

He looked confused, "No."

"Well, you can sleep. Or write a letter to your family," I shrugged. "I thought it seemed a bit lengthy when I first arrived, but now I've come to enjoy it," I smiled.

This seemed to irritate John. "Why?"

"I don't know, an afternoon nap seems very civilized." His irritation seemed to compound. "Is there something wrong with that?"

Anna returned to pick up the last of the dishes. John and I stood to help her. He put his dishes on the counter and went to his room without a word. Anna nodded her head like she did when she spoke, but this time she wasn't saying anything. She smiled and patted me on the shoulder, "Go get some rest, I'll finish up here."

After rest hour we piled into Malcolm's truck and zoomed back home to Fada. I followed Anna while she showed John to his room in the Guest House and then into the Guest House's kitchen the next-door down. "You and Katherine can share your meals in here." She set down the rules. "It's really not appropriate in this culture for an unmarried man and woman to be in a house alone at night."

Chapter 7

John's face flushed. He didn't like being told what to do.

"But, you can eat your lunches at Katherine's house," she added. John looked at me. "Glory!" he exclaimed and gave his right leg a little kick. I had forgotten about this curious habit. Anna looked at me for interpretation. I shrugged my shoulders.

"Anyway, there are some cinnamon buns and milk in the refrigerator for your breakfast," she pulled open the fridge to show John.

"Wow!" he said, "Those look mighty delicious."

"Well, it's the best we can offer here in the bush," Anna demurred.

"Anna is a great cook," I assured John.

John looked around the kitchen. "Well, when I first walked in I thought this was pretty shabby, you know, country like." I vigorously shook my head but he didn't notice me. "But, it's growin' on me."

I looked at Anna apologetically. The Guest House was her pride and joy. "I think he means everything is lovely."

"Oh," she waved her hand dismissively. "No need to explain." The kitchen door clapped shut behind her but then she pulled it open and poked her head back in, "I'm warming up some frozen soup for dinner if you would like to join us in about an hour?"

"Thank you, Anna." I said. "That sounds great." I was relieved not to have to cook for us tonight.

John leaned into the fridge and eyeballed the cinnamon buns. He was oblivious to his offense. "John, Anna is very proud of this Guest House. You hurt her feelings."

"Why?" He pulled out a bun and stuffed it in his mouth. "C'mon, it's a simple mud brick box infested with termites!"

"She doesn't see it that way."

I sat down at the table and watched him poke around the kitchen. He sat down across the table from me.

"You are comin' home, aren'tcha?" he asked with a nervous laugh.

"Why do you ask that?"

"Because you seem to like it here."

"I do."

The Visit

"Pastor Jay says I should bring you back on the plane wif me," his face reddened. "That enough is enough and I should just take you as my wife." His words were confident but his red face betrayed him. He looked at me expectantly.

"You're joking, right?" He was already irritating me.

He took a deep breath. "Not many men would wait like I have."

"No one forced you to wait, John, it was your choice." Our words were like lines in a play we had repeated them so many times. I sighed and looked down. John exhausted me. We sat in silence.

I stood up from the table and picked up a stack of old National Geographic magazines I had already read that I left in the kitchen to share with other guests. I handed them to John.

"What are these for?" he asked.

"I thought you might want something to read. There are no TV's or radios in your room."

"Where are you goin'?"

"You can put those in your room. Then I thought I could show you the office and we could see if Anna needs any help getting ready for dinner."

The four of us sat for dinner at Malcolm and Anna's dining table. Malcolm asked John about the insurance industry and they chatted at length. Anna and Malcolm then discussed John's activities for the next two weeks.

"The new church is very pleased that you will be building the benches. It might seem a small contribution but wood is very expensive here," Malcolm explained.

"I'm lookin' forward to it," John nodded.

"Tomorrow we can take the truck into Fada and pick up the supplies so you can get started. I must warn you, it's very hot during the day so you need to be careful working outside and definitely stop during rest hour."

"Oh," John dismissed him. "I'll be fine."

Malcolm looked at me and smiled, "Katherine has been a tremendous contribution to the team here in Fada. We feel blessed that she is here."

Chapter 7

I smiled like a Cheshire cat. It felt so good to know they liked me. John didn't say anything.

We helped Anna tidy up and I walked John to the Guest House kitchen. I picked up my flashlight that I had left in the kitchen earlier.

"Can I walk you home?" he asked.

"Sure," I said. "But you need your flashlight."

The kitchen door clapped shut behind us. I waited for him on the path while he went into his room and returned with his flashlight. Our footsteps crunched as we walked across the compound. "That's my kitchen window." I pointed it out to him. "I stand there a lot just watching people and birds."

But John didn't look at the window. He looked at me with what seemed like disbelief tinged with mild concern.

I stepped up on my stoop and unlocked the padlock and pushed through the door.

"Can you show me around real quick?" he asked.

I looked back to Anna's house. I didn't want her to think I was disregarding her request for us not to be alone in my house at night.

"Oh, c'mon. We're adults! You can show me around your house." He pushed in behind me.

I flipped on the light and lizards scurried out of sight. "Yuck! Those things are gross," he shook away a shiver.

"They're not bad. They really do eat a lot of bugs." I headed through my kitchen to the living room and flipped on another light. "That's my little kitchen and this is my living room." He stopped and looked around the room.

"Oh, Louis Lamour!"

"You can take a couple to read if you want."

He took one off the shelf. "I only have two weeks, now." He looked at my writing table stacked with airmail paper and a fresh candle. "Who are you writin' with all that paper?"

"Just friends and family."

His face flushed again.

"What is your problem? Do you want me to be miserable? Anytime I say I like something, or if Malcolm says he appreciates me

— 163 —

The Visit

you get all bent out of shape. Does it bother you that I'm doing a good job and enjoying myself?"

"I don't know. I'm just tryin' to understand what it is you're doin' here. I'm tryin' to understand who you are now," he admitted.

He walked over to the writing table and started rummaging through my stuff. "What are you doing?" I demanded as he picked up notes and letters to see whom they were from. Thankfully my journal and Bible were still packed in my duffel bag from the trip to Ouaga to pick him up from the airport.

His face was flushed as he glanced at each piece of paper and put it back down, not really reading anything. At the beginning of our relationship I had perceived him as the spiritual leader, but I had grown a lot in the past year. I stood in silence and watched him invade my sacred spot. I had nothing to hide, but it offended me that he couldn't respect my privacy and that he was afraid of me as an individual apart from him.

My silence unnerved him and he stopped.

"I think you should go now," I said. Last year we would've gotten in a yelling match and worn one another down. This time I kept my silence, the rules of our game had changed and John looked unsettled.

"Sorry about that, I just want to know you, I want to feel a part of things," he tried to defend himself.

"I'm tired, John. I'd like you to go now, okay?" I turned and walked down the hallway towards my bath and reached for the light. John rushed up behind me and wrapped his arms around me. He turned me around and planted his lips on mine.

"C'mon baby," he smothered my lips and nose with his mouth. "I know you've been lonely. Standin' at that kitchen window like an old widow."

I pushed his head away with both of my hands and stepped back. "No." I turned and walked through my bedroom and back to the screened door. I held it open. "You need to go."

"What is your problem?" he hissed behind me.

"I want to respect Anna's wishes." But that was only a part of it.

"So, are you miss pure missionary now?" he was in my face.

"No, I'm just not ready for all of that, okay?"

Chapter 7

He studied me for a moment. "Well, thanks for the Louis Lamour book." He pushed out my screen door and I leaned out and pulled the tin door shut and latched it from inside. I went to the kitchen window and watched the beam of his flashlight bob across the compound and disappear into his room.

"Lord, help me." I just needed to make it through two weeks.

The next morning I reorganized my table before writing in my journal and praying. Danjou nodded at me as he walked across my back porch to pump my water. I decided to be reconciliatory and walk over to the Guest House kitchen to fix John breakfast.

I unlocked my door and opened it when I saw the back of John's head. He immediately hopped up from the stoop and turned towards me. I don't know why but I felt fearful and quickly latched the screen door before he could reach it.

"What are you doing?" he demanded through the screen.

"Why are you so mad? You're making me nervous."

"Open this door." He pressed his face up against the screen.

"No."

"Open this door." He growled.

I swallowed hard. "No."

"If you don't unlatch it I'm going to rip it off the hinges." His face was purple.

I heard the heaven-sent footsteps of Danjou come around the side of the house having finished pumping my water. "Bonjour, Danjou," I called out.

"Bonjour, Madame," he answered and headed towards us. John stepped back from the door and turned to greet Danjou. I slipped out of the screen door and locked my door behind me. I did not want to be alone with John.

John saw what I had done and shot me a dirty look. I introduced him to Danjou and explained the morning ritual to John. He was curious so he followed Danjou around to the side of the house to see the pump.

"I'll be at the office," I called to John's back.

The Visit

After finishing some correspondence I heard Malcolm's truck leave the compound. I hopped up and went out to the drive to see the truck pull through the opened gate and turn left onto the Fada Road. Danjou closed the gate.

"Anna?" I asked through her curtained kitchen door.

"Yes?"

"Where did Malcolm go?"

"Oh," she pulled open the door. "He and John went to the market to buy the material for the benches."

"Oh." I must've looked confused.

"Are you okay?" She cocked her head to the side.

"Yeah, I guess," I tried to act nonchalant about the tension I was feeling with John.

"C'mon in for a snack," and she held the door open for me. I settled on my stool and she resumed punching her bread dough.

"How's it going?" she asked with a smile.

"Fine." I said but tears welled up in my eyes. She dampened a kitchen towel and covered the bread. She pulled off her apron and hung it on its hook and came to me.

"What is it, Katherine?"

I put my head in my hands.

"Come," she said and took my hand. We walked into their bedroom and she closed the door. She sat me down on the bed and sat next to me.

"I don't want to marry John, and I'm kicking myself for not breaking up with him earlier so that his visit could've been cancelled. He's acting so desperate he's scaring me." I took the tissue she handed me and dabbed my cheeks. "I'm just exhausted."

We sat on their bed in silence for a few moments.

"It takes a lot of courage to end a relationship," she nodded. "But it's so much better in the long run, for the both of you."

"I just have this tremendous pit in my stomach. I've felt nauseous since he got off the plane."

She laughed. "Well, that certainly doesn't sound like a passionate bride-to-be!"

I smiled "Clearly."

Chapter 7

"Let me ask you this: What has kept you engaged?"

"Guilt. I've sincerely struggled with the commitment thing. I told you that John believed the Lord had put us together. And, I believed him. I guess as a new believer I respected him and I've felt a bond to him because of that."

"That somehow you'd be disobeying the Lord almighty if you didn't marry him?"

The way she put it made it seem ridiculous. "You make everything seem easy."

"No, no," she waved her hand. "These are difficult, life changing decisions. But, I believe that God gives us each freedom to make them. In marriage more than anything there has to be agreement and unity. You don't marry someone out of obligation."

I sighed. "I'm afraid of his reaction. He's acting really weird."

"Do you really think he'll be surprised?"

I pondered this for a moment. "Unfortunately, yes." I laughed. "He's not the brightest bulb on the planet."

She tried not to giggle but it slipped out.

"Marriage seems so easy for some people and so elusive for others." I said absently as I looked at Anna's nightstand that held two teacups and two plates with crusts of toast. Behind the plates stood a framed black and white picture of a very young Malcolm and Anna on a motorcycle. Her arms were wrapped around his waist and he gripped the handlebars. They both smiled at the camera.

"Oh, Katherine." She scoffed and rubbed her hands on her knees. "There's no such thing as an easy marriage. But, there are plenty of marriages that become true partnerships. I always told my children that there were two things to look for in a potential spouse: friendship and trust. Because if you don't really like the person or trust them marriage will only heighten those feelings, not cover them up."

I nodded in agreement, "I stood and watched John rummage through my writing desk last night and realized that there was no trust between us. He seems afraid of me doing or being anything apart from him."

"There must be room to change and grow in marriage. The key is to have enough space to grow without growing apart. It's a daily

The Visit

balance." She pulled her legs up underneath her on the bed and continued. "We have a good marriage, but it's become a marriage over time. We married young but we were committed to making it work. But I tell you, when our second child came along when we were on furlough in Canada and my husband decided to hop in a car and drive north to spend Christmas with his family leaving me in the hospital to endure a difficult birth by myself I was angry. But, I had to let him go because he needed to work out those ties by himself." Tears welled in her eyes remembering. Tears welled in mine, too, because somehow I thought they weren't capable of hurting one another.

"Thankfully, his own mother took him aside and she told him, 'Son, your place is with your wife now,' and she sent him back to me. And I did the same for both of my sons. I let them go and I said it before I meant it, but you have to do that." She nodded. "But, I had to forgive Malcolm for that. And, I've had to forgive him for a lot. And, he's had to forgive me." She nodded to herself and swiped away a tear. "But, that's what marriage is, there are no perfect people."

She picked up a roll of toilet paper and pulled off some for me and some for herself. She blew her nose and dabbed it lightly.

"I think you already know what you have to do, Katherine. And my prayer for you is for courage and sensitivity. There is no reason why this can't still be an important experience for John and we really do appreciate him building the benches."

"Yeah, I'm glad he has an activity."

She patted my knee and stood up. "Enjoy the time as a single woman to see what God has in store for you as an individual before you worry about marriage. The more confident and mature you are as a woman the better your eventual partnership will be," she nodded to herself. "No doubt about that."

I blew my nose. Somehow it was easier to hear these words from her than my own mother, who had been banging on the same drum since I could remember. I stood up and followed her back out to the kitchen to eat my snack.

Chapter 7

The next few days settled into a comfortable pattern of activity without in-depth communication. Things were tense between John and I but it seemed neither of us had the courage or the energy to talk. I busied myself in the office and John sawed and hammered together twenty benches for the new church. I stood at the office door watching him do his handiwork in Anna's yard. After four days in the sub-Saharan sun his nose was smeared with zinc and he wore a floppy white hat like Gritty's.

John looked up from his work. "You think I look sexy, babe?"
I giggled. "I guess some people consider snowmen sexy."
"Oh, shut up. You try bein' out here in the sun all day."
"Maybe you could work in the evening."
"What, and miss my evenings with you readin'?" he sneered.
I laughed. "There is nothing wrong with reading, John."
"I didn't come to Africa to read." He slammed the hammer onto a nail. "Anyway, I've read more in the past three days than I have in the past 10 years."

I would've laughed but I knew it was true which made it pathetic. I rolled my eyes and walked back into the office.

That evening we were all invited over to the churchyard for a Christmas Eve celebration dinner dedicating the new mission church, which included the new benches John was building. When we arrived the bonfire was blazing in front of an arc of woven chairs set up for the dignitaries, which included us.

John sat down next to me. I smiled and waved to Sarai who was standing with her friends in the choir in their new matching skirts. I could now appreciate how much effort it took to have such a fire and serve food for the whole church community. This evening represented hours of collecting sparse wood and preparing mounds of food for people who often went hungry. George McDonald described a Highland family as "gracious as only the poor can be," in one of his fiction books I had just read, and I was beginning to understand that sentiment.

Once Philippe and his wife, Miriam, arrived and sat down in the last two woven chairs the choir kicked off the celebration. The recital began with a few missionary hymns but the choir looked desperately

The Visit

bored. Quickly they delved into African spirituals and the choir came alive!

John clapped his hands and punched his arm the air, "Glory!" he laughed; "They've got soul." We all laughed appreciating his enjoyment.

The choir moved into a circle around the bonfire and danced and jigged and clapped their way around. They pounded the ground with their bare feet in unison. Dust swirled in front of the blazing fire as they twisted and turned and jumped in a circle.

"Soul train!" John could not contain himself any longer and hopped up and joined the choir's circle dance. The crowd went wild and clapped and cheered him on and many followed his lead.

Malcolm, Anna, Stan and Gritty all laughed and clapped. "I've never seen anyone join the choir before!" Gritty laughed.

"He's got courage!" Stan stood up and jigged around in place.

John was drenched in sweat but he laughed and kicked and exclaimed, "Glory!" all the way around the circle. The choir followed him and kicked and yelled, "Glory!" to the delight of John.

Philippe looked at me and smiled approvingly, "He has spirit."

"He does." I watched his sweaty back disappear around the bonfire one more time.

After a half an hour Philippe stood up to begin the proceedings. The choir stopped and shook John's hand and thanked him. He danced back over to the chair next to me to the enjoyment of the whole crowd. Philippe waited patiently for everyone to calm down.

John looked at me, "Glory! That was fun." He lifted up his shirt and wiped the sweat off his face. He smiled from ear to ear.

"You looked great out there!" I laughed.

He shook his head. "Now that's praisin' the Lord!"

The women of the church walked out in a single file line with voluminous metal bowls balanced on their heads. They held up the food for Philippe to bless it before serving it. One woman handed out tin plates and the next woman knelt down and held the huge bowl in front of us.

John looked at me, "Spaghetti?"

"Yeah." I scooped a portion out with my hand.

Chapter 7

"Don't we get spoons or forks or anything?"

I shook my head, "No, just eat it with your hands."

John scooped up his spaghetti with gusto and let it dribble out of his mouth. He shook his head and let it swing around his head. The choir couldn't take their eyes off this white man who danced with them. They laughed and pointed appreciating his every antic.

After everyone ate their fill the music and dance started up again. Everyone wanted to dance with John and he didn't disappoint a single person. I sat and watched his legs and arms flail and dust kick up all around him.

"He's in his element," I said to Gritty but she didn't hear me.

"This was a night to remember," Philippe said as he closed the evening and nodded toward John. The fire had dwindled and the food was gone.

"Glory!" John said and kicked his leg. Several in the crowd mimicked him to his pure delight.

We walked back across the compound. "Thanks, John," Stan said as he and Gritty turned off to their house.

"Hey, I love praisin' the Lord." John said.

"Good night," Malcolm shook John's hand. "It was great of you to join in, not many people would do that."

"Thanks, Malcolm."

"Good night everyone," I said.

John walked into the Guest House kitchen and I followed him in.

"I'm glad you had such a great time," I smiled at him.

"Yeah, that was the most fun I've had here so far," he grabbed a towel and wiped his forehead. I sat down at the table and ignored the slight.

Anna poked her head into the kitchen door. "Do you want a scrabble game?" she asked.

"Sure!" I looked at John. "Do you want to play?"

"I guess."

Anna walked in and handed me the game. "And listen, tomorrow I hope that you will join us for Christmas dinner after rest hour? I am inviting the Wauken's and Irmgard will be in Fada tomorrow as well so she will be able to join us."

The Visit

I was so relieved not to have to cook or to be alone with John. "Thank you." I smiled at her and then remembered. "Did I meet Irmgard in Mahadaga?"

"Yes, she's coming in to pick up the supplies Malcolm bought in Ouaga for the dispensary," she nodded. "She's got a bright yellow pick up truck that one of the drug companies in Germany bought for her, you can't miss her!" She pushed out of the screened door, "Good night!" she called.

We played a few rounds of Scrabble. I asked him about his business and how things were in Beauville.

"Momma's doin' fine. She wanted me to bring along some ham biscuits for you. She knew those were your favorite."

"That's sweet."

"But I told her they probably wouldn't let me bring them on the plane."

"Probably not," I smiled at him. He really could be kind sometimes.

We finished our game. "Well, Malcolm told me again that you're doing a good job. A real help to him and Anna."

"That was nice of him to say."

"Yeah, I thought I should pass that on."

"Thanks." I looked at my watch. It was late. "Well, I think I'm going to head home." I picked up my flashlight and headed for the door.

"Can I walk you?"

"Sure." I held the door for him.

We walked lazily across the compound and he took my hand. I unlocked my padlock and pushed through the screen door. He followed me in and I didn't stop him. He pushed the door closed behind him and grabbed my arm. He pulled me to him. "I still want you to be my wife. I have to feel you near me." We held each other.

I wanted to feel something. I wanted to see him like the crowd did tonight. I wanted to feel those were the loving arms of the man I wanted to sleep with; have babies with; grow old with. But, it just wasn't there. I pulled away.

Chapter 7

But he pulled me back and held me so tightly it hurt. "Stop," I said.

"Shh," he gasped.

He began rubbing himself against my stomach. I tried to pull away but he held me tighter. "I have to be near you." He rubbed himself faster against my stomach and pushed his hands against the small of my back. "God, I need you." He buried his sweaty head into my shoulder and gave a final push. He fell to his knees and wrapped his arms around my waist and buried his head into my stomach. "I need you."

The moonlight cascaded into my kitchen and spilled on the floor. It didn't reach us in the little pantry.

"You better get up, John," I said.

He stood up with effort and looked at me, "What's wrong? I was just huggin' on you."

All I wanted was to get him out of my house as fast as possible. I unlatched the screen door and held it open. "Good night."

He left. I latched the screen again and walked to the kitchen window. I watched the beam of John's flashlight dart around the compound as he re-arranged his sodden pants. He appeared briefly under the Guest House light and then disappeared again into his room. I shook my head in disgust. Love him? I didn't even like him anymore.

It was Christmas morning. I sat at my writing desk and thought about my family, the sun wouldn't rise over D.C. for at least six hours. They will be relieved to know that John Gruber won't be joining us for any future Christmases. I smiled remembering the annual scene: There were two Christmas trees, one in the family room with every handmade ornament from four children and the other 'designer' tree in the living room. My youngest brother was the present scout. "Santa came in a *big* way," he always assured us as we straggled down the stairs behind him at dawn.

Mom exhausted herself buying, cooking, entertaining, and decorating the entire month of December so that by the time Christmas morning arrived she would sit propped up in a chair with a

— 173 —

The Visit

cup of tea in her hand while we tackled the mountain of gifts. Dad sat next to her shaking his head at the scene. "C'mon, Scrooge!" she would tease him and we would all laugh. We always laughed together.

John and I weren't laughing. I prayed and asked for courage to survive the last 9 days of his visit knowing that I needed to end the relationship today for both of our sakes. It wasn't healthy and every time we were together we were both frustrated. I finished my journal and walked over to the office with my cup of tea. It was locked so I knocked on Anna's kitchen door.

"Come in!" Malcolm called.

I walked through the kitchen to find them both decorating a little artificial Christmas tree in the corner. Malcolm had the short wave radio propped up on the table and it was playing *O, Holy Night!*.

"It's the VOA. They play Christmas carols all day long. It's really wonderful," Malcolm explained as he adjusted the lights.

"Neat," I said and walked over to them. The tree was decorated with homemade ornaments from their children and Anna tied miniature handmade Canadian flags to the tips of the branches. She smiled at me, I could tell that she was enjoying herself.

I put my tea down on the table and sat down in one of their woven chairs. I admired the tree, the lights were varied colors but did not blink. I felt a little flutter of excitement inside and enjoyed feeling "Christmassy". I watched Malcolm and Anna, these people that God had brought me half way around the globe to be ministered by. Together but fully individual, kind and generous but not weak, so unshakable in their faith they appreciated everyone just as they were. Here, tucked away in the tribe of the Gourmas, were the best that God created.

Malcolm took off his glasses and rubbed his eyes. "John's quite a dancer," he mused. "Are you enjoying having him here?"

"Yeah," but I sounded unconvinced, even to the untrained ear. They both glanced at me and snickered.

He put his glasses back on and walked around to the back of the tree. It was only about 4 feet high so I could still see his face. "Anna said you were having some doubts." He nodded his head

Chapter 7

sympathetically. "And, I just wanted to tell you that Anna and I think the world of you." He dropped his voice to a whisper, "It takes tremendous courage to end a relationship, but it's a whole lot easier than being trapped in a bad marriage."

It warmed my heart when they said they liked me.

"I've been praying for you and I just want to encourage you to trust in God's great plans for your life." He walked back around the front of the tree and adjusted the bottom strip of lights. "God loves you and John regardless of whether or not you marry one another."

"Thank you." I got up to leave. "Do pray for me, I'm going to talk to John right now. I think we both need some resolution."

He looked up and winked at me.

"Good luck," Anna encouraged me.

I left Anna's and went to my house and put the ring in its velvet box in my pocket. I walked across the compound and knocked on John's door. He wasn't there so I stuck my head in the Guest House kitchen. He wasn't there. I walked up the path to the Wauken's and ran into Danjou.

"Have you seen John?" I asked him in French.

He nodded and clicked the back of his throat and pointed to the church. "Glory!" he smiled.

I laughed, "Yes, Glory." I walked across the compound to the church and stepped inside. John was in there alone in the front pew. He was bent over in crash position with his head in his hands.

I sat down next to him. I waited patiently for him to finish praying.

"I'm sorry about last night," he said. He shook his head and struck a remorseful pose.

"John, I don't want to marry you." I admitted. I pulled the velvet box from the pocket of my skirt. I handed it to him, "I'm sorry."

His laugh startled me. It was cruel. It crescendo into a cackle, "Oh, that's funny," he slapped his knee. "Right, I fly half way around the world to see you, spend all my savin's on your ring and you tell me in the middle of nowhere that you aren't goin' to marry me?" He slapped his knee again and pointed at me, "That's funny."

"I'm serious."

The Visit

"Yeah, you got me with that one," he forced his laugh. "You got me good."

"John, we can still have a good time together."

"Yeah, right." He shook his head. "Just what am I supposed to tell my family, huh? What am I supposed to tell the folks at church?"

I shrugged my shoulders. "That it didn't work out?"

"I'm goin' to be the laughin' stock again. First Mary and now you."

I didn't know what to say.

"I'm ready to be married, dammit! I'm ready to be married!" he dropped his head and bawled. "I'm a good Christian man, dammit." He punched his knees.

He got up and tripped over my feet as he left. I turned around and watched him storm out of the church. I sat for a moment wondering if I should chase after him but decided not to. He had left the ring box on the bench. I put it back in my pocket. Suddenly he reappeared and marched back down the aisle. He leaned over the pew.

I pulled the box out of my pocket. "Are you looking for this?"

He grabbed it out of my hand and stormed out again.

I couldn't help but smile. "Thank you, Lord." I admired the simple wood cross that hung above the altar. I felt I should kneel and pray or something. But, I couldn't. I was elated. An elephant had just climbed off my back and sat down next to me on the bench. I was giddy. "Thank you." I couldn't stop smiling.

After rest hour I changed into one of my African dresses for the Christmas dinner. I took some ribbon from a package my Mom had sent me and tied it around a batique I had purchased in the market for Malcolm and Anna. I left my house and went to knock on John's door but there was no answer. "John?" I asked through the window. Silence.

I knocked on Anna's kitchen door. "Come in," she called. I went in and sat on her stool.

"Merry Christmas!" she had a little Christmas tree pinned to her apron.

"It smells wonderful in here," I said.

Chapter 7

"Thank you," she pulled open the oven and leaned down to inspect her meat. "Where's John?"

"I'm not sure. I saw him in the church before rest hour and told him I didn't want to marry him. He stormed out and I haven't seen him since," I told her. "I assumed he would be building benches."

"Oh, bless you, Katherine," Anna cocked her head to the side. "That took a lot of courage."

Anna looked at Malcolm as he walked into the kitchen. "Is John building benches?" She asked him.

"No, we decided not to work today," he said.

"Maybe you could knock on John's door and see if he's okay?"

Malcolm looked at me.

"I'm sorry for all of this," I apologized.

He held up his hand to stop my words. "No need." The screened door clapped shut behind him.

Malcolm returned two minutes later. "Danjou said that John left through the gates before rest hour in funny shoes."

"Funny shoes?" I looked at Anna.

"Should we drive around to look for him?" Anna asked.

"Maybe we should," Malcolm nodded and we headed out to the truck. Danjou opened the gate for us and as Malcolm pulled through he slammed on the brakes. "Look who it is." We looked up to see John, a candy cane vision in his white floppy hat, white T-shirt, white sneakers with flashing lights and unwise white running shorts heading towards the gate. His legs and arms were so sunburned they glowed in the afternoon sun. He waved and flashed his salesman smile as he jogged past us into the compound.

Malcolm and Anna shook their heads. "He is going to be hurting tonight."

Malcolm pulled the truck back under the Flamboyant tree and we all got out. John jogged in place.

"Howdy folks." John was all teeth.

"We were worried about you, John." I said.

"It's really not very wise to jog in the afternoon, John." Malcolm explained. "The afternoon sun is extremely harsh and I can see how sunburned you are."

The Visit

"Nah." John stopped jogging and dabbed his sweaty forehead. "I'm from Norf Carolina, I'm used to the heat."

"Well, make sure you drink plenty of fluid," Anna advised.

"John, you need to shower." I told him, "Anna has made Christmas dinner for all of us."

"Thanks for your concern, y'all." He walked towards his room, "I'll be there for dinner in five minutes."

The Wauken's and Irmgard joined us in Anna's living room around the Christmas tree. John walked in shortly after and everyone looked at him. His face was already swollen from the sun and his lips looked curiously enlarged.

"What are you lookin' at?" he asked me under his breath as he sat down next to me.

Malcolm invited us all to sit at the table and asked the blessing. Anna darted in and out of the kitchen placing serving dishes of canned green beans, mashed potatoes and a beef dish with a heavy brown sauce on the table. She finally set a basket of rolls on the table and sat down. Everyone complimented Anna on the delicious food. It still astounded me what Anna was able to create from such meager supplies. We made small talk and ate.

"You got too much sun today, John," Gritty commented. "You should put some warm compresses on your face tonight to try and hold down the swelling."

"I'll be fine," John hadn't said much tonight.

We finished dinner and all gathered around the tree to sing Christmas carols. Stan darted back to his house and returned with a guitar. We sang a few songs before John excused himself.

"I'm sorry, Anna, but I'm not feeling so well." He stood to leave and I stood up with him.

"I'll walk you to your room," I said.

"Good night, I hope you feel better," Anna called and the others wished him Merry Christmas. I followed him to the Guest House.

"I'm tired," he said as he pulled open the screened door to his room.

I stood in the doorway and watched him. "Can I get you anything?"

Chapter 7

"I think you've done enough for one day," he laid back on his bed. He didn't look well.

"Have you been drinking the filtered water from the Guest House kitchen?" I asked.

"I've tried to remember, but I get thirsty and just drink out of the faucet in my bathroom."

"It's not filtered!" I said, "It can make you really sick."

Suddenly he hopped up from the bed and ran into the bathroom. I heard him throw up and I dry heaved myself. I listened to hear if he would puke again before approaching the bathroom door. His forehead was covered in sweat. He glanced at me. "You're sick," I stated the obvious. "Let me go get Anna."

I went back to Anna's and told her what happened. She and Malcolm came and we helped him into bed. Anna wetted two washcloths.

"It's probably heat stroke of some kind," Malcolm rubbed his chin.

"He has a fever," Anna stated. "I will get him some medicine for his tummy but he needs to rest." She left and returned with Gritty. She felt his head and neck.

"Let's hope it's just heat stroke," she said.

"He said he had been drinking the water from the faucet," I added quietly.

She shook her head. "Well, if he gets diarrhea that should be the best thing for him. It does a good job of flushing out the system," she nodded. "I'm more concerned about the fever."

John seemed disoriented. His pillow was soaked with sweat but his teeth chattered.

We made him feel as comfortable as possible and finally we turned out the light. "He needs rest," Anna nodded. "He overdid it today." We walked back into Anna's house and sang a few more carols but I wasn't really into it. I was tired and out of sorts.

After *Silent Night* I stood up to leave. "I think I'm going to wrap it up tonight," I said. "Merry Christmas everyone," I hugged everyone and thanked Anna. I walked to John's room and pulled open the screened door. His breath was labored but he was asleep. I flipped on

The Visit

my flashlight and walked across the compound to my house. I made a cup of tea and stood at the kitchen window. I didn't want to marry him, but I certainly didn't wish him any ill will. I prayed that he would recover in time to finish building the benches and that would help to redeem his mini-mission. I was exhausted and went to bed.

John was in bed for six days. Not only did he have extreme sunburn and heat exhaustion but he also had a bad case of dysentery. In a word: bedridden. Gritty and Anna nursed him. I would slip into the room to watch Gritty monitor his temperature and help put wet compresses on his forehead but for most of the week he sat on the toilet or slept.

"There's really nothing you can do," Anna said. "Go home and rest."

I paced the back hall of my house. I tried to write but couldn't. I tried to pray but could not focus. I was restless. I felt responsible.

I went to seek solace from Anna again. She looked at me. I could tell that she was tired, too.

"Go home and pray, Katherine. Let God give you His peace," and she gently prodded me out of her kitchen door.

The sixth morning I watched from my kitchen window until I saw Anna go to check on John. I hurried across the compound and waited outside the door for her to come out. There were seven little tin pots of various stews lined up outside the door. The families from the compound had heard that John was sick and brought him food to show their concern. "How is he?" I asked as Anna let the screened door gently close behind her.

"I think his fever is finally coming down," she nodded. "He seems stronger and in better spirits."

"What should we do?"

"If it doesn't break by tomorrow Gritty said we need to consider taking him to a hospital in Ouaga or at least moving his departure time forward. He still isn't able to keep much food down."

"Oh, no," I burst into tears. "This is all my fault."

Chapter 7

Anna squeezed my shoulder. "It's not your fault." She jammed her thumb in the air towards his door. "He was stubborn and didn't listen to our warnings. He just wants you to feel guilty."

I searched her almond eyes.

"He's going to be fine once the fever breaks." She consoled me. She mustered a reassuring smile and headed down the path to the Guest House kitchen.

I slipped into John's room and looked at him. His swelling had gone down but he look exhausted He stared out the window.

"How are you doing?" I asked.

"How does it look like I'm doing?" his voice was croaky.

I went and sat on the edge of his bed but he still wouldn't look at me. He had heat blisters all around the corner of his lips. "John, I'm sorry you're sick. But, Anna said your fever is coming down."

We sat in silence.

"You've ruined my life," he stated.

"No, I haven't John."

"Well, you've definitely ruined my mini-mission."

I nodded, "Okay, I'll take some of that responsibility."

Silence.

"Malcolm says that God has great plans for our lives. He can still have great plans for us even if we aren't together," I said.

"You don't really believe that, do you?" He scoffed.

"Don't you?" He stared out the window. "You're the one who told me you felt that God had put us together."

Silence.

"I have really struggled with the weight of those words. They were powerful and it made me feel committed to you whether I felt that or not."

Silence.

He looked at me with a blank expression when a light in my mind blinked on: "You didn't really believe that when you said it, did you?"

"No!" he shouted and clutched his neck. He reached for his glass of water and took a life-saving sip.

"And I believed you."

The Visit

He put his water down. "No, I meant that, that you were an answer to prayer."
"You're backtracking."
"No! I meant it when I said that."
I stood up. "You didn't know what you were saying! You wouldn't know what God wanted for you unless Pastor Jay sat you down and spelled it out for you!"
"Hey, now, Pastor Jay is a good man," he wiggled his swollen finger at me, "I was ready to be married again an' I kept prayin' and prayin' an' then you walked into church," he trailed off realizing that explanation somehow lacked a supernatural experience.
"And that was it? That led you to believe that because a single woman walked into church you believed that God had put us together?"
"Well, I-"
"Do you know how strong those words were?" I got in his face. "Do you have any idea!" I backed off and paced the room.
He pulled the covers up around his neck. "Well, look at you, I mean, you could've at least told me you didn't want to marry me before I flew half way around the world to see you."
"No, I wanted to see you," I walked towards him and he covered his face with his hands. "I believed you when you said that God had put us together and I wanted to honor that." I exploded. "Do you know that I have laid awake at night pleading with God to tell me if that was true or not because I didn't feel it myself! But, I was still ready to marry you if that's what He wanted me to do."
He looked away from me. For once, he was speechless.
"You manipulative coward." I took a deep breath and walked away from him. I wanted to hit him.
"You owe me money."
I looked at him in disbelief. "For what?" I demanded.
"A lot of your expenses to get out here. A lot of gifts-n-stuff."
"So, they weren't gifts then?"
Silence.

Chapter 7

I looked out the window across the compound. My kitchen window seemed so small and distant from where I stood. The guinea fowl cackled as they ran around the Flamboyant tree.

"I want to learn how to say 'hello' in three languages," he broke into my thoughts.

"What?" I wasn't sure I had heard him correctly.

"When I get back, Pastor Jay wants me to stand up in front of the whole church an' give a report. I want to be able to greet everyone in three languages." A smile broke across his face no doubt cherishing his fifteen seconds of fame.

I stared at this man to whom I almost gave myself; my life. Who was he? Balding, blistered: a complete idiot. "That's great, John." And I walked out.

John's fever broke that night and he was back in reasonable form the following day. Malcolm had recommended we drive into Ouagadougou for John's last few days in the country. After dropping John off at the airport we would then stay on in Ouaga for the annual missionary conference.

"It's wonderful," Anna enthused as she loaded her basket of goodies into the truck. "All the missionary families from around the country come together for a week. We have a guest speaker and spend time together."

"I'm looking forward to it." I swung my duffel bag into the flatbed. I looked at John sitting under the Flamboyant tree surrounded by families from the compound who had come to say good-bye.

"Twon-twon-twennee," he repeated the Gourma greeting slowly. "Is that right?"

"Twon-twon-twennEE," another repeated.

I walked over and joined them. Malcolm finally came out and loaded his stuff in the truck. "Are we all ready?"

John got up and hobbled to the truck. His legs were still sunburned. He turned and waved, "Good-bye y'all!"

"Say hello to everyone in your village," Danjou said to John in French. I translated for John.

"In my village?" John slapped his knee and winced. "Hey," he pointed to Danjou, "that's funny."

The Visit

"Glory!" Danjou said in English and kicked his leg beginning a "Glory" pep rally with everyone under the Flamboyant tree. John was delighted.

We pulled out of the compound followed by a crowd running behind the truck yelling "Glory!" I thought ruefully that John had probably a greater impact in Fada in his two short weeks, half of the time in bed, than I would in my full year.

John rolled up his window and sat back in his seat.

"They liked you," I said to him.

"I'm just glad I had the chance to show them how to really praise the Lord." He shook his head, "They're just simple folk, you know?" he nodded his head and looked out the window, supremely satisfied with himself.

8
Back to Ouaga

I sat at the back of the conference room trying to understand our esteemed French speaker at the annual missionary conference but he was from Paris and spoke too fast for me to understand. Malcolm had said that he was a leading Bible scholar and was invited down to the conference to encourage the "laborers." He taught on Moses, and reminded the tired missionaries to take encouragement from that desert Father as his life was a long journey of faith and he did not live to see the fruits of his labor. The teacher contended that the dynamic missionary adventures of St. Paul were hard to emulate.

I looked at my watch and counted back on my fingers six hours. I figured John would probably be back in Beauville now no doubt met by a throng of family and church friends at the regional airport. It had been two days since he left. Malcolm and Anna were so busy preparing for the conference they had little time to sit and chat with me. I knew I had made the right decision but it still hurt. I was lonely for a friend to talk to.

"In First Corinthians," I caught the speaker say. Bible pages rustled as everyone deftly turned their Bibles to that book. I couldn't find it so I looked it up in the Table of Contents and skimmed the words myself even though I couldn't understand his message. It was an exercise in frustration.

I looked around the room at the collection of people. It was neat to put faces with names that I had come to know in the office in Fada N'Gourma. One person I did not recognize was a guy who looked about my age. He wore a colorful Hawaiian shirt with khaki shorts but when I scaled down and saw his black socks with his Birks I couldn't help but smile.

Back to Ouaga

He looked up and caught me looking at him. I looked away.
"Great," I thought. "Just what I need is this guy to think I'm flirting with him at the missionary conference!"

The speaker apparently announced that we would have a break because everyone suddenly stood up and started talking and stretching.

"Hi, I saw you looking at me from across the room," he smiled. "I'm Stuart Miller."

"Hi, Stuart," I stood up. "I should've known you were British," I pointed to his socks. "I'm Katherine Tierney."

He laughed heartily. "For that my sweet, you may call me Stu."

Stu was no taller than I, but like so many short men, he had a giant personality. I was not at all physically attracted to him, but I was very pleased to think I might finally meet a friend.

"And I have to say, I've never seen anyone at a missions conference use the Table of Contents in their Bible!"

"Well, what is it there for then?" Every group has its own set of peer pressure. "I didn't realize there was a contest to see who could turn to Corinthians the fastest."

"Oh, of course there is, my pudding," he laughed. "But, looking it up in the Table of Contents, that was brilliant."

I laughed, too.

"Don't you speak Froggy, then?" he wondered.

"Froggy?"

"You know, Frenchie."

"I do, but he speaks too quickly," I said. "I haven't gotten a lot out of these lectures."

"Nor have I," he looked around. "What do you say you and I skip the afternoon session and tear up the town?"

"Tear up the town?"

"Oh, yes, my little treacle tart. There is excellent shopping to be done, bargains to be had." He bowed. "Anyway, I need a beer after all that spiritual strengthening."

"I thought you couldn't understand him?"

"Shh," he took my arm and led me out the door. "That was what made me so thirsty."

Chapter 8

"Shouldn't we tell someone we're leaving?"

"I shall take care of it, my sweet. Don't you worry." He turned around and went back inside the conference building. On the outskirts of Ouaga the Baptist Church had recently built the conference center and they rented it out to various groups for conferences. There were four simple one-story cement block buildings situated around an open area in the middle. One building held a conference room and kitchen facilities and the other three were dormitories with communal bathrooms.

I looked up at the gray sky. It looked like it might rain, but Anna said now that January was here we were moving from the "cool season" into the Harmattan season which would keep the skies gray full of dust from the Sahara. "The dust sticks to everything," she had told me. The sun nestled behind a gauze curtain but its warmth still reached me.

I unzipped my money belt and counted my CFA. I had two 10,000 CFA notes and about twenty 1,000 CFA. The exchange rate was roughly 700 CFA to the American dollar so I had plenty of money to purchase some souvenirs.

Stu slipped out of the conference center door. "All sorted. Let's go!"

We walked out through the gates and onto the main road. We started walking towards the city when a cab stopped and offered us a ride to the main market in Ouagadougou.

"Have you been here before?"

"I think we were here for fruits and vegetables with Anna when I first arrived."

"Ah, well you haven't been to SOCOGIB in the arty-farty section. This will be a tasty morsel."

"SOCOGIB?"

"It's a huge outdoor market they built about two years ago, it's supposedly the biggest in WaWa."

"Wawa? Don't tell me: West Africa?"

He pointed at me and smiled, "You're quick, for a Yank."

We walked through the cement gates into the covered market. It was built like a parking garage that sloped up at such a gradual angle

Back to Ouaga

I didn't realize how high we were until I caught a glimpse of the rambling city over a cement wall at one point. Each stall was packed with every conceivable trinket one could imagine. Sculpted ebony and ivory animals posed proudly next to faded T-shirts of Farah Fawcett and the Dallas Cowboys. One stall blared Prince's *Purple Rain* while another was tastefully decorated with bolts of English wax fabric. Muslim prayer mats were neatly rolled up and tied into tubes next to black velvet posters of Michael Jackson. The sights and smells overwhelmed me; I walked along behind Stu absorbing the atmosphere.

Stu was excellent at bartering. He clutched his heart and looked thoroughly offended when someone wouldn't give him his asking price. He hung his head and wiped away an alligator tear. The women were particularly charmed and would call "Monsieur!" and hand over their merchandise.

He looked at me and winked. "Watch and learn from the master."

"I think they feel sorry for a white man in shorts with black socks!"

His laugh was always ready, whether the joke was on him or someone else.

Word spread quickly around the market that two white idiots were walking around looking for reasons to spend money. Suddenly our leisurely exploration became frantic as we found ourselves surrounded by young boys pushing everything from packs of gum to knives with elaborate sheaths into our faces. One boy stood in front of me and unrolled a poster of Brooke Shields.

"Is this you, Madame?" he charmed me in French.

"Nice try," I smiled at him. "But, I'm still not going to buy it." He moved away undaunted. The cleverness and confidence of the young vendors always impressed me.

"Madame, Madame!" Another boy held up an armful of malachite necklaces in front of me.

"Madame, Madame!" The necklace boy was shoved out of the way by another boy carrying leather bags that dangled from both arms and around his neck.

Chapter 8

I looked over at Stu who was also surrounded by boys selling everything from baguette to wooden stools.

"I actually wanted to buy some of these things," I hollered to Stu. "But, I feel like I'd start a feeding frenzy if I do!"

"I hear what you're saying my duck," he waded through the boys towards me. "How 'bout we take a refreshment break and return incognito later in the day?"

"Good idea."

The boys followed us until they realized we were leaving and went in search of other customers. We left the market and hurried across the street to a café and sat down at the white bistro tables outside.

"Well, this is all rather civilized," Stu said looking around.

"They even have fresh squeezed orange juice!" I pointed to the menu taped to the outside window.

Stu laughed at my delight. "A few months in the bush can really make you feel like a peasant."

A French woman came outside and took our orders. Stu ordered a beer. I ordered orange juice. I could barely hear the Bob Marley song *Buffalo Soldiers* over the street noise, it was emanating from a boom box plugged into the outside wall.

"Bob Marley," I stated. Stu nodded. I remembered the little city park along the Pitt River in Beauville where we would all go hang out on Sunday's to nurse our hangovers. We would doze in the sun listening to Bob Marley while the more mobile of us played Frisbee.

"So, are you the one I heard about who invited her unsuspecting fiancé here for Christmas only to tell him to sod off?" He smiled.

"Sod off?"

"Ya know, bugger off?"

"I didn't tell him to bugger off." I sighed.

The waitress returned with our drinks and left. Stu swigged his beer. "Well, you might as well have done."

"It was the best thing for both of us—but it was the longest two weeks of my life!"

He smiled, "And his as well, I imagine, my cream cake."

I savored a gulp of orange juice. "Do you refer to everyone as a dessert?"

— 189 —

Back to Ouaga

"Only you," he winked.

"I draw the line at Spotted Dick pudding," I teased, I had read that in one of my novels of late and laughed out loud. Stu burst into laughter while trying to contain his mouthful of beer but leaned over and blew beer out of his nose. He wiped his nose with great flourish. We laughed together for a long time. It felt so good.

"So, how long have you been out here?" I asked after we had composed ourselves.

"Two summers ago I arrived to help set up the Street Kids project. We try to keep the kids off the street at night and keep them out of prostitution and gangs."

"Do you have a safe house or something?"

"There is a house next to the church that the mission rents. We open it up at night as a place for them to come and eat, sleep and hang out. We're beginning to outgrow it so I'm heading home to try and convince the wise, and may I add wealthy, people of my church to give us money to buy our own house dedicated to the project."

"Sounds neat."

"And," he stage whispered. "I need to go home and marry the woman and bring her back with me."

"You miss her?" I smiled.

"Sarah?" He patted his heart. "You see this?"

I smiled at his enthusiasm. "I think I'm going to give myself a break from romantic relationships."

He shook his head, "If it's not right it hurts too much. If it is right you don't mind the hurts."

I looked at him. "That was profound."

He looked around for the waitress. "That earned me another." The waitress pulled open the door. "Another beer and," he looked at me.

For a brief moment I considered ordering a beer. But I blurted out, "Café au Lait."

"Bon," she nodded and let the door close.

We were the only ones seated outside.

"You don't imbibe, then?" he asked me.

"Well, I don't know about you, but I signed a no-drinking statement to come out here," I teased.

Chapter 8

"Ah," he waved his hand, "Yanks are too uptight about that sort of thing."

"Well, I think I've reached my lifelong quota of beer anyway."

"Reached your quota? How old are you?"

"Twenty-three."

He raised his eyebrows. "That's an impressive quota to have met by twenty-three."

"Yes, well, it kept me busy," I teased.

"I imagine so, because I'm twenty-four and no where near my quota!" He thought for a moment. "So, you're telling me you'll never drink again. Ever?"

"I don't know. I've been thinking about that—I haven't made a decision but I feel like maybe God is asking me to make that commitment." I shrugged. "And, frankly, when I think about never having a hangover again I feel giddy. I feel free."

He smiled, "Well, I can assure you my dear that the Creator of wheat and barley is asking me to do no such thing."

"I'm glad," I smiled. "I don't feel that my personal revelations are necessarily universal revelations."

The waitress returned with our drinks.

"A toast," Stu lifted his bottle and I lifted my coffee. "To your freedom from all sorts of nasty habits, including that bloke you sent packing home."

"To freedom," I tapped my coffee against his bottle and turned to watch the street so he didn't see the tears well up in my eyes.

The market from whence we had come towered above us across the narrow street. Mopeds whizzed past bleating their horns at chickens, goats, and small children that meandered past. I watched a man pedal his bicycle pass us with a dirty mattress balanced precariously on top of his head. Stu and I shook our heads and smiled as we watched him make his way through the crowded street hollering at everyone in front of him.

"Ah, the blue men of the desert approach," Stu said. I followed his gaze to see three men approach draped in cobalt blue robes and turbans.

"The Tuaregs?"

Back to Ouaga

Stu nodded at them as they stepped up the cement stoop into the café area. They knelt down next to us.

"Madame?" The first one pulled a scarf out from somewhere inside his robes. He cupped it in one hand as he gently unfolded it with the other revealing several pairs of silver earrings. They were shaped like an anchor with a delicate floral design carved into the bottom.

"They're beautiful." I gushed.

Buoyed, the second man held up two large leather bags which were unique because they were striped red, black and yellow. I had only ever seen natural leather colors in the market.

I took one of the bags and inspected it. A perfect beach bag, I thought. But, boy did it smell! I handed it to Stu.

"Camel," he smelled it and handed it back to me. "Uncured. It will smell for years to come, what a charming memory."

The first man showed Stu his scarf of earrings. I had heard Malcolm talking about the Tuaregs, the nomadic tribe of the desert, who were traditionally tradesmen and guides across the Sahara. He had said that as descendants of the Africans and Arabs they were not accepted by either culture. This man's face was long and narrow and his skin was leathered. He smiled when Stu reached for his wallet revealing three lonely teeth. I watched his long narrow fingers choose two earrings for Stu. He let them dangle from his index finger for Stu's approval. He seemed so delicate and yet rugged at the same time. He looked back at me and held up the earrings.

"I'll take both," I told him in French. I pointed to a pair of earrings and the bag.

He smiled in approval. We paid for our purchases and they left. We finished our drinks and Stu was on the edge of his seat ready to go.

"Am I keeping you from something?" I smiled.

"Bargains! Treasures! Let's go." He stood up and dropped several bills onto the table.

I followed Stu back into the market but my mind was elsewhere. I thought about my drinking problem and what a relief it had been not to drink these past six months. I had not had a hangover, or been late

Chapter 8

to a meeting or done anything humiliating since last July. Would I consider a life without drinking? The thought seemed radical! I grew up in a household that regarded knowledge of red wine as something akin to divine wisdom and no celebration complete without champagne. I belonged to a denomination that relished in all fortified creations and yet the 12 Steps were birthed from its own membership. But, I was tired of wrestling with alcohol. The only way for me to free myself was to stop drinking. I pondered these things before Ouaga's most aggressive salesmen accosted us.

This time they changed their approach. They began guessing which nationality I was and then displayed their language prowess in French, English, German, Italian, and the last one must have been Dutch. I kept shaking my head, "Non, non," as to which tribe I might belong to.

After we finished browsing Stu and I took a taxi back to the conference center in time for dinner.

"Say, are you going to the 'do' at the American Embassy tomorrow night?"

"What 'do'?" I asked.

"Ellen probably has your invitation at the Guest House in Ouaga. Every year the Yanks host a Holiday party, a sort of Christmas slash New Year's party at the embassy. Every Yank in the country is invited and you can bring a guest."

"Really? That sounds like fun! I will ask Ellen about my invitation and if I have one you can definitely be my guest."

The missionary conference ended the next morning and everyone set off in their Land Rovers back to far flung villages up and down the eastern portion of the country. The Catholic missionaries were the first to arrive with the French colonists so they worked with every tribe all around the country. The later Protestant missionaries established themselves with specific tribes and tried not to overlap their resources by working in the same places. PMI traditionally worked with the Gourma tribe and to a lesser extent with the Fulani, two of the smaller tribes in the east.

I packed my stuff and rode across town with Malcolm and Anna to the Ouaga Guest House where Malcolm needed to stay an extra day

Back to Ouaga

to take care of some administrative work. Ellen did have my invitation to the Embassy party. Thus, I found myself with a free day before Stu and I went to the party the following night.

"What should I do?" I asked Anna.

"If I were you I would go to the Hotel Independence. They have a lovely pool and shops and you could treat yourself." Anna said conspiratorially. She would never go herself as she believed it wouldn't seem befitting as a missionary leader to be lounging poolside. But, she still thought it would be fun and wanted me to enjoy myself.

I exchanged several more vouchers for cash before Malcolm dropped me off in front of the Hotel Independence on his way to the bank. "I'll pick you up around 3:30," he said. I glanced at my watch. It was 11:30 a.m.

"Okay," I hopped out of his truck and slammed the door shut. I dodged a large steer pulling a boy standing in a rickety cart wildly flinging his whip around and then scattered a flock of guinea fowl before stepping safely onto the steps of the hotel, shaded by flowering Bougainvillea trees. Once I entered I felt I had walked through a time machine. The hotel was air-conditioned, the patrons were dressed in "Safari" fashions, and the staff in sleek black uniforms. One woman walked by in a white leopard skin pants outfit, white stiletto heels and bleached blond hair smoking a cigarette with an elongated plastic holder. Clearly she had not spent too much time outside the hotel because white really doesn't work when you live in a mud hut.

But, I looked down at my long khaki skirt and dusty Doc Martens and felt like a peasant. I quickly stole into a boutique and purchased a chic black one-piece swimming suit with a matching cover-up, sunglasses, and flip-flops. I regarded myself in the dressing room mirror and decided that I hadn't gained or lost any weight since arriving. I tied the cover-up around my waist as it was a necessity being that I had not shaved properly.

The owner was French and stood outside my dressing room holding my dusty clothes at arms length. "Everyone needs a break from the bush," she sniffed. "From whatever you do out there."

Chapter 8

"Can you bag those clothes, please?" I would definitely need to change before Malcolm picked me up. I used several 10,000 CFA notes on the purchase but I had spent very little in the Fada market. So, I could justify one extravagance!

I bought several magazines from another shop, including *Paris Match*, the French magazine dedicated to popular culture, and *Time International* from the prior week. I headed out to the poolside. I settled into a lounge chair and delighted in the break from my routine. A man stood under a cabana playing a buzuq and singing in Arabic and the waiters delivered oversized glasses of Mango punch with large slices of oranges and mangoes floating on the top. Most of the patrons were European but there were many Burkinabé there as well. They were like the ones I had seen in Charles De Gaulle airport many months ago, obviously from the intimate ruling class of the country, they were fantastically robed, jeweled, and exuded a real confidence.

"Have you come to Burkina for FESPACO, Madame?" the waiter asked me as he took my used glass and set down my third Mango punch.

"FESPACO?" I asked.

"Yes, Madame, Burkina hosts the Panafrican film festival every other year. It brings people from all over the world to judge the best of African cinema."

"When is it?"

"It is the last two weeks of February this year," he said.

"I am living in Fada N'Gourma this year so perhaps we will return to Ouaga?"

He smiled at me just like a Washingtonian would smile patronizingly at someone who said they were from a little town in the Blue Ridge Mountains. "You live in Fada N'Gourma? *Pour quoi,* Madame?"

"I am serving this year with PMI, a mission's group."

"Ah, PMI," he nodded. "*C'est bon.*"

The pool thinned out during rest hour and the singer disappeared but I was not the only one left poolside. I dozed off. It was 2:30 when I awoke. I returned to the boutique and changed back into my bush uniform. I wandered around the hotel and looked in the shops, some

Back to Ouaga

were still closed from rest hour and others looked as though they hadn't closed at all. One shop had the same malachite necklace I had bought in the outdoor market for five times as much as I had paid for it. In the newsagent's I spotted a basket of Kit Kats and bought all six of them.

I walked outside sat on a bench outside the Hotel Independence munching on my Kit Kat's and waited for Malcolm to pick me up. The Harmattan made the sky gray and sand dust was constantly crunching between my teeth but it was still warm.

Malcolm pulled up exactly at 3:30 p.m. I climbed into Anna's seat in the front.

"Did you have a good time, Katherine?"

"I did, thank you."

"We're taking the long way home tomorrow," Malcolm explained as he pulled into the fray of mopeds and general chaos of Ouaga traffic. "The LaFargue's didn't make it to the conference so I want to stop in and see how they're doing."

"Oh, of course, Bev and Jim weren't there." I had been looking forward to seeing Bev and the baby at the conference.

"We'll drive out East to stay with them in Diapaga tomorrow night and then head back to Fada the following day."

"I am supposed to go to the American Embassy's "Holiday Party" tonight. But, if Stuart doesn't show up I think I'll skip it."

Malcolm nodded in response but I could tell he was distracted. We rode the rest of the way back to the Guest House in silence.

"I think you'll be going to the party," Malcolm stopped the truck in front of the compound gate. "I can see Stuart's truck in the parking lot," he said and got out to open the gate.

We pulled in and there was Stu in a Hawaiian shirt, jeans, and his sandals with white tube socks on. He shook Malcolm's hand and walked around the truck to greet me.

"Aren't you a little early?" I asked. "I don't think the party is until 7:30."

"I had some business to attend to with Charles," he said. "But, I also wanted to meet with the Falk's before they leave to talk about the

Chapter 8

Street Kids Project. Of course, if that's acceptable to you, princess?" he bowed deeply.

"Sorry." I felt silly for being presumptuous. "I need to shower and get ready."

Stu and I climbed in his truck at seven p.m. and bounced through the uneven residential streets to the embassy compound. It was almost dark and hard to see because of the high compound walls but once our passports were checked at the gate we walked into a beautifully manicured and torch lit courtyard. We stopped at a table and wrote nametags on which we were asked to include the organization we represented. The residence was a two-story white house with a veranda that stretched the length of the second floor.

We followed the line of guests up the stairs inside to a large living area that had four French doors that opened onto the balcony. A candlelit buffet table was set up on the balcony. Stu and I helped ourselves to punch and stood admiring the view.

The sparse mercury-vapor lights of the city blinked in greeting from their important posts above the few landmarks against the night sky.

"It's won't be bad once they finish it," Stu commented.

"What's that?"

"Ouaga," he said wryly. But I watched him breath in deeply to smell the smell of Africa and it was clear to me that he would not want to be anywhere else.

The Ambassador was probably in his mid-forties, he was tall and clean cut and had a boyish Mid-Western persona. He introduced himself as William Barnes and invited the group to join him in the living room. The couches quickly filled up so we sat on the floor. It was carpeted and I found myself running my hands through it while the Ambassador spoke. It felt so soft and luxurious after months of hard cement.

"As you all are well aware, the January 15th deadline is fast approaching for Saddam Hussein to retreat from Kuwait," Ambassador Barnes explained. I watched many of the people sitting next to me sigh and shake their heads. "Now, I know many of you have voiced concerns to us about the potential war and the Muslim

Back to Ouaga

community's response to it. And, I assure you we are working at every diplomatic level in the region to reassure the leaders of America's goals in this military effort." He held his hands out and looked around the room waiting for a response. "If you have any questions, please feel free to talk to me later. But, for now," he slid behind the white baby grand piano, "it's time to sing!"

We sang *Jingle Bells, Silent Night, Rudolph the Red Nose Reindeer*, and the first verse or two of other familiar favorites. After a few requests and a repeat of *Silent Night* he stood up from the piano and bowed. We clapped and he invited us onto the porch for refreshments.

Stu knew many of the people there and we stood in a circle listening to most everyone voice concern about the pending crisis. Stu stepped back from the circle and explained to me, "Many of these people fled your country in protest of the Vietnam War and still have a deep distrust of the government. And, the Europeans, well, we are supposed to be against whatever the American government offers up—that's just the EU spirit!" Stu laughed.

There were university researchers, teachers from the International School, Peace Corps personnel, medical workers, and several aid agency staff represented in our chat circle, as I could conveniently read on their nametags. Several in the circle represented a unique breed of older single women that I had encountered in every sector since arriving in Burkina. I remembered Elisabeth Luder, Fiona Keys, and others who seemed to discover a niche in the developing world where they could excel as strong independent women. Perhaps in the developing world they had more freedom to pursue their dreams not hampered by the rules of western society. And although Africa has very definite expectations for its own women, because these women were white they were exempt from African rules. They were respected scientists, doctors, nurses, teachers, missionaries, nuns and others who were not married and therefore they had the freedom to be single-minded in their work plus they were able to operate outside societal constraints. They were women of abiding faith and passionate convictions and I found the bar they set in life very high.

Chapter 8

"It was either move into Ouaga and send the girls to the International School or head back to the States," a man from one of the aid agencies explained. "And, Jeanie and I decided that we just couldn't go back there," he shook his head in dismay.

Several in the group sympathized with his concern so he continued. "Every time we return home after an extended period I always feel as though I have stumbled upon a circus tent in the middle of the desert."

"What do you mean?" a young teacher from the International School asked.

"I mean that Americans live in a bubble in the midst of a hurting world. Most people I meet don't have a clue where Burkina Faso is and frankly don't care," the aid agency man explained. "And not to mention the last time I was home on a domestic flight the guy sitting next to me actually spent 10 minutes complaining to me that his breakfast cereal had fewer raisins in it than it used to!" Everyone laughed heartily.

"That's rubbish," said another man from the diplomatic corps at the embassy. "Honestly, I get so weary of Americans who spend time living or traveling overseas that decide they need to reject where they've come from. It reminds me of petulant teenagers who have to reject their parents before they can appreciate them." He looked around the circle, "I do not agree with all of the policies passed down by the State Department but I have lived and worked at length in six different countries, with six different governments, and I have become ever more appreciative of America. It's not perfect but show me someone who is doing it better."

The aid agency man became defensive, "I'm just voicing my frustration with the isolationist mentality of most Americans."

"But, given that isolationist mentality how do you explain the fact that individual Americans still give proportionally more to charities, including overseas agencies, than any other country?" the teacher asked. "And American dollars are no doubt funding your salary," she winked at me, perhaps because I was the only other young woman in the circle, or perhaps because she knew that reminder would effectively end the conversation.

Back to Ouaga

It ended the conversation. Everyone moved to the refreshments table, including Stu, and the young teacher approached me. "Hi," she held out her hand, "I'm Fred Lewis."

"I'm Katherine Tierney." I shook her hand. "Fred?"

"Frederica, the beauty of family names," she smiled. She was probably in her thirties and wore an African dress with Birks. Her dark hair looked hurriedly twisted in a scrunchie and she carried an oversized leather bag that was so full of paper it was sticking out of the top. "Every time I come to one of these parties we end up standing around, eating food funded by the American tax payer, bashing Americans. I do agree with some of their assessments but I've gotten tired of it lately, I guess I'm just in a mood. Anyway," she looked more closely at my nametag, "you're with PMI?"

"Yes, I live in Fada N'Gourma."

"Oh, I've been to Fada. I grew up in Nigeria where my parents teach at the international school in Jos. My Dad is an avowed atheist who fled the States during the Vietnam War. As you can imagine, he is not a fan of missionaries. Anyway, there is a point to this story," she assured me with her hands. "Many years ago we were on a trip driving from Ouaga to Niamey and we blew a tire just outside of Fada. Some people walking by told a missionary couple of our trouble when they got to town and the man came and picked us up and we stayed at their Guest House overnight. Not only did he fix our tire but I'll never forget sitting on their porch eating this fabulous meal!"

"Was that Malcolm and Anna Falk?"

"Yeah! That was their name," she shook her head. "It seemed like anytime we traveled deep in the bush we would run into some kind of trouble and there would always be a missionary family that bailed us out. That really irritated my father," she smiled.

"Well, the Falk's are still in Fada doing their good work," I said. "And, I have eaten many excellent meals on the same porch."

"Good work is debatable," she raised her eyebrows knowing her words were a challenge.

"No, I live with them," I shook my head. "I see how they care for the people in the community. There is no debate."

Chapter 8

"I won't debate you on the Falk's, but the Gourma tribe has had their own animistic religion for centuries. Why do they need a new religion?"

"Well," I tried to get my thoughts together. I had been on the mission field for seven months and never had to explain my existence. "I think the Falk's would say that they aren't there to share a religion, or a way of life, but Truth."

She guffawed, "Only a missionary would have the arrogance to stand there and tell me with a straight face that there is Truth!" She shook her head in disbelief.

"Well, I'm not *really* a missionary," I mumbled and then was horrified that I had denied it. I didn't hear a cockcrow, but I did feel a pit in my stomach. Buck up, Tierney, I chastised myself.

Her head was too full of her own thoughts to have heard me. "Do you really *believe* all that?"

I took a deep breath. "I don't know about 'all that', but honestly, if you had asked me a year ago I doubt I would've said I believed. But, in the past months I have had certain spiritual experiences that I can't deny, many I can't explain, but I know they point me to one thing…" my voice trailed off and I looked at her. "Yes, I do believe."

We stood regarding one another when Stu walked up and handed me a napkin with two Snowmen cookies. "Hi ladies," he looked from me to Fred. "Frederica," he nodded, "never been a fan of nicknames."

"Thanks, Stu," I took a bite of one cookie.

Fred looked at Stu and back to me and walked away.

Stu watched her and then looked at me, "What was that all about?"

"Oh, I had to come clean and admit that I not only was I a missionary but I actually believed," I sighed. "And she didn't like that."

"It's a freeing feeling, really, my pudding. But, Frederica, she's happy for you to believe anything as long as it's *not* Christianity," Stu took my second Snowman cookie.

"I think I'm ready to go," I said and we walked back into the house.

"For my part, I stood over the beverages debating the UK versus American health care systems with a few of your compatriots."

Back to Ouaga

"And the verdict?" I asked.

"The consensus is that as long as you're never sick and only need to give birth every so often or break a bone or two, the UK's National Healthcare System is better hands down. But, if you develop a terminal illness or anything that can't be cured by aspirin and a hot compress, the US system comes out ahead."

We descended the stairs and walked out across the lawn. The Ambassador and other colleagues stood at the gate shaking everyone's hands as they departed. "Thanks for your service," he said to us. We walked out into the dark street where bats swooped in front of us. Stu drove me back to the Guest House.

"Do you want to come in and have a Coke or Fanta?"

He laughed, "No, I need to get back to open up my house for the kids."

"It was great to meet you. And, all the best with Sarah," I said.

"Thanks," we hugged. "You're alright, for a Yank and all."

I slid out of his truck and he waited in the drive to make sure I was safely inside. I waved from the kitchen window and I watched him reverse his truck back out onto the street. He got out to close the gate and waved again and was gone.

The next morning we loaded up Malcolm's truck and set off for Diapaga. It was nice to be in my familiar spot in the back seat listening to Anna and Malcolm talk about everyone they had seen and the overall success of the conference. I only listened with one ear as I rolled down the window. We left behind the last tin stall and baguette seller and headed out into the bush. The familiar sites of termite mud mountains, Baobab trees, and low rolling brush filled the landscape. Every few miles we passed a mud hut compound with young children and women busily tending to their chores to run their bush estates. They always looked up and waved as we drove by. I waved back.

I had dozed off when Malcolm pulled the truck into the LaFargue's compound at dusk. The boys were in the middle of a soccer game with some African boys and cleared out of the way to allow the truck through. Jim jogged out of the house and waved.

"Well, this is a surprise," Jim shook our hands. He seemed to have boundless energy.

Chapter 8

"We were worried about you when you all didn't show up for the annual conference this past week, Jim."

"I'm sorry, Malcolm. But, with Pete's birth and the boy's schooling Bev just didn't feel she could afford the time away."

Malcolm rubbed his chin. "Were you not here?"

"I thought I told you about my work with the Fulani tribe?"

"Oh, yes. How is that going?"

"It's exciting. My last meeting with them lasted about two weeks, which is why I didn't come to the conference. But, I really didn't want to miss the opportunity to build bridges with that community."

Malcolm nodded. "Where's Bev?"

"C'mon inside," he turned and we followed him in the house.

We walked up a few stairs into a large screened-in porch area. The porch was decorated with the typical woven chairs that one finds in the market but it was also strewn with brightly colored Fisher Price boats and trucks. We walked through into the living area where we found Bev sitting at the kitchen table nursing Pete. She looked exhausted.

"Anna!" she smiled. Anna leaned down and kissed her on the cheek. Malcolm did the same.

"Hi, Katherine!"

"Hi, Bev," I kissed her cheek. "It's good to see you again."

"I'm sorry I can't get up. She waved her hands towards the chairs, "Please, sit down."

"Hon, before we sit down I want to take Malcolm in the back to see the garden." He turned to Malcolm. "We're almost self-sufficient here. So much so we've had enough vegetables to open a stall in the market and fund a new teacher for the school."

"Excellent," Malcolm followed Jim out the screened door and it clapped shut behind him.

Bev switched Pete to her other breast. She brushed her fingers across his cheek and smiled at him as he suckled contentedly.

"How's the nursing going, Bev?" Anna asked.`

"Oh," she sighed. "The nursing is fine."

Anna cocked her head to the side. "Sounds like Jim has been busy?"

Back to Ouaga

She nodded. "Jim is always busy."
"He's got the Protestant work ethic?" Anna smiled.
"I call it the Calvinist guilt, but I guess it's the same thing," she smiled at her own joke. I burst out in hearty laughter, my Mom had always made similar jokes about my Dad. She looked at me and smiled.
    Anna stood up. "I'm going to step outside to see the garden, okay?"
"Sure," Bev smiled at her.
"You look tired," Anna smiled at Bev.
"I am."
"I know it's a lot of work, I had four, remember?"
I thought Anna's comment was kind of thoughtless!
"I know," Bev said. She looked at me again. I smiled at her.
"Do you want to come, Katherine?" Anna asked me.
"No, that's okay. I'll sit here with Bev."
Anna slipped out the back door. I tried to avert my eyes from Bev's breast but it was fascinating to see the baby nursing. It seemed so sensual and natural at the same time. "It must be fun having all these little kids around," I said absently; the Fisher Price toys reminded me of my brothers when they were young. The colors seemed brighter and 'other worldly' on the cement floor of a bush house.
    I turned back to see Bev's face crumple in pain. "It is," she burst into tears. "Oh, I love them, I do." She took the burp cloth off her shoulder and blew her nose with it. She tossed it on the floor. "But, I am so miserable."
    "What's wrong?" I asked, sincerely baffled.
    "Oh," she sighed. "I am just so overwhelmed. I feel as though I have everything I've ever wanted and yet nothing," she looked at me: "Does that make sense?"
    I opened my mouth to respond but she continued.
    "When Jim and I were in graduate school we did our research on the Fulani tribe. We were so excited about our ministry, we just knew that God was calling us here, together. The first few years were like a dream. We would drive our Land Rover anywhere in the country to

Chapter 8

do ministry work and study Fulfuldi, the Fulani's language. We made a special mosquito net tent that we could pop on the roof of the truck and we'd make love and sleep under the stars."

"That's neat!" I enthused, longing for a great relationship.

"I know," she didn't deny it. "It even has a built in shower and refrigerator that Jim set up to run on a little generator. It was awesome." She dislodged her breast from the sleeping Pete. She pulled her shirt closed and pulled a blanket over the baby. "Then I found out I was pregnant with our first son and we were so excited. But, I naively thought I could continue with the ministry work but I couldn't. And then our second son came along I could barely make it out of the house. And now, I have a third son and I'm lucky if I get a bowel movement and a shower on a regular basis!"

I must've looked horrified.

"Sorry," she added quickly. "You probably didn't want to know that."

I shrugged, "It's okay. I've just never thought that much about what it's like to care for babies, I guess."

"Well, Jim's ministry hasn't stopped and it kind of angers me, you know? I mean, he still goes and spends two weeks with the Fulani tribe. He's continuing his relationships and learning their language. He's progressing. And, I'm not. My language learning has stopped and I haven't been out of this village aside to give birth."

I opened my mouth and shut it again. Clearly Bev needed to vent.

"And it just really seems unfair that Jim is still considered this great father and all he does is breeze in and out doling out hugs and kisses and reading a few bedtime stories. When I was pregnant with our first son I used to say "we" were pregnant. Then, during an 18-hour labor I remember looking over seeing him sitting in the same clothes he was wearing 9 months prior, eating a baguette smeared with butter, reading a book! And I yelled, "I'm pregnant, *I'm* pregnant!"

I smiled to myself picturing the scene in my mind. She smiled, too.

"And, of course, Jim thought I had totally lost it."

Back to Ouaga

"I saw him brush your hair when you were in labor—I'll never forget that. It was so gentle."
Tears brightened the green of her eyes. She sighed and softened her tone, "Jim is a great husband and I love him. I just feel the burden of raising these kids without any community, no family or support. And when I've mentioned going home Jim is hurt because I know how much this ministry means to him." She shrugged. "I know that being Mom to these kids is more important than any contribution I could make to the Fulani tribe. But, I am just struggling with the reality that Jim can do both. He can be a great Dad and work with the Fulani. But for me, as Mom, I have to choose."
I didn't try to say anything, I was just there to listen.
"But what's even more strange is that Jim can leave for two weeks at a time and he'll miss us. But, I just don't think I could physically be away from the boys that long. I need to feel their skin near mine. And Pete. I swear I feel a sensation when his skin touches mine, I don't think I can even describe it. I can't make a move without considering them," tears refilled her eyes. "I am bound to them, they've captured my heart and my life."
We sat in silence and watched her heart lay bare on the table between us.
"You'll probably never want to have children after hearing me go on!" She wiped away her tears.
"I just can't imagine feeling that way about anyone."
"I couldn't either," she assured me which gave me a glimmer of hope that I wasn't a completely selfish cad.
Suddenly Bev looked at me, "Weren't you engaged?"
"Yes."
"Didn't I hear that he visited for Christmas?"
"Yes," I rolled my eyes and she giggled.
"And?"
"We broke up."
She resettled herself on the chair for some girl talk. She leaned towards me, "What happened?"

Chapter 8

I liked her, she seemed happy for an excuse not to wallow in self-pity. "I met him at a turning point in my life and I think I associated my faith in God with John, as if they were linked somehow."

She nodded, "Yeah? Go on!"

"Well, I realized after months of emotional torture that I didn't have to marry him. It was a great revelation and a relief."

"How did he take it?"

"You mean after spending several days in bed with severe sunburn and dysentery? He was thrilled."

She laughed heartily. "Ouch!"

"I do think he was relieved. But, he would never admit it."

"Do you miss him?"

"No," I admitted. "I really don't, I'm just relieved, unburdened, whatever you want to call it. I was drowning under a frozen pond and after feeling my way under a lot of ice I finally found the hole."

She smiled and cocked her head to the side.

"I have no idea where that came from," I felt embarrassed and regretted being so honest, but remembered that Bev had been honest with me. "Well, actually, I do know where that came from, I had that dream a lot. Or, the one where you fall in a ditch and try to climb out but the earth keeps collapsing in your hands."

"Girl! That's intense," she shook her head. "So, you're pretty confident about this decision?"

"Oh, I have no doubt. I mean, after six months of sweaty nights and emotional turmoil, I am now pleased to announce that I am fully confident," I laughed and she laughed with me. It was nice to be with someone who appreciated my humor.

Anna returned from the garden. "Well, the garden is wonderful, Bev. How nice to have fresh veggies. Thirty years ago things were certainly a lot harder," Anna walked into the bathroom and latched the door.

I glanced at Bev and she whispered, "I think Anna misses having all her kids around, she always wants to remind me of how hard she worked."

"She still works hard," I shrugged, thinking of her shuffling up and down the path to the Guest House freezer with trays of baked goods. Bev smiled at me with that smile that says, 'I'm being lifted up and torn down at the same time by motherhood and you haven't a clue,' but she didn't say that. "I think being here reminds her of when her kids were young. It makes her a little prickly."

We gathered around the LaFargue's table for dinner. It was piled high with fresh veggies from the garden and a selection of breads. The boys laughed and teased one another. Jim quieted them down, "Let me ask the blessing, please." We bowed our heads.

"Lord, we thank you for your abundance: In grace, in food, in love, that you bestow upon each of us. I thank you especially for Bev, my friend, for the woman and mother that she is. Amen."

"Amen!" the boys giggled and hopped out of their seats. Pete lay on her lap while the two other boys covered her with kisses and hugs. Her heart smiled through her tired eyes. I smiled at her delight and couldn't help but think that she was a woman blessed.

We headed back to Fada early the next morning. I never thought I would be so happy to see those burgundy gates! We settled back into our routines and before long I was sitting on my stool in Anna's kitchen waiting to be fed my morning snack.

I had thought a lot about Bev and our conversation in Diapaga. I watched Anna put her oversized reading glasses on and smooth a crumpled page to make out a recipe in her cookbook.

"How was it raising four children out here with no extended family or community, Anna?"

She held up her finger and measured her baking soda and powder. She took off her reading glasses and nodded to herself while she considered the question. "When the kids were young, especially the boys, I made myself sick with worry over their safety. They ran all over the village with their African friends. I worried they would get Ringworm, or be bitten by a snake or whatever. But, the girls stayed closer to home," she nodded, remembering.

Chapter 8

"I've never doubted our call to the mission field. But, I longed to be home in that wonderful Canadian prairie community where there is so much support. The snow falls deep and everyone depends on one another.

"One day I was crying because we missed Malcolm's family reunion—it was once every ten years—and I yearned to be there. I was angry with God and I bargained with him, I said, '"Well, if we have to be here at least keep my children safe."' The next morning I walked outside to check on my youngest, she was three at the time, and I saw her squatting in the sand in front of our house. I walked up behind her and saw that she held a baby scorpion in her hand. I feared that if I startled her, it would startle the scorpion and it would sting. So I stood still and watched.

"I'll never forget her little trusting eyes looked up at me and smiled, she was proud of what she caught and wanted to show me. Meanwhile my soul screamed out to God to protect her. Then, without a word, she made her hand into a ramp and the scorpion scurried off and under the house." She shook away a chill and wiped a tear off her cheek. "I will never, ever forget that."

She looked at me. "There are few times when I've felt the Lord speak to me directly. But, that day I did. And, I've never doubted our call since then. I had to give those fears to God and then I was able to enjoy the unique upbringing we were able to give the kids. And, I've never bargained with God again either."

"Wow," I said. "You should tell Bev that story."

Anna shook her head. "Bev's kids will grow very quickly and her life will open up again. She will be able to do great work with the Fulani. But, it's hard to have that perspective when you are tired and overwhelmed by the relentless needs of little children. There is no quick cure for the angst that Bev is feeling right now."

"That's kind of harsh, isn't it?" I took another swig of my Fanta.

"It's all part of being a Mother, it's the process of becoming one." She nodded to herself, "I call it a glorious entrapment."

"A what?" I demanded. "That's sick!"

"It's not," she giggled at my outrage. "You'll only feel it when you're there. Women who love their children are captured by

— 209 —

motherhood. Their lives are forever changed. Sacrifice is natural." She shook her head. "It's a glimpse of the love God has for us. It's holy, really."

I was profoundly uncomfortable with this notion of self-denial. It must've shown on my face.

"That's definitely why you shouldn't do it until you're ready or it will drive you crazy with inner conflict."

I considered her words. She measured some flour and tossed it in her bowl.

"Do you miss them?" I asked her, remembering Bev's comment.

She turned to adjust the temperature on her oven and returned to smooth the pages of her cookbook, an action more of habit than of necessity. She smoothed them again, and again. Her lipped quivered before she spoke, "I spent twenty years longing for a moment's peace," she nodded. "And, I've spent the last ten years trying to fill the quiet they left behind."

She swished passed me to the refrigerator, she checked something in the freezer and made busy in the fridge. She shut the fridge and returned to smooth the pages in her recipe book. It was the first glimpse I had ever caught of Anna's hurt. The things we all have that wake us up in the dead of night, fill our daydreams, and give us fodder for righteous anger. It was her children.

"I can't even find a mate," I mused out loud. I wanted to make light and let Anna know that I didn't expect anything else from her.

She waved her hand dismissively, "That's the easy part."

"Thanks." I deadpanned and she managed a smile behind her tears.

9
Root Canal Near Timbuktu

It was bloody hot. March set in marking the beginning of "hot season" and the end of my energy. Before bed I would drench a towel under the shower and lay down on top of it. For a few minutes I enjoyed a cool reprieve before the dry air sapped its moisture and the towel became a bed of prickles.

Malcolm and Anna moved their bed onto the porch and slept outside. They hung a mosquito net from the light fixture on the ceiling, the white gauzy material cascaded down and widened over the beds making a delicate tent. It seemed awfully romantic to me. I did not have the nerve to sleep outside. But, I was so hot I did leave my mosquito net bundled over my bed and that allowed me to think I felt a breeze during the night. Anna lent me an oscillating fan that shut off with the generator at midnight. Then, at 6 o'clock in the morning when the generator came back on it would start back up again on its own. But I couldn't tell if it helped or not, every time the fan whizzed by me it felt like an oven door was opened and then shut as the fan continued on its way.

I watched Danjou walk across my back porch on the way to the water pump. He glanced in the window to make sure I was at my writing desk and nodded. I smiled. I had been sitting there watching the sunrise and praying but I didn't have the energy to write. It wasn't just the heat, I was a little bored.

The kettle whistled and I made a cup of tea. Malcolm said the Tuaregs, the desert nomads, drank hot tea. He swore by the theory that drinking a hot drink cooled the body. I drank hot tea at every opportunity. I shuffled across the compound with my hot tea and settled behind my desk to finish the French correspondence I had been working on with Malcolm.

"Katherine?" Malcolm said from his adjoining office.

"Yes?"

"Good morning."

"Sorry, good morning."

"Is everything alright, Katherine?"

"Oh, fine."

"Why don't you come in here for a minute?"

I got up from my desk and went into his office. I sat in the little wooden chair in front of his desk and waited for him to finish writing a note. "The war ended quickly," I said absently, there was a copy of the Economist on his desk.

"That's an understatement. But, there is a lot of unrest in the Muslim world I'm afraid," he shook his head and sighed.

"What's up?" I asked him.

"I wonder if you might be interested in doing us a favor?" He took off his glasses.

"Sure."

"Gritty needs to see a dentist. She is in terrible pain. But, no one is free to drive her. I wonder if you would mind driving Gritty to have a root canal?"

"Of course," I figured the dentist would be in Fada or Ouaga.

"You will need to drive Irmgard's truck because I need mine."

"Oh?" Irmgard, one of the nurses stationed in Mahadaga, had the coolest truck, it was a safety yellow Toyota Forerunner with a 16 valve engine. She worked closely with Gritty and Stan in the pharmacy and often came to Fada for supplies. She always pulled in and out of the compound in clouds of dust.

"And, you'll need to pack some clothes because you need to drive her to Timbuktu."

"Excuse me?"

"The Swiss have a mobile dentistry unit, and one of their annual stops is on the border of Burkina into Mali, on the road to Timbuktu. Some years they set up shop on the Mali side of the border and other

Chapter 9

times on the Burkina side. But, it's always on the Timbuktu road. You'll just have to ask around when you get up there.

"You and Gritty can stay in PMI's Guest House in Sebba, which is near the border as well. I will try to phone them today but the phone rarely works. Anyway, I can't imagine they have a lot of company in the Guest House."

I stared at him. "Let me get this straight, you want me to drive Irmgard's truck, with Gritty in it, to Timbuktu?"

"Well, it's just south of Timbuktu. Like I said, you'll have to ask around when you get there to find the Swiss. They aren't too hard to find," he assured me. "Is that okay?"

"Yeah!" I tried not to gush. "When do we leave?"

"Whenever you're ready."

"I'll pack now."

"I'll need to sit down with you and show you the maps."

"Okay." I was on the edge of my seat.

"You need to be careful."

"I will." I promised him. I stood up.

He smiled at me. "Go get your stuff together. I'll talk to Gritty."

I darted back to my house and quickly threw a couple skirts, shirts and underwear into my bag. I tossed in my Bible and journal and toothbrush and zipped it up. I locked the padlock behind me and went to stand under the Flamboyant Tree. I smiled as I looked back at my kitchen window. I was the one leaving this time.

Gritty straggled down the path with her floppy bag and hat. She looked at me. "Have you driven in bush country before?"

"Not to Timbuktu."

Malcolm came out from his office with various maps, car registration, cash, and other information I would need. Anna came out of her kitchen with a canvas bag. She handed it to me.

"Just a few nibbles for the trip."

"Thank you."

"And, plenty of water."

"Thank you Anna. That was really sweet of you."

"I've taken a little Valium for the pain, so I hope you don't mind if I sleep most of the way?" Gritty took a hankie out from her voluminous dress and blew her nose loudly. A couple guinea fowl scurried away.

"No, that's fine." I tried not to smile.

"Katherine, you're driving in bush country. There are no phones, few people, and if something happened to you it would be hard to find out. Please be very careful."

It sounded like he was reconsidering his decision to send me. I opened the door to the truck and hopped inside and rolled down my window.

"I will."

Gritty snapped her seat belt and stuffed a pillow in between her head and the doorframe in the passenger's seat. I settled in behind the leather wrapped wheel. I tucked the maps and the identification papers in the dash, adjusted my seat and started up the engine. Danjou pulled the gate opened for us and I waved to him. I waved to Malcolm and Anna one last time and we turned west on the Fada Road toward Ouaga. Gritty was already dozing off.

Charles and Ellen had lunch waiting for us at the Guest House in Ouaga. "Are you sure you don't want to rest?" Ellen followed me out to the gravel drive after lunch.

"No, thanks," my adrenaline was pumping. I was eager to drive.

"Are you going to be okay, Gritty?" Ellen asked Gritty.

Gritty got in the truck and fluffed her pillow. "I've got my Valium. That's all I'm worried about."

"I'm just worried Malcolm will be angry with us for letting you go." She squeezed my elbow. "Normally the trip upcountry is a two day journey."

"We'll be fine." I assured her.

I waved at Ellen and pulled out of the Guest House compound onto the main road leading north out of the city. Endless rows of mud huts and market stalls dwindled to none as we finally left the last group of baguette peddlers behind. After twenty miles or so the road narrowed into a single paved road and we were alone. The scrubby countryside stretched out to the horizon interrupted only by the endless thread of road. Termite mounds stood six feet high and thorny leafless trees seemed a cruel joke to those who might seek relief from

Chapter 9

the relentless sun. Only the Baobab and Flamboyant trees offered shade under their generous arms. Yet there was something enchanting about this simple countryside, I felt a rush being part of one of the few undiscovered parts of the world. Although it had been traversed by Arab traders and nomadic tribes for centuries only nature had taken a true toll. It had been beaten by the sun and starved of rain and covered by dust from the great desert months at a time. It seemed a barren widow, somehow weakened by the trials of life and yet rich with secrets.

I pushed the pedal down further and sprinted into the netherreaches of the earth. I glanced at Gritty to make sure she was still out and pushed the pedal down further. I rolled my window down all the way and let the wind rip through the truck.

I had dreamed of a day like this when I would lay awake at home thinking about Africa. I wanted to feel free.

The wind grabbed my hair and threw it in every direction. Butterflies swarmed in my stomach, flurried up my chest and into the back of my mouth. I shook my head to let them free and laughed out loud. I felt the crunch of dust in between my teeth. I pushed the pedal down as far as it would go and gripped the steering wheel tighter: we blasted through the countryside.

Some bush grass had grown up in the middle of the road taller than the truck, but I drove right over it.

"Whoa!" I yelled out loud. I spotted a ditch too late and bounded in and out of it and over another pothole. I righted the wheel and pressed the pedal to the floor again. I glanced at Gritty. She was staring at me.

"You trying to kill us?" she hollered over the ripping wind.

"Sorry, did I wake you up?" but couldn't contain my laugh.

She shook her head and lay back on her pillow and closed her blood shot eyes.

I pressed on towards the horizon. Hours later I passed a Baobab Tree with a young boy sitting underneath watching his herd of goats nibble lazily in the sunshine. He hopped up and jumped up and down waving at me as if cheering me on in a race. I smiled and waved and left him in his own world in a cloud of desert dust.

Root Canal Near Timbuktu

I glanced at my watch: it was 4:30 p.m. I drove on, too fast. But it felt so good.

I spotted a thatched roof along side the road in the distance. I slowed as we approached the booth and eventually stopped in front of a freestanding gate. I could easily have driven around it as the road was so flat. I glanced in the rear view mirror. My face looked deeply tanned but it was dust and dirt crunched between my teeth. I took a swig of water and opened the door and spit it on the ground.

An armed gendarmie appeared from behind the hut. "Gritty," I said aloud to wake her. I needed her to speak Gourma to him.

Gritty pulled together the registration and our passports. "Where is that AAA driver's license you've got?"

I unzipped my fanny pack and pulled it out.

"He'll like that because it is written in French." She handed the guard all the papers through my window.

The guard nodded at me but spoke with Gritty. They expected white people to speak French, knowing Gourmantché always surprised and impressed them. Gritty leaned against me as she spoke with the guard through my window. Clearly the discussion led to her ailing tooth and she opened wide and stuck out her tongue so the guard could get a good look for himself.

"Do you mind?" I asked her.

She closed her mouth. "He wanted to see my tooth."

"Is he a dentist?" I teased her.

"No, he's probably very bored and we could well be the only people that have driven by all day so a decayed tooth seems very exciting."

"Well, while you're entertaining the guard I'm going to sneak behind his hut and relieve myself," I slid out of Irmgard's truck and onto the ground. I stretched my legs before meandering behind the hut. I returned and then Gritty went. We both finally settled back into the truck.

We giggled together as we watched the guard struggle to open the gate.

"We could drive around the gate," I stated the obvious to Gritty as we both watched the guard.

Chapter 9

Finally the guard moved the gate out of the way and waved us on. We both smiled and waved. I watched in my rear view mirror as he stood waving and suddenly I felt really sorry for him, that he must be very lonely.

"Watch the road," Gritty fluffed her pillow.

"It's getting dark," I mentioned.

"We're not far from Sebba. We should be there just as the sun sets. That is always a treat out here."

"What's that?" I asked.

"The sun set. It's always brilliant. It's a reminder from God to us that He's still large and in charge."

I glanced at her and smiled. Why had I been so uncomfortable with her? She was fun.

The closer we traveled towards the Sahara the landscape became more sparse, an endless sea of brown with hills on the horizon. Or, was it a mirage of some sort? Thorny trees, termite mountains, and the occasional dry bush were stark against the sun-baked brick of the houses and sand. The sky was streaked with pink as the sun began its descent and the road was a thread laid out ahead of me.

My relationship with John was over. The plans had ceased and the wedding was forgotten. Friends were planning their summer vacations and worried about their own lives. Now it seemed I had everything and yet nothing in front of me. What would I do? Where would I go? Malcolm kept assuring me of God's plans for me but they didn't seem obvious.

"Well they're not going to float down on a little card from heaven," he chided me at our last Sunday night group meeting on his porch.

"Well, how do you know then?" I wanted answers.

"You keep praying, and asking and praying. You knock on doors and some are answered and some are not."

"That's so unsatisfying."

He shook his head and smiled at me. "It's one of the greatest challenges we all face, Katherine," he looked at Anna and patted her hand. "Life is a great journey. But a journey that we can only take one day at a time. We're only given one day at a time, one blank page in our book."

"I feel like I've spent a lifetime of people asking me what I wanted to be.'"

"That puts a tremendous amount of pressure on young people." He shook his head in lament, "Many times in our lives we just 'are' and we need to learn to appreciate those seasons as well."

"It's a balance. If we're so focused on the future we miss today. And life happens today, while we're making all those plans," Malcolm went further. "We have had to learn in good Benedictine style to cherish and find holiness in the dailyness of life, especially out here."

Without warning the sky became a kaleidoscope of color. Streaks of pinks and purples twisted by clouds and refracted by the setting sun. I slowed the truck and pulled to the side of the road.

I marveled at the colors and suddenly, unprovoked by me I heard, "Don't be afraid." The voice I now recognize, so gentle I almost missed it, spoke to me as I watched the glorious sunset.

"It puts things in perspective, doesn't it?" Gritty said. "Listen, if I die at the dentist's I want to be buried here in Burkina under the Flamboyant tree. Don't let Stan pack me off to New York to be covered with a piece of green turf. I want to give that tree a shot of protein." She guffawed at her own joke.

"Gritty, you're just getting a root canal. You're not going to die."

"I'm not worried if I do," she gazed out the window. "I'm tired. I'm ready to see Jesus."

"Well, I'm not too keen on having you stretched out in the cab!" She laughed.

"That's Africa," I thought, the beauty and frustration of it. There's no pretense. Everyone lived at the heart of life everyday. There was no shying away from birth or death. "You're not going to die, Gritty," I added anyway.

I picked up my speed again and shortly came upon an intersection of sorts. The paved road continued north with a simple signpost that read 'Timbuktu' and another smaller sign that read 'Sebba' pointed to

Chapter 9

the left. I turned off the paved road onto a mud path towards the small bush market town of Sebba, on the Mali border.

I glanced at my watch: it was 7:30 p.m. We had left Fada about twelve hours earlier. By the time we arrived at the mission's Guest House it was dark. The guard pulled opened the gates for us and I parked the yellow monster under the one tall vapor light that lit up a corner of the compound. I stepped out of the truck and stretched, my knees were like jelly.

A slight man gently pulled the door of one of the mud houses closed behind him and almost tiptoed to meet us at the truck. He held out his hand, "Welcome."

"Hi, Robert," Gritty said. "This is Katherine, our short-termer down in Fada."

"Hi, Katherine." We shook hands. "I have to say, I wasn't really expecting you until tomorrow." He looked from Gritty to me. "But, we have a room ready for you anyway."

Gritty nodded towards me, "This one was eager to drive." She looked back at Robert, "How's Philippa?"

"Oh, she's wonderful," he smiled to himself and shook his head. "Just gave birth to number seven last week. So, she's resting."

Gritty looked at me. "His wife."

"Well I didn't think he was talking about his horse, Gritty." She laughed way too hard and then cupped her jaw in pain. I looked at Robert, "Congratulations." He had neat, trim hands that he pressed together when he spoke. He seemed too gentle to have seven children!

"Thanks. Let me show you to your room. I'm afraid there isn't a lot to do at night in Sebba," we followed him to the second mud house that stood to the right of theirs. Gritty carried her pillow and her purse.

Except make babies, I thought with a smile.

"And, the generators go off at 8:00 p.m.," he stepped onto a small porch and pushed open the door for us. I heard several scurrying sounds before he flipped on the overhead light, a single light bulb hanging from a wire. The room was typical of bush Guest Houses: two single beds with a makeshift table between them. On the table sat a candle with a lighter next to it. The floors were cement. Anna used starchy white sheets and blankets on her Guest House beds, these just had a simple blanket and no pillow or sheets. No wonder Gritty brought her own pillow.

"We did clean out in here today, but watch out for scorpions and spiders, we do have an abundance of them I'm afraid," he flipped on the bathroom light for us, too. "The desert really cools at night, there are two blankets in the closet," he stepped out of our room. "We'll see you at our house for breakfast at seven or so? Good night."

"Good night," I said as retrieved my flashlight from my duffel bag. I had been through this routine before. I pulled both beds out and shined my flashlight in every corner. I went into the bathroom and looked in every nook. I didn't see any snakes.

"All clear, Captain?" Gritty teased me. She lay down on top of her covers in her clothes. "A scorpion sting isn't all it's cracked up to be. I've had several."

"Don't expect me to be surprised," I shook my head and she giggled. I went into the bathroom and changed into sweats and a t-shirt and brushed my teeth. When I returned Gritty was already asleep in her clothes and lay sprawled on her back with her arms flopped over either side of the bed. I laid down on my bed and the generator shut off a few minutes later leaving me blinking into the night.

It wasn't that Gritty snored like a horse, I just couldn't sleep. If they had let me I would've hopped back in the truck and kept driving. But, there were no such things as streetlights or rest areas, so driving at night was not a wise option. Unless of course one drove an 18-wheeler full of illegal arms, then driving under cover of darkness was apparently the only option.

The windows in the Sebba Guest House were rectangular slots at the top of the wall. Because they were so high there was no need for thief-proofing but consequently I couldn't see anything out of them but a few lonely stars. I pulled my sweatshirt and sandals on and slipped outside. I sat down on the brick wall that formed a front porch, it was slightly lighter outside than it was in the room. There were no lights, no tall buildings, and no airplanes, just a hazy half moon. The air was cold and yet there was little breeze. I heard the cry

Chapter 9

of a new baby carry from Robert and Philippa's home and as quickly as it came it was gone, silent. Comforted.

I sat. I watched. I prayed. I had felt over the last few months the need to make a commitment to myself, and to God, to stop drinking. I still felt giddy when I thought of making such a radical commitment to sobriety. I was tired of the control that alcohol had over my life, the control I had given it, the mistakes and embarrassments I had endured in the name of alcohol. Alcohol had been nothing more than a thief of my self-respect. I said out loud, "Lord, I commit to a sober life for my own health." I looked around but there was no earthquake, no shooting star or great sign from heaven. Just the quiet assurance of peace.

The next morning I drove Gritty over to the Swiss dentistry unit that sat outside of town. It was a new mud-brick single story structure painted white with light blue trim. Even in the middle of West Africa it still had the clinical air of a dentist's office.

We pulled behind the office and were greeted by a group of young African boys. They moved back to make room for us to park the truck. Gritty burst into laughter. "Look at their shirts." She pointed, "Oh, that's great. That's priceless."

Each of the boys had a little picture of a blond, blue-eyed topless woman pinned to their shirts. Some of the boys' shirts were so worn they were attached by threads but the picture managed to perch proudly on their chests.

We got out of the truck. "Bonjour," we said.

"They are those prizes you get from a piece of bubble gum." Gritty realized.

"Oh," I laughed.

The tallest boy took his off and handed it to me. "American," he said in English.

I smiled and handed him back the prized picture.

"500 francs," he offered.

"No, thanks."

"Cadeau?" the shortest one asked and rubbed his tummy. I took out my change purse and gave them each a few coins and went inside with Gritty.

Root Canal Near Timbuktu

The dentists were from a Swiss medical charity, and came to this particular dental unit two months every other year. On the off year they were across the border in Mali, closer to Timbuktu. There were two dental chairs and what seemed to be very modern and clean supplies. I sat on the windowsill of the opened window and watched Gritty.

"We bring all the supplies with us," the dentist explained in French. "Enough to treat people for eight weeks. Sometimes we see 200 people a day, and other times we see 20," he shrugged.

"You have a welcome wagon outside with photos of nude women on their shirts," I teased him.

"Yes," he smiled, "You know we gave them the gum last time we were here and they have kept those little photos all this time?"

I shook my head, "I have to say that doesn't surprise me anymore."

Gritty survived the root canal in good form. "Are you sure you don't want to stay another night in Sebba?" she asked.

"No, I would rather head back to Ouaga." I was eager to drive again and it was still early in the morning.

"Well, I'm putting my foot down about staying in Ouaga tonight. This is supposed to be a two-day journey. Malcolm is going to have my hide."

I giggled. "We can definitely stay in Ouaga tonight."

Gritty took slightly less Valium on the trip home so I couldn't drive quite as fast. But, she indulged me and we hit a few potholes and sped south back to the capital city. I think she was enjoying a little break from her routine, too. We stayed at the Guest House in Ouaga and then left for Fada early in the morning. We arrived home at lunchtime.

Gritty and I pulled through the burgundy gates. I waved and smiled at Danjou as he ran up and closed the gates behind us. I parked under the Flamboyant tree.

I immediately heard the familiar clap from Anna's kitchen door.

"I'm glad you made it back safely," she said but her red and puffy eyes betrayed her.

Chapter 9

"What's wrong?" I asked. Gritty walked around the side of the truck and joined us.

"Little Pete LaFargue is seriously ill. They took him to the hospital in Niamey the day before yesterday. But, PMI decided to go ahead and med-evacuate him with the family to Atlanta yesterday."

"You're kidding!"

"The baby?" Gritty asked.

"Yes," Anna nodded.

"Is he alive?"

"Barely. They think it's cerebral malaria."

"Oh, no," Gritty gasped.

"They took him to the center for tropical disease in Atlanta, PMI doesn't mess around with malaria. It's their standard practice to evacuate immediately."

Gritty nodded in approval. They glanced at one another in a knowing way.

"What does that mean?" I demanded of the silent exchange.

Gritty looked at me. "We've seen this before, Kath. Babies don't have a well enough developed immune system to fight such an attack."

I looked at Anna. "How's Bev?"

She shook her head and whispered, "Not well." She pulled a crumbling Kleenex from her apron pocket and wiped her nose. I looked back at Gritty who watched the Guinea fowl investigate the warm wheels of the truck.

"Put your stuff away and come to my house for an early dinner," she looked at me and then Gritty. "We can eat on the porch and have our meeting afterwards."

It was Sunday, I had forgotten about our weekly meeting. I pulled my duffel bag out of the cab.

"How was Sebba?" Anna asked as an afterthought.

"Fine," I said.

She looked at her watch, "You made quite good time."

"Yes, I enjoyed the drive and we didn't run into any trouble. I'll see you in a little while," and I hurried to my house. I unlocked the padlock and pulled open the tin door. Three lizards scurried away. I pushed open the screened door and walked inside. I dropped my duffel bag on my bed and went to stand in front of my kitchen window.

Was it possible that the same God who had given me peace was allowing Pete to die? Where is the justice in that? I drank my tea and freshened up for dinner. I was relieved to be eating at Anna's and yet I felt angry.

We ate in silence and then gathered our chairs around in a circle on the porch.

"I hope the soup was alright?" Anna asked.

"It was delicious, Anna," I said, still nibbling on my bread. It was warm and satisfying.

"I didn't feel like cooking tonight, it was something I had frozen."

"It was kind of you to invite us, Anna," Gritty nodded. Everyone was weary and distracted.

The compound's phone rang from Malcolm's office. The French had their influence there, too, with the double ring. Malcolm hopped up and went through their house to answer the compound's only phone.

We sat and waited for Malcolm to return. I watched Anna adjust her apron and re-cross her legs from one side to the other. Gritty leaned her head back on the chair and closed her eyes. Her eyes suddenly opened and she stared at the ceiling. Stan leaned forward on his elbows and kept sighing. I tucked my legs up under me on my chair and spread my dress out.

I could see my house from my seat on Anna's porch. The fluorescent light strip that hung outside above my kitchen window illuminated the front of the house. It would like to have stretched further but the night was too thick. It surrounded the light and kept it contained like a firefly's perfect circle of light in a darkened room.

When I first arrived I was afraid of the night but now I'd come to enjoy the reprieve from the heat. The noises and activities that filled the night were so strange to my "white noise" suburban ears, but I had come to relish in the otherness of it. The night felt like I do after a bath when I slip on a silk robe: sensual, clean, and yet vulnerable.

Chapter 9

"I'm going to check on Malcolm," Anna stood up and walked into the house.

"Thanks for driving me to get my root canal done," Gritty said to the ceiling and then flopped her head down to look at me.

"It was fun." After spending two solid days with Gritty I knew her a little better and was less threatened by her abrasiveness.

"Fun for you, I had the root canal," she countered.

"And you survived it," I teased her.

"Yeah," she sighed and leaned her head back on the chair.

"Will the baby survive?" I asked her.

She sighed again.

Malcolm held the door for Anna and they joined us again on the porch. Anna dabbed her eyes with a cloth hankie. Malcolm's eyes were watery. He took off his glasses and rubbed his eyes.

"That was Jim," he swallowed and looked down. "The baby died in route to Atlanta. Bev has been hospitalized for shock and distress. They will stay with her parents in Atlanta for a while."

I stared at Malcolm and wondered if I had heard him correctly. From somewhere deep within Gritty a well of hurt ripped open and out spewed raw pain. She moaned as if she were in deep physical pain.

My vision blurred as tears filled my eyes. They streamed down my face and I wrapped my arms around my waist, I physically ached for Bev, my friend.

Stan came to Gritty's side and tried to help her out of her chair. At first she pushed him away but he persevered. She finally relented and he helped her to her feet. Malcolm put out his hand to Stan and he grabbed it and nodded as they stepped off the porch together and crunched through the gravel towards their home.

Malcolm looked at Anna and tilted his head to the side, "Mother?" he whispered. She went to him and sat in his lap and they held one another. Malcolm lifted his eyes to hers and she responded by pressing her face into his as if she could draw strength from his touch. He wrapped his arms tighter around her and it was if they had become one in the chair in front of me.

I looked away from their intimacy. I cried because I hurt for Bev and Jim and it was so unfair. I couldn't begin to understand the pain that they must be experiencing. And to top it all off I was sure I would never find anyone that would love me like Malcolm loved Anna.

I stood up to leave. Anna stood up and held out her arms for me. She held me. "Are you going to be alright?" she tickled my ear when she spoke.

I stepped back. "I'll be fine."

Malcolm stood up. "I'd like to pray, Katherine. Will you join us?" I nodded yes and we held hands.

"Lord, we come to you weakened by tragedy. We pray that the LaFargue's feel your presence. Let them find comfort in one another's arms and healing in you, most merciful Lord."

Merciful Lord? I thought to myself. I looked up and saw their heads still bowed. What a crock! People who had dedicated their lives to serve God in the middle of nowhere and that's the thanks they get for their ministry? What a cosmic joke! I felt defiant. I knew that I needed to leave before I said something I regretted.

"Good night," I mumbled and stepped off the porch leaving them in their silent prayers.

I set across the compound to my house. I realized I had left my flashlight but I didn't care. The gravel crunched under my feet as I walked down the beaten path to my front stoop. The fluorescent light that hung outside my kitchen window illuminated the front of my house. I unlocked my padlock and walked inside. I flipped on the kitchen light and looked back at Anna's porch. Their light was still on, but they had gone inside.

I was angry. "How could you let Bev's baby die?" I demanded out loud of God. "It makes a joke out of their calling! It mocks them and their mission!" I was indignant on their behalf. I stood at the kitchen window and watched myself cry in the reflection. I decided to take a walk.

I locked my padlock behind me and stepped off my stoop. I had no flashlight with me but I hoped the path was now familiar. I walked past the church tripping over the uneven ground. Small potholes filled

Chapter 9

with unnamed liquids splashed on my feet. Scurrying sounds answered my approach. I circled around towards Gritty's house. It always surprised me how dark it could be when there was no moon.

I glimpsed the fluorescent light above the Guest House through the bush grass. The wind blew and I lost sight of the light but I walked towards it. It comforted me to know it was there even if I couldn't see it. I reached Gritty's house and stepped up onto the cement path and walked down to the Flamboyant Tree.

The heat of the day lingered in the air. It was hazy and I could see few stars.

"Are you alright, Katherine?"

I jumped at Malcolm's voice.

"I'm sorry," he held up his hand to comfort, but did not touch me. "I didn't mean to startle you." The fluorescent light from the Guest House gave him a blue hue like that of a Haunted House at an amusement park.

"How did you know I was here?" I asked.

"Danjou came to tell me. He heard noises and thought it was an animal before he saw you."

I hadn't even seen Danjou. "I forgot my flashlight so I was tripping around near the church."

He nodded and smiled, "He said to tell you that your eyes aren't good enough to hunt at night." He relished Danjou's perspective. I smiled in spite of my anger.

He leaned against the tree and crossed his arms. We were silent in our own thoughts. "How do you feel?"

"I think it's really unfair that Pete died. The LaFargue's dedicated their lives to God's service and then they were crapped on, excuse my French, but I think it's really awful!"

"Katherine, God promises us His presence as we journey through life and death. Belief in Him does not excuse us from life, but enables and guides us." He regarded me for a moment and then looked into the night. "If only it were so easy, but it's not."

His gentleness diffused me. "If what were so easy?"

"Life," he shrugged. "Life is not so easy. We all suffer, even the saints like Bev and Jim. Dedicating your life to God's service does not make us impervious to sin, or its affects."

"So what does our faith give us then?"

"Hope."

"Is that it?"

He shook his head, "Hope is no small thing. Healing, peace, hope—all of these things are gifts that God graces us with in the midst of suffering. The 'peace that passeth all understanding,' that is the gift I pray for Jim and Bev right now."

Whenever I found myself standing next to him I was surprised by his short stature. He presence made him seem taller. I sighed and looked away.

"It's still unfair," I said.

"It is," he agreed. "But I do believe that Pete is with Jesus in heaven, healed and whole. And, Jim and Bev and his brothers will know him again."

The image of reuniting in heaven and the connectedness we have to one another eternally struck me again as it had the day of Pete's birth. I thought about my own brothers and sister and parents in a way that I had never done before.

"Get some rest," Malcolm said.

"Thank you for checking up on me," I said and headed across the compound towards my house.

"Good night," he called over his shoulder.

Danjou had been in my yard earlier with his machete hacking away at some grass that had grown in his path to the water pump and as I walked across it I caught a hint of fresh cut grass. I stopped and breathed more deeply to try to catch it again. A yearning for home gripped me so powerfully I ached inside.

I closed my eyes and smelled fresh cut grass and hamburgers cooking over a charcoal grill. I could hear the water running while Mom stood at the kitchen sink peeling potatoes for her salad. The window was opened and occasionally she would call out, "What was that?" to my sister and me sitting on the patio gossiping about mutual

Chapter 9

friends. We were both home for the summer from different colleges. My Dad flipped the hamburgers.

"Diane, could you get me another beer?" he called.

"Sure," she answered through the window. The water stopped and a moment later she struggled to open the sliding screened door with a beer in her hand. The door came out of its track and my Dad helped her put it back in. He took his beer and returned to the grill. She stood in the doorway and regarded the scene in the backyard and smiled.

My brothers were running around with the dog, Bonnie, a Scottish terrier. They threw an old tennis ball back and forth and laughed when Bonnie would jump twice her height to try and catch it.

"I just can't tell you how nice it is to have you all home," she giggled in delight. "My heart is about to burst!"

That day I rolled my eyes and dismissed her as a crazy, overprotective Mom. Tonight I understood her enthusiasm and her desire to have her children safe at home, to touch them. Tonight I longed to see her face again.

Tears blurred my vision as I opened my padlock and went in my house. I threw myself on my bed with such force that I wheeled it into the wall. I didn't bother to right it. It startled the lizards on my wall and they scattered.

I cried for Pete and Bev and Jim; I cried because I missed home and my family; I cried because I really wanted a cigarette but I really didn't; I cried because I had entered into a relationship with Jesus that I realized would take eternity to understand. But through my tears I knew that there was truth in Malcolm's words and in the crevices of my heart I felt the hope he spoke of. "Well, I'm still sick of taking cold, lame showers!" I called out to God in one final act of defiance before falling dead asleep.

10
The Next Chapter

It was Saturday morning, June 29th. I checked off the date on the calendar Anna had made and hung on a nail to the left of my kitchen window before my arrival. I lifted it off the nail and flipped through it. I had jotted down all the visitors that had come through Fada and the various excursions I had made. Last fall I had doodled wedding bells and practiced writing my would-be married name: Katherine T. Gruber. John's two-week visit over Christmas had giant red slashes through each day's box with exclamation marks blotting out his departure date. By January I was doodling the view of the Flamboyant Tree outside my kitchen window. In March I tried to sketch the African Roller's that graced my yard in swooshes of pastel. I had also written Peter LaFargue's name on the date of his funeral in late March in Atlanta where the family remained to mourn with Bev's parents. My drawing was lamentable but my spirit was free.

    I took the calendar into my room and tossed it in my opened trunk. I had decided to leave all of my clothes for Anna to divvy up between whomever might need some newish skirts and shirts. I kept the African dresses that I had tailor made in the market and one outfit to wear on the plane. My trunk was neatly packed with correspondence that I had received throughout the year and souvenirs.

    My cosmetic case had served me well but I had either used all of my toiletries or they had melted and gone awry in the heat. I had decided to give it to Anna, I was confident she would use it for something creative.

    I pulled open the middle drawer of the dresser and checked my purse. My wallet was bulging with several crisp 10,000 CFA notes along with many smaller, more well used, 500 and 1000 CFA. I had also exchanged my vouchers for roughly 100 US dollars worth of

Chapter 10

French francs and 300 American dollars for my upcoming travels home. Even after that hefty exchange I still had leftover vouchers to return to the head office. They were tucked in next to the American dollars looking distinctly like green Monopoly money. My passport and open-ended plane ticket were there as well. It took out one 500 CFA note for Sarai and closed the drawer again.

When I last checked on Sarai she was outside helping me hang up the last bits of laundry on the line. We had soaked the sheets and the mosquito net in the oversized metal laundry drum so that I could return them to Anna freshly cleaned before my departure.

I picked up a pile of correspondence that I had decided not to keep, along with a t-shirt, and walked outside to toss them in my half-buried metal drum to burn. I had an assortment of sorority T-shirts that I slept in but I decided that this one in particular would not be appropriate to give away and I didn't want to use the space in my trunk to take it home. It was safety yellow with a screened image of a dancing beer can in a bikini with generous cleavage wearing Wayfarer sunglasses with the words "Party University" written across the top. "Spring Break 88" was scrawled across the bottom.

I smiled at Sarai as I walked by and tossed my stuff in the drum. I had more discarding to do so I did not burn it yet. I walked over to Sarai who was tossing the sheets over the clothesline.

"Ca va?" I asked.

"Oui, ca va," she said and went about her work. The sky was cloudless so she squinted into the sun when she looked at me.

I went back into my kitchen and put the 500 CFA note on the counter. I took a Fanta and a Coke out of the refrigerator and walked back outside. I handed her the Fanta while I sipped on the Coke. She stood up and wiped her brow.

"Merci," she said.

"I was invited to Irmgard's for lunch," I told her in English. "But, I will be back."

She clicked the back of her throat and nodded.

I had been invited to Irmgard's apparently infamous luncheons as a way to say thank you for my contribution to Fada during my tenure. I had driven Irmgard's truck to Sebba and had met her several times

The Next Chapter

but I hadn't had the opportunity to work directly with her. She was German, a nurse and split her time working in Mahadaga and whilst in Fada she worked mainly with the Wauken's in the pharmacy. While she was in Fada she stayed in a house outside the compound walls.

"I am leaving on Tuesday for Ouaga with Anna and Malcolm. I fly out next Friday," I said to Sarai.

She nodded and clicked the back of her throat.

Malcolm and Anna were driving me to Ouagadougou on Tuesday where we would stay in the Guest House for three days before my flight left on Friday morning for home.

"You can buy some souvenirs while we stock up on supplies," Anna had said when I was over at the office earlier exchanging my vouchers with Malcolm. She seemed excited to be getting away for a couple days. None of us had spoken of my departure.

Irmgard's rented house was very posh by bush standards. It was cement but the floors must've had some kind of sealant on them making them very shiny. She had curtains and the inside doors were painted blue. Several boys helped her serve the nine of us that gathered around the table. It quickly became apparent that there were six different nationalities and the normal common denominator of French did not work because five of the visitors did not speak French. Thus, I watched Irmgard shuffle around the table heaping large spoonfuls of rice on everyone's plates, often slightly off-target, and translate back and forth for all of us. I knew that she was conversant in several languages but this Herculean feat of serving lunch and translating in Dutch, English, Italian, German, French, and Gourma was astonishing.

Her 'boys', as she called them, served a delicious chicken stew over the rice and we were all happily eating. But, Irmgard had gotten into such a rhythm that each time someone made comment, no matter how off-handed, she would quickly translate it into three or four different languages for the rest of us to enjoy.

Towards the end of the meal Irmgard turned to me and said in English, "So, you like my truck, yes?"

"It's a great truck."

Chapter 10

"One of these big companies gave it to me, they gave me a, how do you say, *magnetic* sign to stick to the door to give them promotion. But, it fell off in the bush many months ago."

I laughed, "I think the color is promotion enough."

"Yes, yes," she regarded me. Her eyes had a smile behind them. "Gritty said you drove too fast. But, I told her that truck asks to be driven fast."

"I don't think it would work as well driving slow."

We stood to leave and said our goodbyes. Irmgard double-kissed my cheeks and nudged me out of her door. "Go home and raise funds and come back, yes?" she nodded once as if that settled the issue.

"Thanks, Irmgard," I appreciated the vote of confidence.

I left Irmgard's house and walked down the Fada road amidst the foot traffic. I smiled and nodded at everyone as I meandered along the outside of the compound wall. There were enough expatriates in Fada that seeing a white person was not a shock as it often was in the deep bush. No one tried to lift my skirt to see if I was 'the same', as others had experienced, but my cats eyes and freckles still looked different.

I walked behind two women chatting as if they were strolling through a shopping mall. Never mind the fact that they were barefoot, each had an infant tied to their backs by a swath a fabric, and they were balancing a small forest of trees on the tops of their heads. They both carried large metal bowls full of a root vegetable that had just been pulled from a garden no doubt miles outside the village. Surviving is a full time job.

They noticed me, the unencumbered white woman, at the same time and greeted me in Gourma.

"Twen-twen-twenee," they said.

"Twen-twen-twenee," I nodded and slipped into the compound gate.

"Bonjour!" I called out to Sarai.

"Bonjour," she called back from the other side of the house. I walked around the back to find her stoking my metal drum with a stick. She had burned my trash while I was at lunch.

"Do you want to go to the market today?" she asked me in French.

The Next Chapter

"No, thanks. I only have a few more days so I'll try and use the food I have left."

She clicked the back of her throat.

"I think we're finished. Will you come and see me on Tuesday before I leave?"

She nodded and smiled at the ground. I could never tell if she found it hard to express her feelings or if she was humoring me.

"Let me run inside and get your money." I went inside and immediately noticed the 500 CFA note I had put on the counter was gone.

I went directly to my dresser and pulled my purse out of the middle drawer. I opened the wallet to find all the CFA notes were gone but the other currency remained.

I stood and looked around in disbelief. Would Sarai have taken the money? Had someone been in the house while I was gone? Sarai had been outside the whole time but I had left the house open. I pulled open all the other drawers and looked in my trunk. But, I knew it wasn't there because I had just arranged the money earlier in the day.

Having exhausted my search, I walked back outside and called to Sarai from my stoop, "Sarai, did anyone come to visit me while I was at lunch?"

She looked at me briefly and went back to stoking the fire. "Non."

All of my CFA had been taken so I had nothing to pay her with. I regarded her for a moment. I just couldn't believe that Sarai would have stolen all that money from me. Not to mention she would raise a lot of eyebrows trying to spend new 10,000 CFA notes in the local market. Most local business was done in 500 or 1,000 CFA notes. I watched her from my stoop and wondered what to do.

I went back inside and took another voucher from my wallet. I needed to talk with Malcolm and Anna about what happened and cash another voucher for final expenses before my departure next week.

"Sarai, why don't you come back after rest hour and I'll pay you then?"

She stoked the fire one last time and dropped the stick on the ground. She glanced at me and looked away which roused my

Chapter 10

suspicions. But, then I checked myself because Sarai always looked away when she spoke to me.

"Oui," she said and we walked out of my yard together. She turned left and headed past the church towards the family compound and I hotfooted it through the dust to Anna's kitchen.

"Anna?" I asked from outside her kitchen door.

"Yes? Come in, Katherine," she recognized my voice by now.

I walked inside to find her slicing cinnamon buns and placing them carefully on a baking sheet.

"I like them to touch so you can pull them apart to eat," she explained.

"Anna, someone stole my money!" I told her how I returned from Irmgard's to find all the CFA missing.

She nodded as she listened to me, "You need to speak with Malcolm. And, he will need to speak with Sarai, too."

"I just can't believe that Sarai would take the money."

"She probably didn't. There are several thieves around who probably knew you were preparing to leave and then saw you go to Irmgard's. They could've snuck in while Sarai was outside and she probably didn't even see them."

"How would they know my plans?"

"I have no idea, I just know that it's possible."

"I hate to leave on a bad note."

Anna shook her head, "You were right to say something."

I found Malcolm standing next to his short wave radio. He held his right elbow with his left hand while rubbing his chin. It was just after one o'clock and he was listening to BBC World Service headlines.

I waited for the news to finish and we sat down in his office. I told him the story.

"How much was stolen?"

"Well, I cashed several vouchers this morning. I think there were five 10,000 CFA and several smaller notes."

"That's roughly 80 US dollars. There are very few people in this village that would have a 10,000 CFA note," Malcolm rubbed his chin and nodded. "It would raise some eyebrows if someone tried to use it in the local market."

The Next Chapter

"Anna said someone might have known that I was leaving and would have cash. That maybe they saw me leave for Irmgard's?"

"It's entirely possible," he nodded. "I'll send for Sarai so that we can talk about this."

"I really don't think she stole my money."

"She probably didn't. But, we need to talk to her and see if she saw anything. And, if she saw someone near your house she might be frightened to admit it."

Malcolm asked Danjou to find Sarai in her compound.

I handed Malcolm another voucher to exchange for more CFA. "I need at least one 500 CFA note to pay Sarai for her work today."

"I'm going to speak to Sarai in Gourmantché, Katherine, so that she feels more comfortable. I will tell her about the theft and ask her if she knows anything about it."

"Okay."

Danjou returned with Sarai. She stepped into the office and sat down in the folding chair next to me. She looked at me and then at Malcolm sitting behind his desk.

I sat and listened to the conversation. Sarai looked increasingly uncomfortable and wouldn't look in my direction.

"Non, non," she nodded her head. "Non, non," she repeated several times.

I looked to Malcolm for interpretation. "She said she didn't see anything," he said.

"Sarai," I said and held out her 500 CFA note. She took it but wouldn't look at me. I felt horrible. "Sarai?" I asked again.

Malcolm came around the desk and held out his hand, "If you hear of anything, please let us know," he said to her. She turned and quickly left the office.

"I hate that this is our final meeting! She wouldn't even look at me."

"I'm sorry, Katherine. I'm not sure why she wouldn't look at you. I made it very clear that we were not accusing her."

We sat together in silence. I heard Anna's kitchen door open and the flip-flop of her sandals walk around to the back of their house where she kept a pantry of dry goods.

Chapter 10

"How's the packing coming along?"

"Fine," I nodded. "I'm leaving my clothes if you know anyone who might be able to use them."

"The entire set of animal shirts, too?" he teased me, but I knew the clothes would be well used.

"Yes, even the Ostrich."

He smiled. "I will weigh your trunk before we leave for Ouaga. I can tell you that in order to board in Ouaga and to get that trunk through Paris it can not weigh more than 35 kilos."

"I don't think that will be any problem."

"Well, I would like to enjoy some of rest hour. We will see you tomorrow for church? And then we will have our Sunday evening meeting and I think Anna is planning a going-away dinner for you."

"That's very kind, thank you."

I felt weighted down as I walked back across the compound to my house. It saddened me that my relationship with Sarai had suddenly fallen apart and probably would not be mended before my departure.

The Fada Road behind the compound wall was unusually quiet. I glanced at my watch. It was 2:30 and rest hour only had a half hour left. I decided to slip out of the compound and take a walk along the bank of the shrinking lake.

I pulled the burgundy gate back and slipped out onto the Fada Road. I turned left but instead of crossing the bridge I made an immediate left at the corner of the mission's compound wall. I could see the top of Anna's house over the wall as I walked between that and the lake. Now that the lake had shrunk since rainy season the footpath became a levy.

The lake was normally bustling with activity. Naked kids would run in and out of the water while the women waded in to wash clothes. Further down young boys would be urinating while another filled a 5-gallon plastic jug to capacity.

Full, green trees with hardy wax leaves grew around the lake making it look surprisingly picturesque. The sky was cloudless leaving us without a buffer from the relentless sun.

I stopped and picked up a small discarded toy. It looked to be an airplane constructed from tongue depressors. I smiled as I inspected it

The Next Chapter

when a wave of appreciation and respect for the Burkinabé washed over me for all that they had taught me. Their comparative poverty did not hinder them from the joys of this life, if anything their need seemed to forge community and familial interdependence that was simply foreign to me. I tried to give the plane a good flight into the lake but it nose-dived only a few feet away.

A few hundred feet ahead a group of five vultures had landed and were jostling at something on the ground. I continued toward them figuring they would scatter at my approach. But, they did not. They stood their ground. I stepped off the path and circled around them. Their red, wrinkled heads and beady eyes followed me closely until I was safely past their dead lunch. They were big birds, probably more than three feet high standing up, but they were sloppy with their gray feathers all askew. I turned back to look at them.

I judged myself to be about 15 feet away. Four of them resumed picking apart the remains on the ground. The fifth and closest eyeballed me. I stared back. It was a standoff.

I charged the bird. "Boo!" I yelled and froze in my best Kung Fu stance 10 feet away.

He backed up. I had surprised him. But then he charged me with his wings spread out!

"Ah!" I turned and sprinted a couple hundred safe feet away. I looked quickly over my shoulder and took comfort in seeing that my nemesis had resumed lunch.

Suddenly I had this image of my parents being phoned because I had been pecked to death by a vulture. 'The only thing left was this shirt with the Ostrich on it,' Malcolm would lament to my Mom. I laughed uncontrollably.

I stepped off the path and circled behind the compound wall through the dusty outlying neighborhoods until I came to Gritty's pharmacy. She and Stan were opening up after rest hour.

"What are you doing out here?" she asked me as she unlocked the padlock on the outside of the pharmacy door.

I was flushed with sun and laughter. "Oh, just walking along the lake."

Chapter 10

She eyeballed me. "Ya know, you really shouldn't be outside during rest hour. The sun is potent and can make you crazy."

I grinned under her watchful eye and continued my journey through the compound to the shade of my mud brick abode. Maybe, just maybe, I considered the possibility that I had a little too much time on my hands.

The next morning I got up early to attend the entire church service. Normally they lasted three to five hours with a series of preachers, singing, and praying.

Also, Sarai was in the church choir and I wanted to try and speak to her before my departure for Ouaga on Tuesday.

I walked down the path from my house to the compound's church. How familiar it was now! A young boy passed in front of me pulling a cardboard tea box with 4 red plastic can covers for wheels attached by twigs.

"Bonjour, Madame!" he waved and smiled. I was familiar to them, too.

"Bonjour," I smiled as I watched the boy pull his truck through the dips and pools of unidentifiable liquids and into the church courtyard.

I entered the crowded church and was accosted by the smell of raw body odor. It was only 7:30 a.m. but it was already hot and the little mud brick church had few windows and one lonely oscillating fan to churn the thick air. I sat down on the corner of the backbench.

A man spoke in what I recognized as Gourmantché but I couldn't understand him. I spotted Malcolm in the front row listening attentively. A chicken wandered in the door and pecked around until it discovered there was no food and eventually wandered back outside.

I watched a boy who was at least 8 or 9 years old walk down the aisle and lift his mother's shirt to suckle on her left breast while a baby, tied by a swath of fabric, slept nuzzled against her back.

Anna had told me how many African women, at least in the rural bush areas, had babies every three years throughout their reproductive lives and consequently nursed for 20 to 30 years. The woman caught my eye and nodded. I smiled at her.

The Next Chapter

The preacher eventually finished and asked everyone to pray. We all bowed our heads and when I looked back up the choir had assembled at the front of the church.

I spotted Sarai and my stomach sank in disbelief! There she stood in front of the church proudly squeezed into the T-Shirt with the dancing beer can that I had tossed in my drum to burn yesterday. I waited for her to look in my direction but she didn't. She clapped and sang her heart out while I watched her. Had I totally misjudged her? I wondered. I felt uneasy so I left the church and walked to Anna's.

"Anna?" I called through the ruffled curtain.

"Yes, Katherine, come in," she called.

"I hope I'm not disturbing you?" I asked. She was twisting an ice cube tray. I didn't have a tray in my freezer so ice cubes had become a luxury.

"Would you like a drink? I was just having a quiet time but you can join me."

"Yes, please." She fixed me a drink and handed it to me. I sipped it. "What is it?"

"Oh, just some mint tea. I iced it and put a lot of sugar in it."

I followed her into the living room and joined her at the dining room table. The table always reminded me of a 1950's greasy diner with the Formica top and thick metal band around it. The chairs had red plastic seat covers accented with sparkles.

"I saw Sarai in church this morning wearing an old T-Shirt that I had thrown in my metal drum to be burned."

She sipped her tea and nodded. "The Africans don't like to waste anything."

"Well, the reason I was burning it rather than giving it away was because it has a dancing beer can on it and says 'Party University' across the top. It's innocuous but I was worried I might offend someone, mainly you guys," I admitted.

She giggled. "Don't worry about it. They drink beer from bottles and they don't speak English," she waved her hand. "You should see some of the second hand t-shirts that are sold in the market."

Chapter 10

I was relieved by her good humor. "I just feel like things have deteriorated with Sarai in the past day. Sarai wouldn't even look at me this morning and it hurt my feelings."

Anna nodded.

"It made me feel like I had misjudged her and I felt foolish to think we had a friendship."

"I think you have had a friendship. But I think there are some cultural misunderstandings going on between both of you and the language barrier exacerbates it," she took a sip and continued. "For one, when you tossed your shirt in the trash to be burned then it's open for the taking. That's not considered stealing. And, if you haven't noticed, Africans are not confrontational people at all. Sarai was no doubt deeply offended, or maybe embarrassed, yesterday to have been asked about the theft, even though no one accused her of stealing.

"So, I think you guys just ran into some cultural miscommunication. It's always a challenge, even for us, to this day."

As always, she was non-plussed. It reassured me. She went back to reading her Bible and I sat with her in comfortable silence. The window next to the table looked out over the compound. Through the thief-proofing I could see the Guest House and Malcolm's truck parked under the Flamboyant Tree. The Elephant Ear plants in front of the window were static as there was no breeze.

"We are inviting everyone for dinner tonight for a little going-away party for you before our meeting."

I nodded and smiled. "Thank you, that's very kind of you."

She reached across the table and squeezed my forearm. "I have appreciated your friendship."

My eyes filled with tears. "I have been forever changed by yours," I admitted and then looked down, embarrassed by my honesty.

Her hand rested on my arm. "Always remember that God is the source of your strength," she gave me one last squeeze and went back to her reading.

It wasn't an admonishment, I recognized it as the truth that had carried her through the challenging and isolated life that she was called to. I stood up. "I'll see you this evening."

The Next Chapter

She smiled and went back to her reading.

I spent the afternoon arranging and re-arranging my trunk. I stood in the front of the kitchen window and prayed. I tried to etch in my mind the view out of my window so it could always be a sacred space for me to close my eyes and retreat to in the future.

I was due back at Anna's for dinner on the porch and our final compound meeting afterwards. I arrived early to help Anna. I knocked but there was no answer in Anna's kitchen. I knocked again.

"Yes, come in please." Malcolm called to me through the house.

I walked through Anna's kitchen into their living room to find them sitting next to one another on a woven love seat. A cassette with a gravelly tape of children singing filled the room.

Malcolm motioned to me to sit down. I sat and listened. I felt embarrassed that I had interrupted them and made to get up but Malcolm waved me back in my seat. Anna clutched a hankie in her hand and occasionally dabbed the corners of her eyes. Malcolm would squeeze her hand in response and she looked at him and smiled. I dropped my head to at least allow them some privacy.

When I looked up Malcolm whispered to me. "It's our girls singing when they were five and seven."

"Oh, that's neat," I looked at Anna who stared elsewhere. She suddenly remembered something and smiled to herself. She dabbed the corner of her eye to stop a tear.

It always took me off guard when I was reminded that Malcolm and Anna 'sacrificed' to be missionaries. It seemed to me that they belonged here.

Anna looked at me. "Our daughter Sarah just phoned to let us know that she's pregnant. It's their first child, she's due next spring."

"We leave on furlough in two years so we won't be able to meet our grandchild until she's over a year old," Malcolm added. "And do we ever miss Sarah and her husband Lonnie. They are wonderful kids," he pursed his lips and shook his head.

She nodded. "We wanted to feel close to her tonight."

I bowed my head, embarrassed that I had intruded on their time. And I struggled with feeling jealous of their love for their daughter.

Chapter 10

Their faces lit up with pride and the smile in their eyes was unmistakable. I didn't want them to see the selfishness in me.

"I just know she'll be a terrific Mom," she added and caught another tear with her hankie.

I looked up and smiled at her. "How could she not be?" with a Mom like Anna.

The tape came to an end and the cassette recorder flipped off automatically. Anna stood up and smoothed her dress, "Katherine, can you help me with dinner? Gritty and Stan should be here shortly. And, I think Irmgard may come as well."

I followed her into the kitchen. I sat on my stool and watched Anna tie her flowered apron around her waist. She put her hands on her hips and surveyed the territory. She sighed and went to work.

"What's for dinner?" I asked.

"Just spaghetti with tomato sauce and baguette. I did make some donuts for dessert, too."

"Oh, those are my favorite."

"I know," she winked at me and then turned to fill up a Dutch oven full of water to boil the spaghetti.

Eventually everyone gathered on the porch. I helped Anna carry the food out to the table and set it for six. Gritty spoke first, "So, you're leavin' already?"

"It's been a year!" I laughed.

"That's nothin'."

The elephant ears swayed gently in the evening breeze. I could see my kitchen window from where I was seated on Anna's porch. I was afraid to leave, I didn't know what the future held for me. Here I felt needed. I caught Malcolm's eye.

"Don't be afraid, Katherine," he smiled at me.

"I just don't know what to do next." I admitted.

"The Lord will guide you, I promise you that," he nodded to himself and opened his Bible. He stopped and smoothed a page with care and looked back up at me. "I was thinking this morning about your leaving and I came across this passage and thought it was so true."

"Oh?"

The Next Chapter

"Do you mind if I read it to you?" he asked.

"Not at all."

"It's from the first chapter of Joshua."

I looked at Anna and she smiled and nodded at Malcolm. I looked back at Malcolm. He put his glasses on, cleared his throat and began, "Be strong and courageous. Be careful to obey all the law my servant Moses gave to you; do not turn from it to the right or to the left, that you may be successful wherever you go. Do not let this Book of the Law depart from your mouth; meditate on it day and night, so that you may be careful to do everything written in it. Then you will be prosperous and successful."

He looked up briefly and continued, "Have I not commanded you? Be strong and courageous. Do not be terrified; do not be discouraged, for the Lord your God will be with you wherever you go."

He closed his Bible and patted it gently.

I awoke at dawn on Tuesday morning, July 1st, and sat at my writing desk to watch the sun rise over the compound wall one last time. I etched my name and the date into the table with a knife to document my tenure there, a small footnote in comparison to Elinor's. I made a cup of tea and walked through the house saying good-bye one last time. It was time to go. I carried my trunk outside and placed it under the Flamboyant tree and returned to retrieve my purse. I locked the padlock for the last time.

I sat down on my trunk and looked around. Isn't it odd how four relatively obscure buildings can come alive, infused with personality by the people that live in them? I saw Danjou walk around the side of my house. He stopped and looked around until he spotted me under the tree. He waved his machete in greeting and went about his work. He was always watching out for me.

Several elderly Gourma women came down the path from the church. One shooed me over and sat down next to me on the trunk. They had come to see Malcolm. They only spoke Gourma so we didn't have a lot to chat about but that didn't stop us from greeting one another. I marveled at their crow's feet and calloused hands, like the rings and knobs of majestic trees. Their breasts were skinny and long, sapped of everything they had to give. They were old friends

Chapter 10

and when they laughed they pressed their hands together and leaned forward in a graceful way.

Malcolm came out and greeted us. "You can go ahead and put your stuff in the truck, Katherine."

"Thanks, Malcolm."

"We'll be ready to go in a few minutes."

He spoke with the women in Gourmantché and listened to their concerns. After they were finished talking they stood to leave. Malcolm must've told them in Gourmantché that I was leaving because they all turned and looked at me and began clicking the back of their throats and nodding.

I slid my trunk into the flatbed and then opened the right rear door behind Anna's seat. It was my spot and I would miss it. Danjou and his family came to say good-bye and the Wauken's and Irmgard. Anna and Malcolm loaded their stuff into the truck. I hugged everyone and we piled into the truck. I rolled down my window and turned to wave when I spotted the yellow t-shirt. It was Sarai. She was standing under the Flamboyant with everyone else. I waved and she smiled as we pulled out of the compound. That was all I needed.

After a few restful days in Ouaga Anna and Malcolm drove me to the airport. They could only walk me into the entrance as only ticketed passengers could go through the initial passport and boarding check. We hugged and stood looking at one another. How many times can you say good-bye? How do you say good-bye to people who are a part of you?

Malcolm broke the silence, "Call us when you get in. Or, write us. We want to know you're okay."

"I will."

He handed me a brown folder. "You need to give this to Harry when you meet with him in Raleigh."

I raised my eyebrows. "What is it?"

"It's your review. But, don't read it," he winked. "God's blessings on you always. Thank you for everything."

We hugged again and I left them. I worked my way through the line and when I came through the other side of the glass partition I looked back at them. They stood side by side as I had seen them so many times. They nodded and Anna smiled her gentle smile, a slight wave from Malcolm, he nudged her shoulder, and they were gone.

I sat on the edge of the double bed in the mission Guest House in Raleigh, North Carolina, and curled the white carpet between my toes. I had just taken the most glorious hot shower and was swathed in fuzzy blue towels. I had not felt so clean in a year. The room was comfortable but sterile. The AC kicked on and drowned out the outside noises. Suddenly I felt strangely claustrophobic: I couldn't smell or hear anything outside. I walked across the room and pulled open the curtain. There was a small square window with a hand crank in the bottom right corner of the larger picture window. I cranked open the window and sat down on the carpet. I wrapped my arms around my knees and breathed in the warm July evening air. I could hear the birds and smell the mulch beneath the window and it calmed me.

Across the grassy compound was the two-story administrative building where I had taken most of my training sessions last summer. In some ways it seemed a lifetime ago and in other ways it felt like I had never left.

An early firefly lighted up in front of my window. After a wink of fluorescent light it disappeared into the bushes. I shook away a chill that ran down my spine, it felt good to be home. But, I sensed that my time in Africa had forever changed me although I couldn't articulate it.

The last time I had spoken with my parents they had arranged a flight for me from Raleigh to Dulles airport. I needed to phone and let them know I had arrived safely and make our final arrangements.

Harry, the short-term missionary coordinator, and his wife had picked me up from Raleigh's International airport and settled me into the room. It was early evening and they offered to take me to their house for dinner but I declined. I was dirty and tired. They dropped me off and I made plans to see Harry the following morning at 7:45 a.m. to begin my de-briefing session in his office.

Chapter 10

"You'll probably be awake and ready to go at 4 a.m. because of jet lag, but try to get some rest," he said as he closed the door after dropping me off in my room earlier.

I stood up from the floor and sat on the edge of the bed. I needed to phone my parents and find out the arrangements they had made for me to return to Virginia tomorrow. I phoned the operator to place a collect call.

"Hello?" it was my Mom. She accepted the charges. "Katherine!"

"Yes, it's me!"

"Oh, it's so good to hear your voice," she sighed. "I just can't tell you."

"It's good to hear yours, too." I smiled. We were silent for a few seconds.

"Where to begin?" she laughed.

"Were you able to book tickets for my flight tomorrow?"

"Of course," she said, a hint of defensive that I would question her organizational abilities. "Can someone drop you off at the airport tomorrow?"

"Sure, Harry will be able to do that," I was confident.

"We have a USAir flight booked for you to arrive at Dulles at 4:50 p.m., so you'll need to be at the airport by two o'clock to catch the 2:50 p.m. flight."

"Okay."

"Is there something special you would like to eat?"

I smiled. I didn't know that she had ever asked me that before. "Surprise me," I said.

She giggled, "Okay."

"I'll see you tomorrow."

"Okay, sweetie. We're all very excited to see you."

"Me, too."

"I love you. We all love you."

"I know. I love you, too."

"Goodnight."

"Goodnight."

I hung up the phone and crawled under the covers in my towels. I was too tired to dig for my sweats and t-shirt in my trunk. I set the

The Next Chapter

alarm next to the bed and flipped out the light. I stared up at the ceiling and allowed my eyes to adjust to the dark. The curtains and my little window were still opened. I heard crickets chirp and the swoosh of traffic from the highway beyond the compound. I fell asleep.

I awoke with the sun before the alarm had a chance to wake me. I leaned over the side of the bed to tip my slippers but only felt carpet. I looked around for a moment and then remembered where I was. I dressed in one of my Burkinabé dresses as I had given away all my other clothes. No one at the mission agency would mind but I relished the look on my brother's faces when they picked me up at Dulles dressed in my tailor made fashions from Fada N'Gourma. I was jet-lagged but I felt good.

I was ready by 6:30 a.m. so I walked around the mission grounds. I prayed and enjoyed the warm morning. Cement pathways winded through neatly manicured flowerbeds and plush green grass, it was definitely different from Fada. I walked up to Harry's office on the off chance that he would be there. He was.

"You start early," I said as I walked into his office.

He stood up and waved me into one of the black chairs next to his desk. "Old habits die hard. After many years in Liberia we still awake at dawn and sleep in the afternoon," he smiled. "Welcome back," he sat down in the chair next to me.

"Thank you. Malcolm and Anna send their regards."

He smiled, "Wonderful, Godly people. Did you enjoy working with them?"

"Oh, yes," where could I begin? " I learned a lot from them."

"And you'll keep learning. It will take years to appreciate all you've seen and learned. It has a way of changing you."

I nodded while he spoke. I believed him.

"We were a little worried about you before you left."

I looked at him, his honesty surprised me but I appreciated it, "Oh, yeah?"

"We have a mold here and you seemed to come straight out of the blue," he laughed. "But, we've learned over the years not to underestimate God's plans."

Chapter 10

"I'm glad to hear that," I handed him the sealed package Malcolm had given me. He opened it and read Malcolm's note. He looked up at me.

"They loved you," he smiled. "They want you back."

"Well, I need to go home and spend some time with my family. Then I'm thinking of graduate school," I shrugged. "I'm really praying about my next step and it hasn't been revealed to me at this point."

He nodded as he listened. He didn't take his eyes off of mine, he really wanted to hear me. "Be patient with your family. You've changed a lot and often it's hardest for those closest to you to appreciate that but give them space."

"I'll try to remember that," I nodded.

We talked about the compound and who lived on it. I told him about Sarai and our last meeting in Malcolm's office.

"That's difficult," he understood. "Tell me more."

I told him about John's visit and our break up and he smiled. Then I told him about Bev and he nodded again, clearly it was not news to him.

"I think the LaFargue's are coming up from Atlanta for a couple of days. They needed to do some business here on campus and I believe they are spending the night here at the Guest House."

"Really!" I almost jumped out of my seat. It had never occurred to me that I might see Bev.

"Let me check on that for you," he stood up and walked out of his office. "Maria?" he called to his wife in the next office.

I stood up and walked to the window. It overlooked the grassy compound that connected the three main buildings. The Guest House was directly across and the Dining Hall was to the right. People were filing into the Dining Hall for breakfast. I glanced at my watch—it was 8:00 a.m. We had been talking for more than an hour.

Harry returned. "Maria says they should be here." He picked up my file. "Let's go to breakfast and talk some more."

He handed me a packet of forms. "There is some literature in there to help you adjust to American life again. We call it re-entry shock."

I laughed and took the packet from him. "Re-entry shock?"

The Next Chapter

"It sounds dramatic, but it can be tough. The best thing you can do is to keep in touch with friends and other missionaries who share your experience. Also, get back involved in a strong church community where you are able to share your experiences and people are interested enough to listen."

He turned to look at me, "We're very proud of you. God clearly called you and you obeyed and took a risk. I want you to know that we recognize that and praise God for it."

"That's very kind of you to say," I smiled.

"You're sure you're not feeling a call into career missions?" he asked as we headed out the door.

"Not at this point, but you will be one of the first I phone if that situation changes."

He laughed as we walked down the stairs and out of the building towards the Dining Hall.

I saw a woman sitting on the grassy slope in front of the Dining Hall. Her back was towards me but her long, dark hair and the thoughtful tilt of her head, was unmistakable. She wore a white linen dress and her sandals sat in the grass next to her.

"Bev," I blurted out but my voice failed me. Harry looked at me, "Bev!" I called again. "It's Bev," I said to Harry and broke into a run.

She turned towards me, "Katherine?" She scrambled to stand up, "Katherine!"

I ran straight up to her and almost knocked her over. I wrapped my arms around her. "Bev, I am so sorry," I whispered into her hair. "I am so sorry."

"I know, I felt your prayers," she said to me. I didn't want her to see my tears. She squeezed me and stepped back. She held my hand. "Stay with me."

"Uh, hello, Bev," I had forgotten about Harry.

"Oh, I'm sorry, Harry," I said but he waved away my concern.

He leaned over to hug Bev, "We love you," he said to her. Her eyes were tired and she had lost weight but she was beautiful in her white linen. Her suffering made her more vulnerable.

"I'll go in and eat and we can finish up later," he squeezed Bev's arm and went into the Dining Room. "What time do you need to be at

— 250 —

Chapter 10

the airport?" he called to me as he held open the door to the Dining Hall.

"Two o'clock."

"Okay, I'll see you later," and he disappeared inside.

"Where's Jim?" I asked. She let go of my hand and picked up her sandals.

"He and the boys are still eating," she said. "Let's walk."

We headed across the grass and walked in the shade along the forest's edge.

"I'm so sorry, Bev," I blurted out again. I didn't know what else to say.

She grabbed my hand and squeezed it. She didn't look at me.

"At night I still feel him, snuggled next to me in the crook of my right arm. He would nuzzle me until I nursed him and then fall asleep with the nipple hanging out of his mouth. He slept with his mouth open and would breathe the smell of breast milk back to me. I woke up last night because I smelled him, but it was my milk, it had leaked, even though it had dried up months ago, and I cried out for him and God!" she burst into tears and buried her head in her hands, "God, I miss him! God, I miss him! I can still smell him and taste him and feel him."

I pulled her towards me and held her and she cried on my shoulder. Her hair was wet on my cheek from my tears.

"Lord! Who is taking care of my baby?" she sobbed. "Who is taking care of him?" I held her.

"Jim grabbed me and held me but the pain choked me and I couldn't catch my breath." We stood there until her soul quieted again. The wind blew and I watched the pansies dance in the nearby flowerbed.

"Malcolm believes that you will know Pete in heaven, healthy and whole," I said.

"Yes," she stood up straight and wiped the tears from her face. "It's my only consolation right now."

"Do you think he'll grow up in heaven or will he remain a baby?" I wondered out loud.

The Next Chapter

"Oh," she licked a tear off of the top of her lip and nodded emphatically, "He'll be strong and handsome, just like his dad," she almost smiled.

We walked along the forest's edge and then turned around and headed back.

"What about you?" Bev asked. "Did you ever hear from John?"

"No," I shrugged. "I think he was as relieved as I was to be out of the relationship."

"God has something better for you."

I nodded, "Well, I think I can only move up from that particular spot," and laughed at my own joke. Bev laughed, too, and it was good to see her smile.

"Enjoy your singleness. Marriage and family are blessings in their own right but enjoy your singleness while you have it. It's a freedom that you'll never have again."

Witnessing her suffering had certainly dampened my romantic images of marriage. But, it had also increased my conviction that a good marriage was one of the great blessings, and mysteries, of our lives. "I spent a long time looking for peace and contentment in other people. But, I know now that it doesn't work that way. Anyway, I think I'm going to swear off relationships for a year."

She laughed, "Not all of us are so confident that we'll have the opportunity to turn down the offer."

I laughed, too. "I don't mean to sound too confident. I'm just trying to simplify my life."

"Bev!" Jim called out and walked towards us. The boys raced passed him.

"Mommy!" they called out and ran towards her. They jumped in her arms and smothered her with kisses.

"Hi Jim," we shook hands.

"You've finished your term in Burkina?"

"Yes," I nodded. "I'm going home to spend some time with my family and I'm not sure what my next step is at this point," I glanced at Bev. "Maybe graduate school?"

"Are you interested in becoming a career missionary?"

Chapter 10

"I don't think so. Maybe that will change, but I think it was time for me to come home even though it was hard to leave."

"God reveals plans on a 'need to know' basis sometimes," he smiled.

"I'm sorry about Pete," I said to him.

He nodded and looked at Bev. "Thanks. We're going to give it another month or two before heading back to Burkina."

"You're going back?" I looked from him to Bev.

"We still feel called, Katherine," Bev said. "But I do want to make some changes so I don't feel so isolated. And, I want to start my language training again."

Jim and Bev regarded one another. He held out his hand and she took it. Jim finished her thought, "I think we will live in Fada or maybe even Ouaga and travel out to the Fulani. But, we need more community and we will probably send the kids to the International School in Ouaga."

"Good," I managed to say at last. Why should it surprise me that they would return? Should they stay in Atlanta and sulk the rest of their lives?

"We have a meeting in 15 minutes, Bev." Jim turned and shook my hand. "It was great seeing you. Thanks for being such a great friend to Bev."

"My pleasure," my heart swelled.

"We'll meet you back in the room, Bev. I'll take the boys for a quick potty stop before the meeting." He grabbed both boys and carried them to the Guest House.

"Keep in touch?" Bev asked me.

"Of course," I said.

"Stay away from older men?"

"Definitely."

"God bless you," she hugged me. "Thank you," she whispered in my hair. She turned and walked up the grass towards the Guest House.

I watched her walk away, "Lord, give her strength," I prayed.

Printed in the United States
61841LVS00002B/445-468